FLY

LEWIS
TRONDHEIM

PAPERCUTZ™

NEW YORK

THE FLY
By Lewis Trondheim
© Editions du Seuil, 1995
All other editorial material © 2021 by Papercutz.
www.papercutz.com

Martin Satryb — Production
Jim Salicrup — Translation
Joe Johnson — Translation (Preface)
Jeff Whitman — Managing Editor
Jim Salicrup
Editor-in-Chief

Special thanks to Jennie Dorny, Dirk Rehm, Anton Heully, and Laetitia Gely

ISBN: 978-1-5458-0708-8

Printed in China
October 2021

Papercutz books may be purchased for business or
promotional use. For information on bulk purchases
please contact Macmillan Corporate and Premium Sales
Department at (800) 221-7945 x5442.

Distributed by Macmillan
First Papercutz printing

PREFACE

Not being very good at drawing, I often hid behind the dialogue in my stories. So, starting in 1992, to break that habit, I gave myself a kick in the butt and drew four wordless pages in a comicbook grid: it was about the adventures of a fly buzzing around, that goes into a house, bangs against a window for a good bit till it can get out. That story appeared in the second issue of L'Association's magazine *Lapin*, in June of the same year.

That's when Pierre-Alain Szigeti turned up. Back then, he was working for the Japanese publisher Kodansha, which was wanting to freshen up its graphic styles and stories. Pierre-Alain's job was to find European authors capable of creating stories, long or short, and Edmond Baudoin and Baru would inaugurate this Franco-Japanese "exchange." Well, "exchange"—Kodansha's rather obvious goal was to test out European stories and then do them over to his liking with Japanese cartoonists and get rid of awful *gaijins*.

So, Pierre-Alain showed up in our Paris studio. He looked left, right, flipped though *Lapin* #2, saw my four pages, and asked me to do a sample for Kodansha, using that fly. But once he got instructions from Japan, he came back to me and specified: "So, the fly, not black. They don't like black characters. And no teeth showing either. They want 'kawaii,' something cute." I responded that it would lose a little of its personality, that there would just be a smiley with wings and shoes. "No worries. The Japanese know what their readers want."

Out with black and the teeth. I did up a first story that was published in the Japanese magazine *Monthly Afternoon*. Then a second one.

What you've got to know is that every month the readers had the chance to vote for their favorite character, their favorite story, their favorite page, panel, and so on, in the previous issue.

So, in come the results about The Fly's first appearance: out of the magazine's thousand pages, it came in eighth place. It was unhoped for.

Sensing they had a success on their hands, the Japanese publisher decided to take charge: the next story was to end with the fly meeting a girl-fly and the final panel, which would take up the space of four panels, would show the two flies kissing.

As much as I'd been completely free for the beginning of my story, they imposed almost everything on me for the rest. "But," Pierre-Alain repeated to me, "don't worry, they know what they're doing."

I gave in, already picturing a TV series, big-time merchandising, giant stuffed fly-toys.

The voting results concerning the story about the girl-fly and the kiss tumbled along with my hopes: "Thanks, goodbye, Mister Trondheim. We don't need you anymore. People don't like your stories."

On the heels of that experience, I redrew those pages, transforming the *kawaii* fly back into a black fly with teeth poking out. I continued the story up to hundred pages and submitted it to the Seuil publishing house, which published it in 1995.

Immediately afterwards, a French producer bought the rights and made a TV series out of it in France and internationally, which was a success, no doubt because it was still wordless.

There weren't any giant stuffed flies, but my desire to do only the stuff I wanted to do, without paying much mind to other people and not looking for greener pastures elsewhere was greatly strengthened.

Lewis Trondheim, April 2021

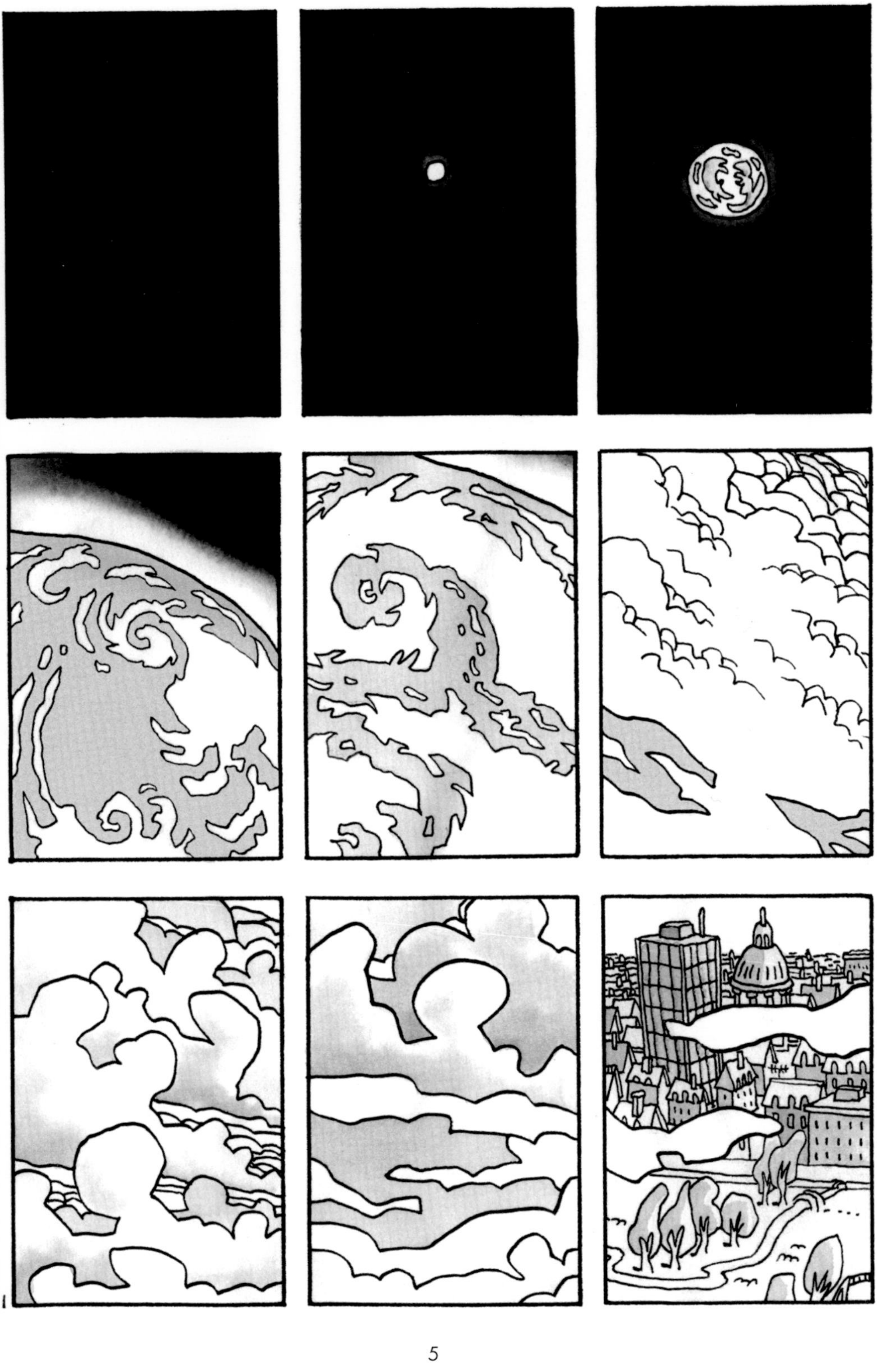

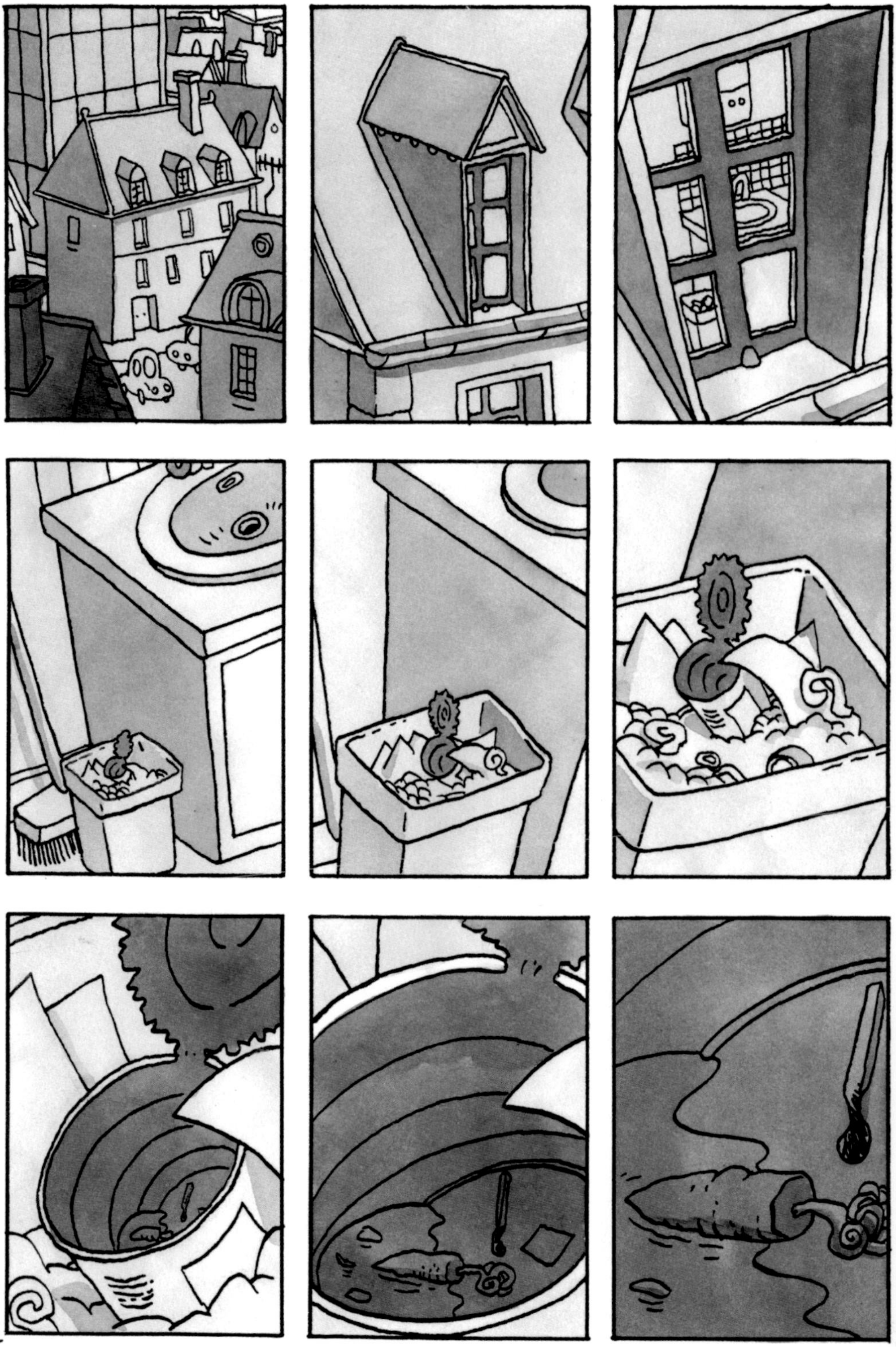

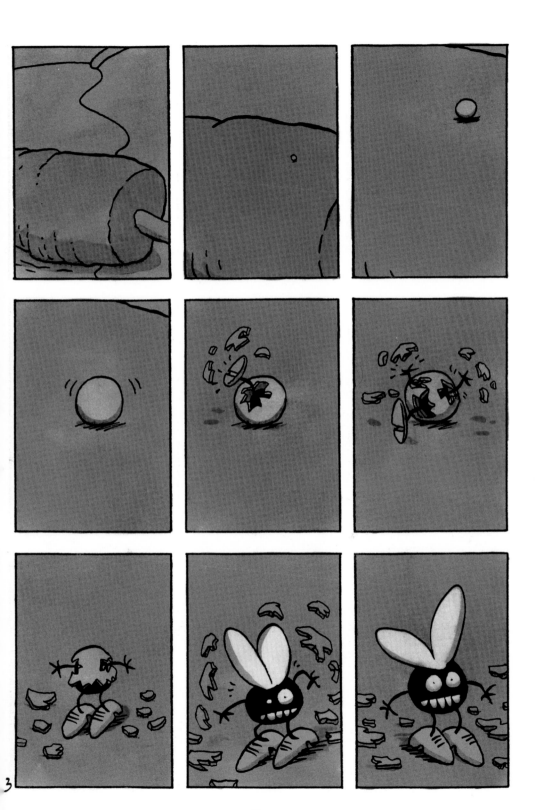

3

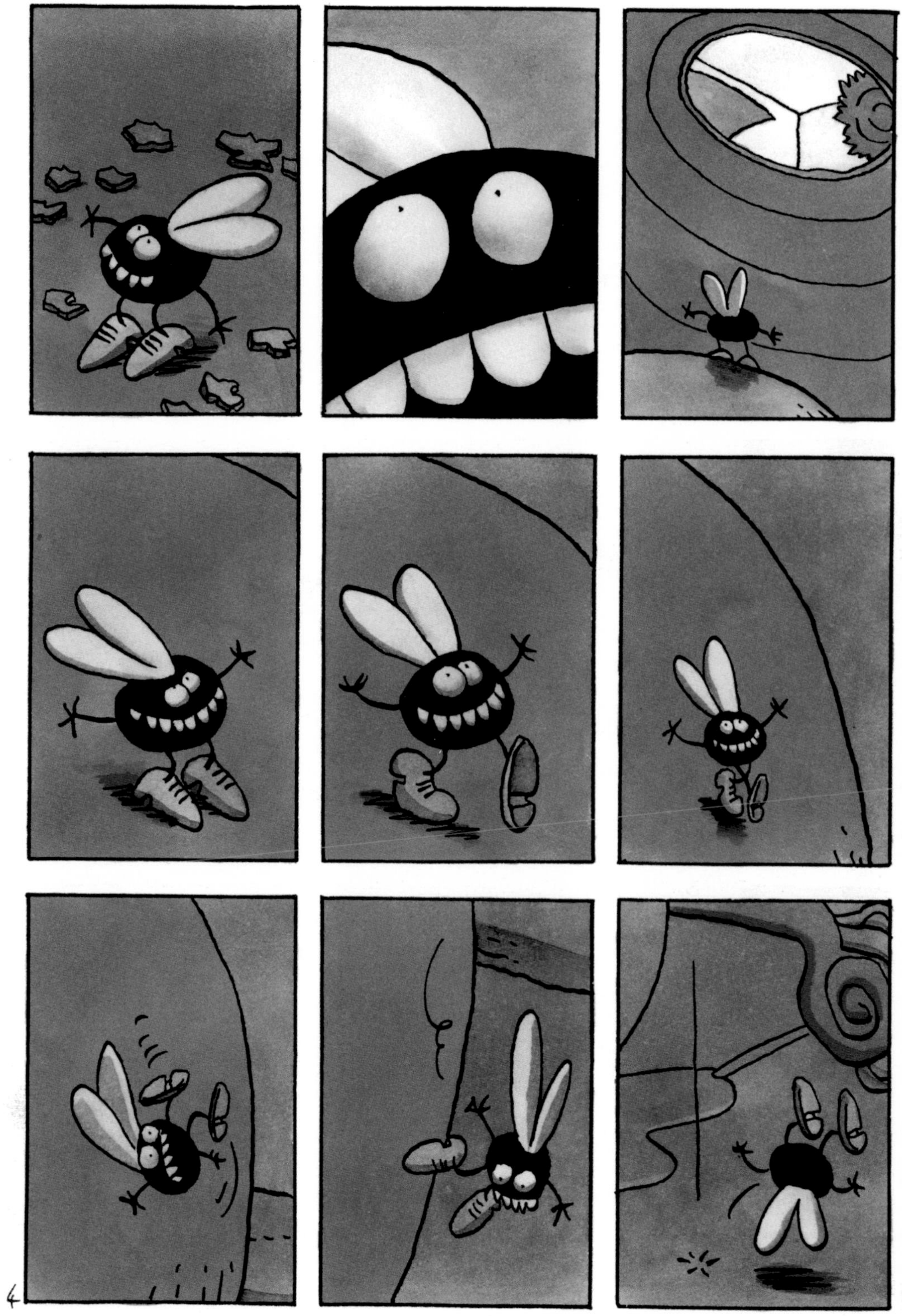

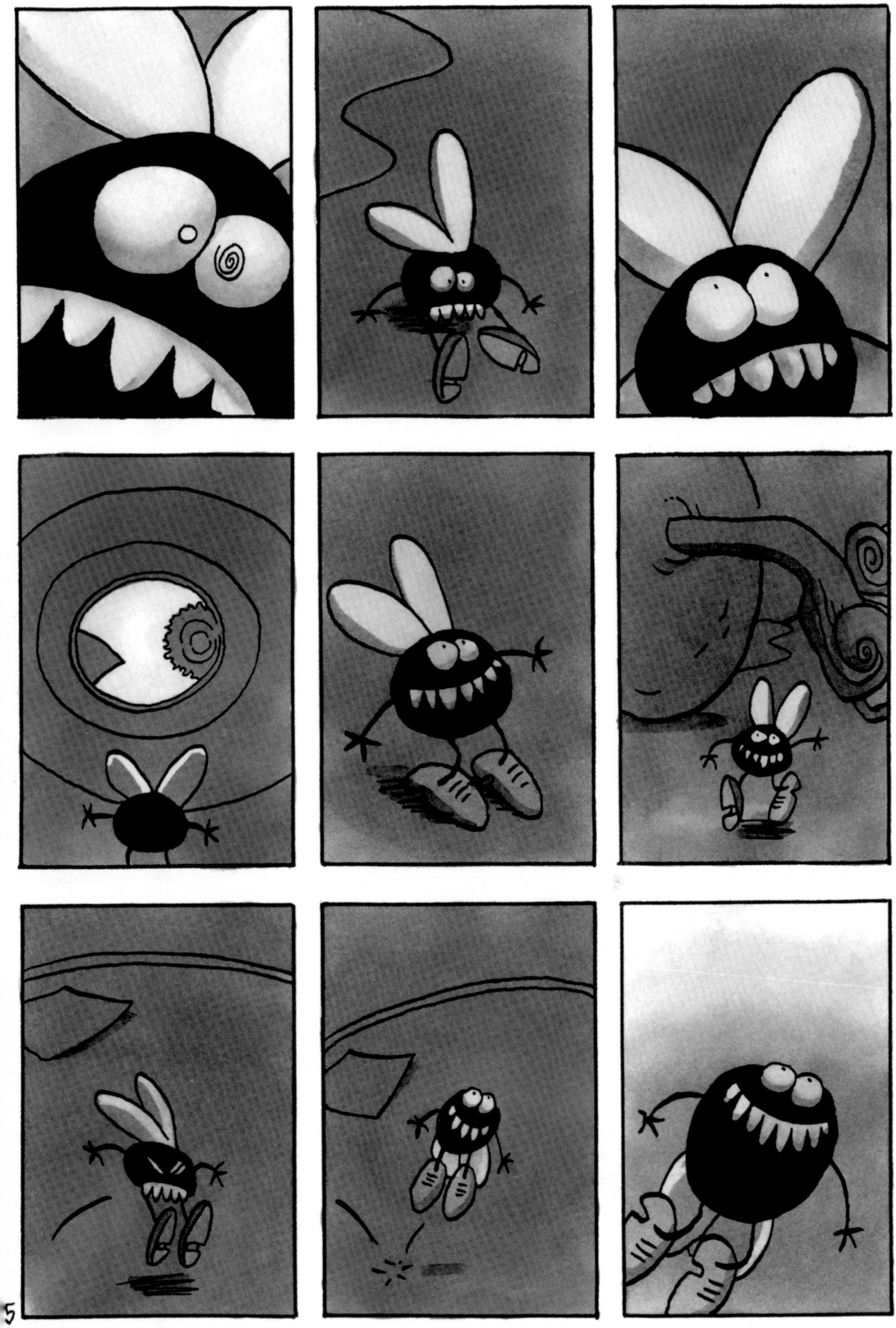

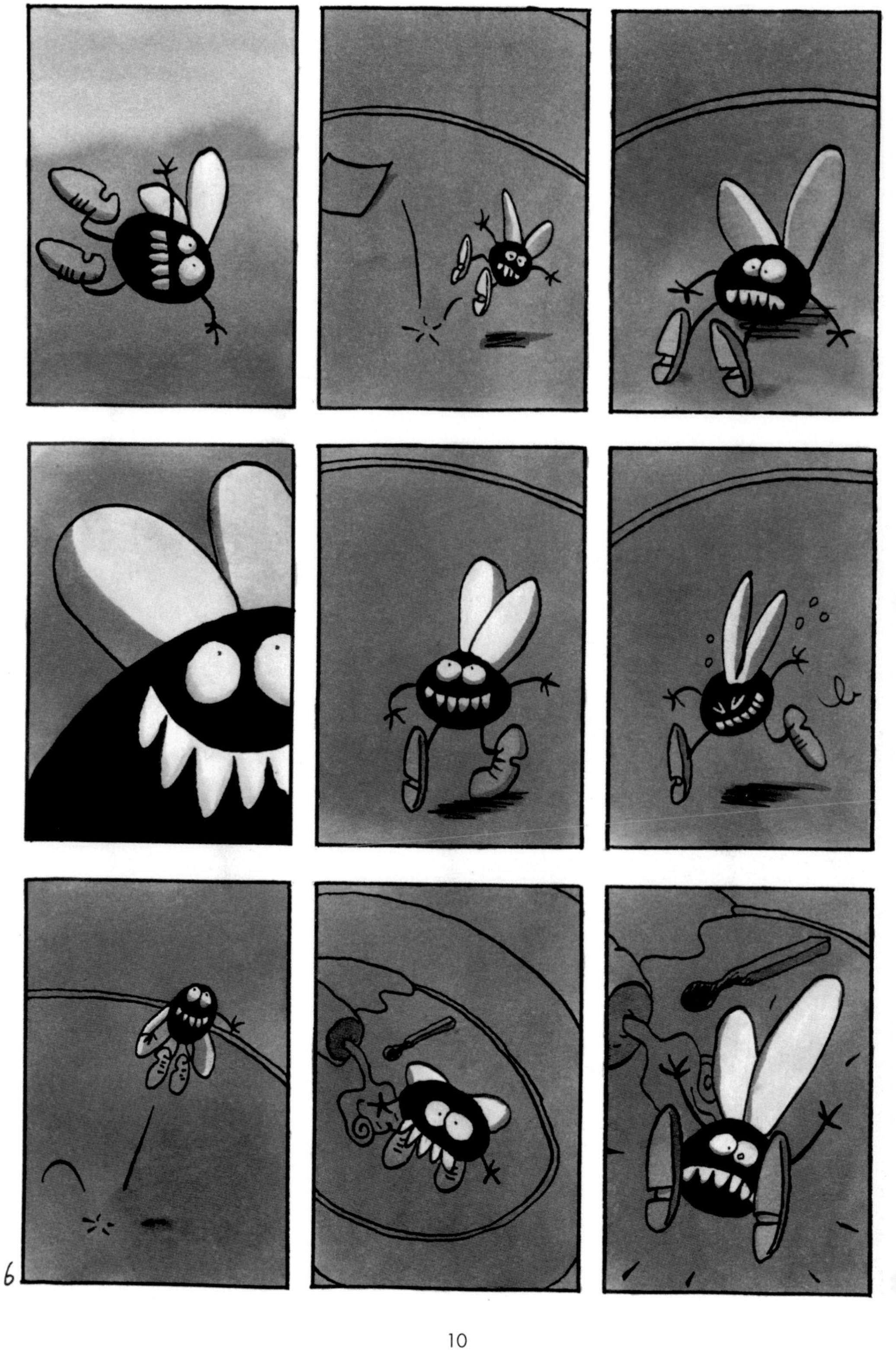

6

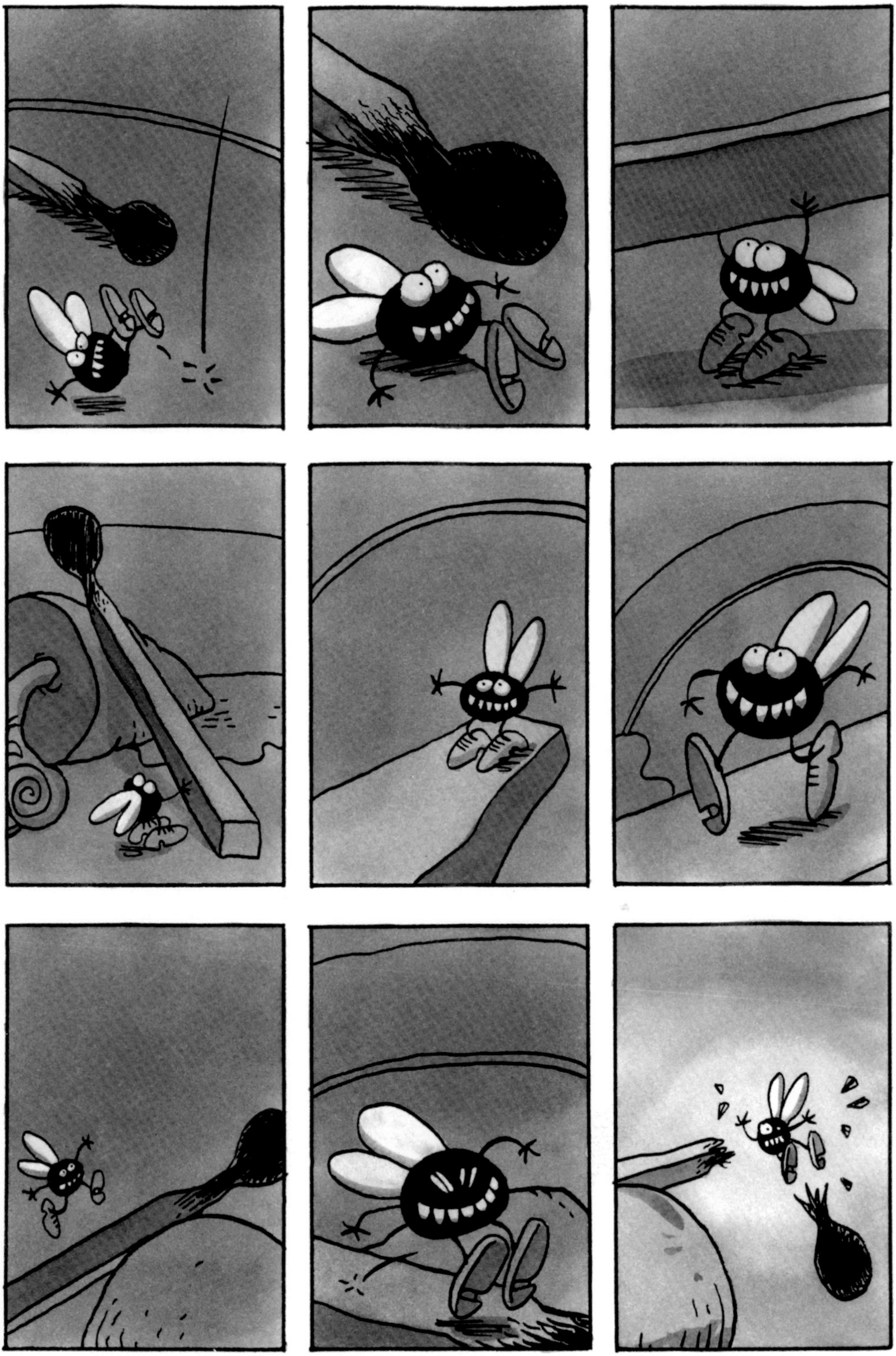

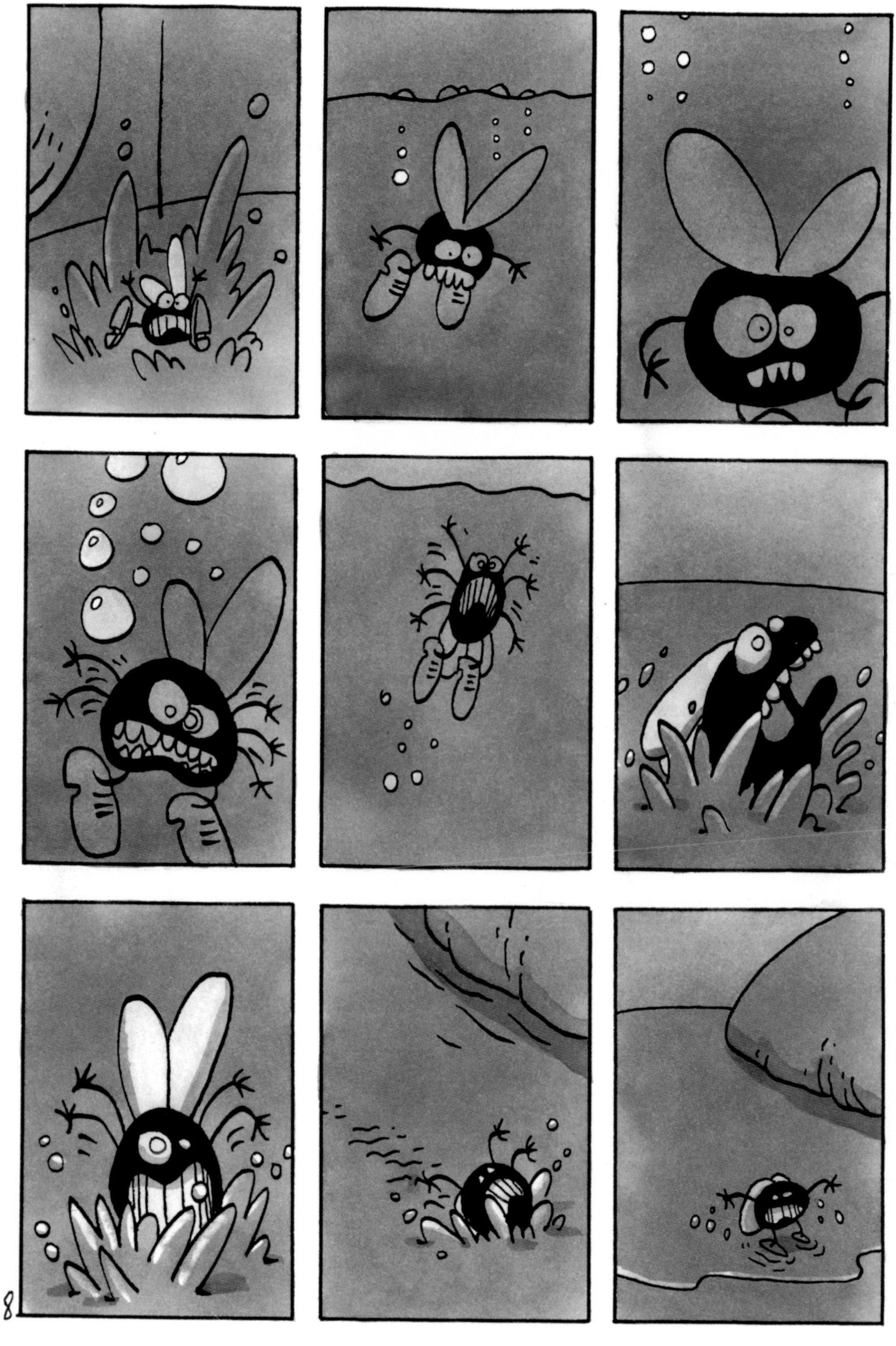

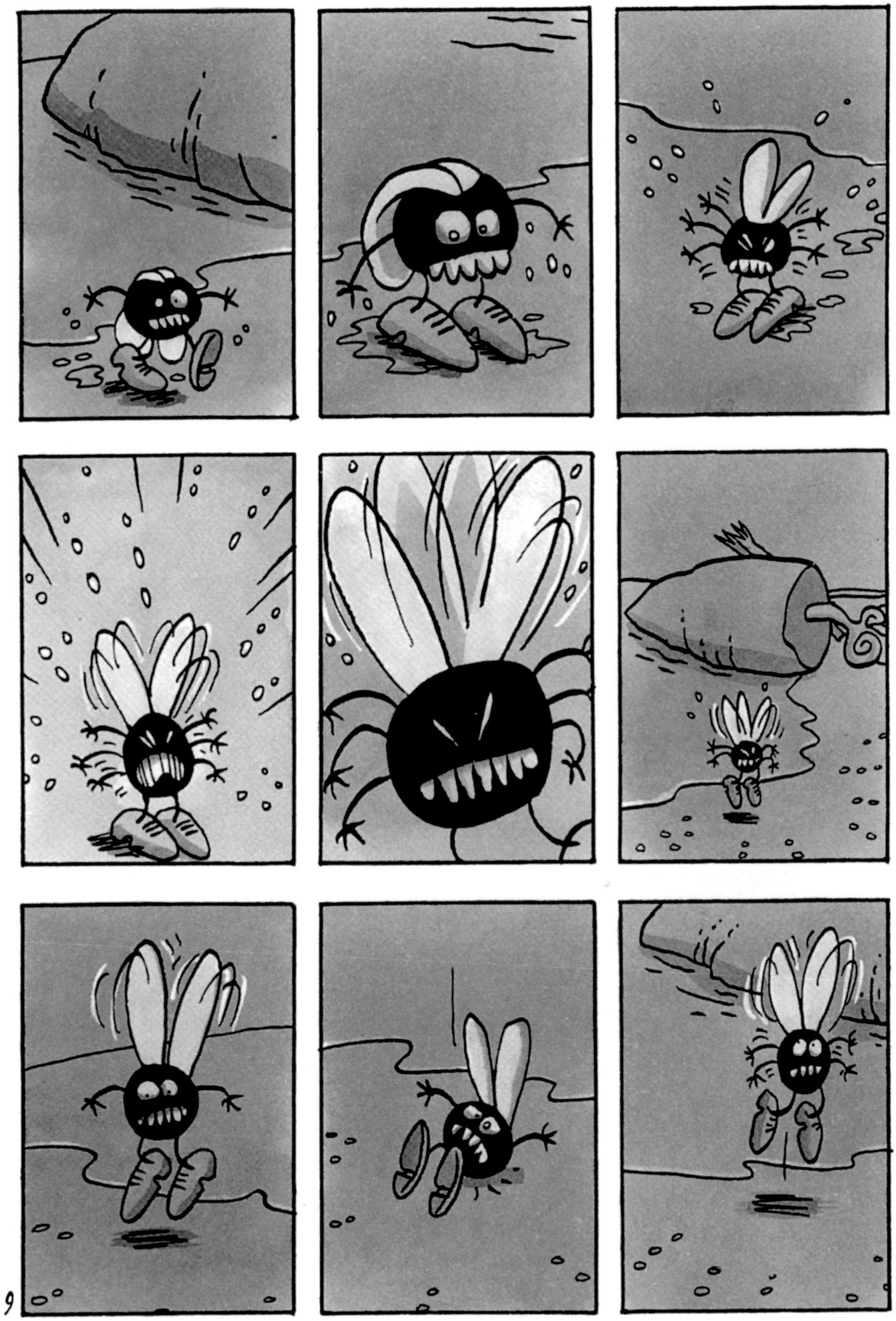

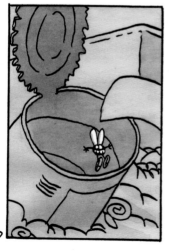

10

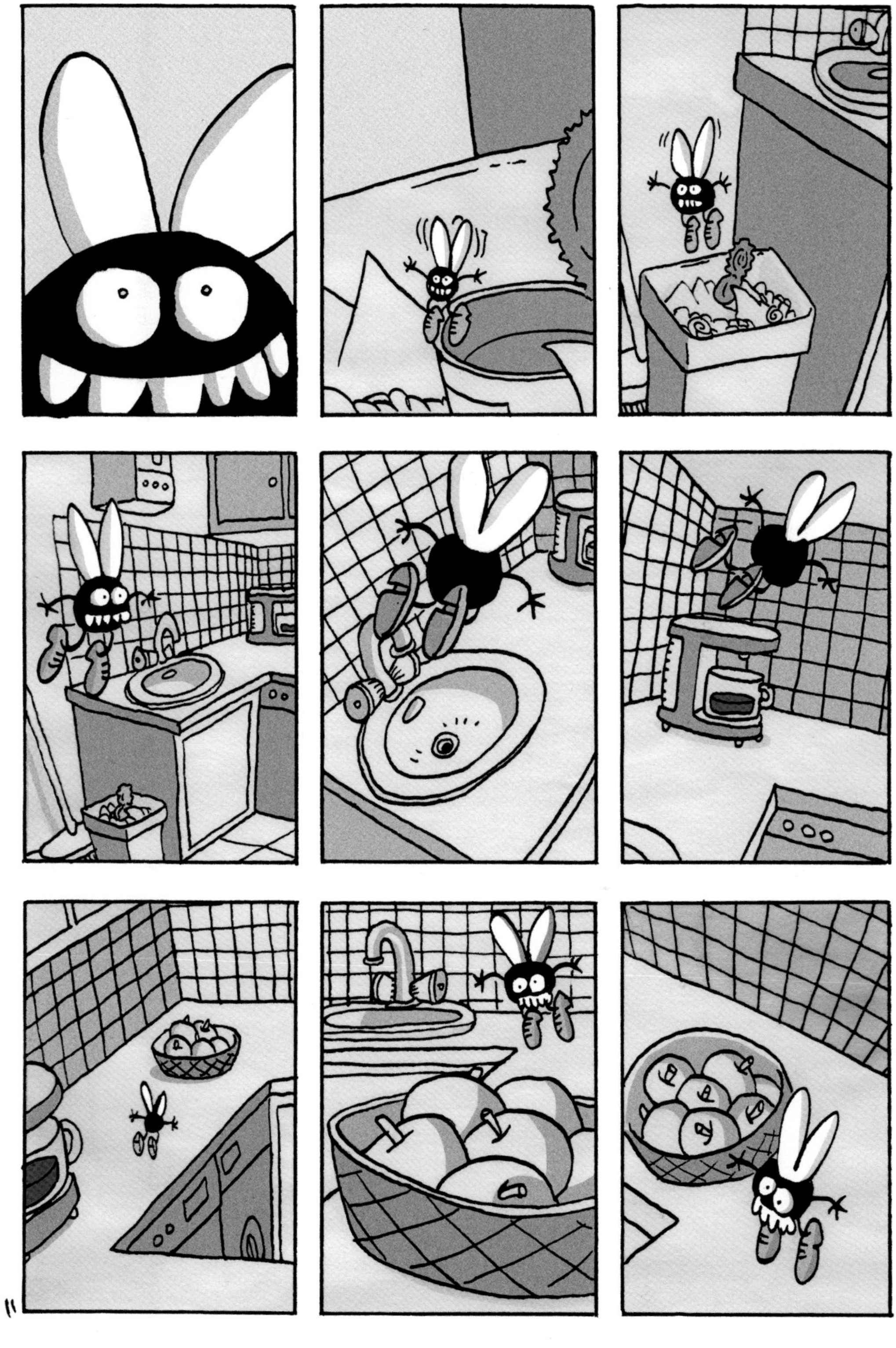

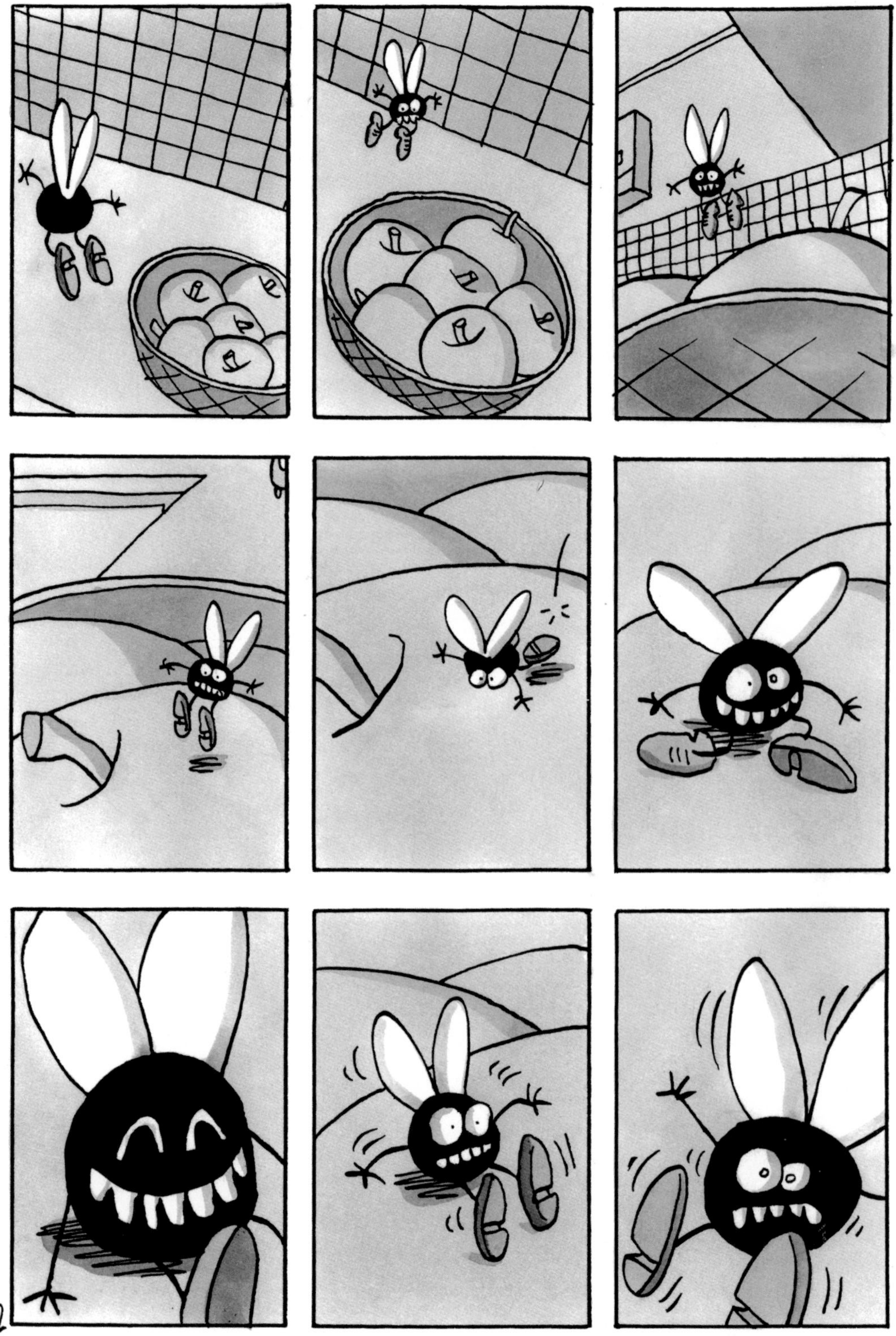

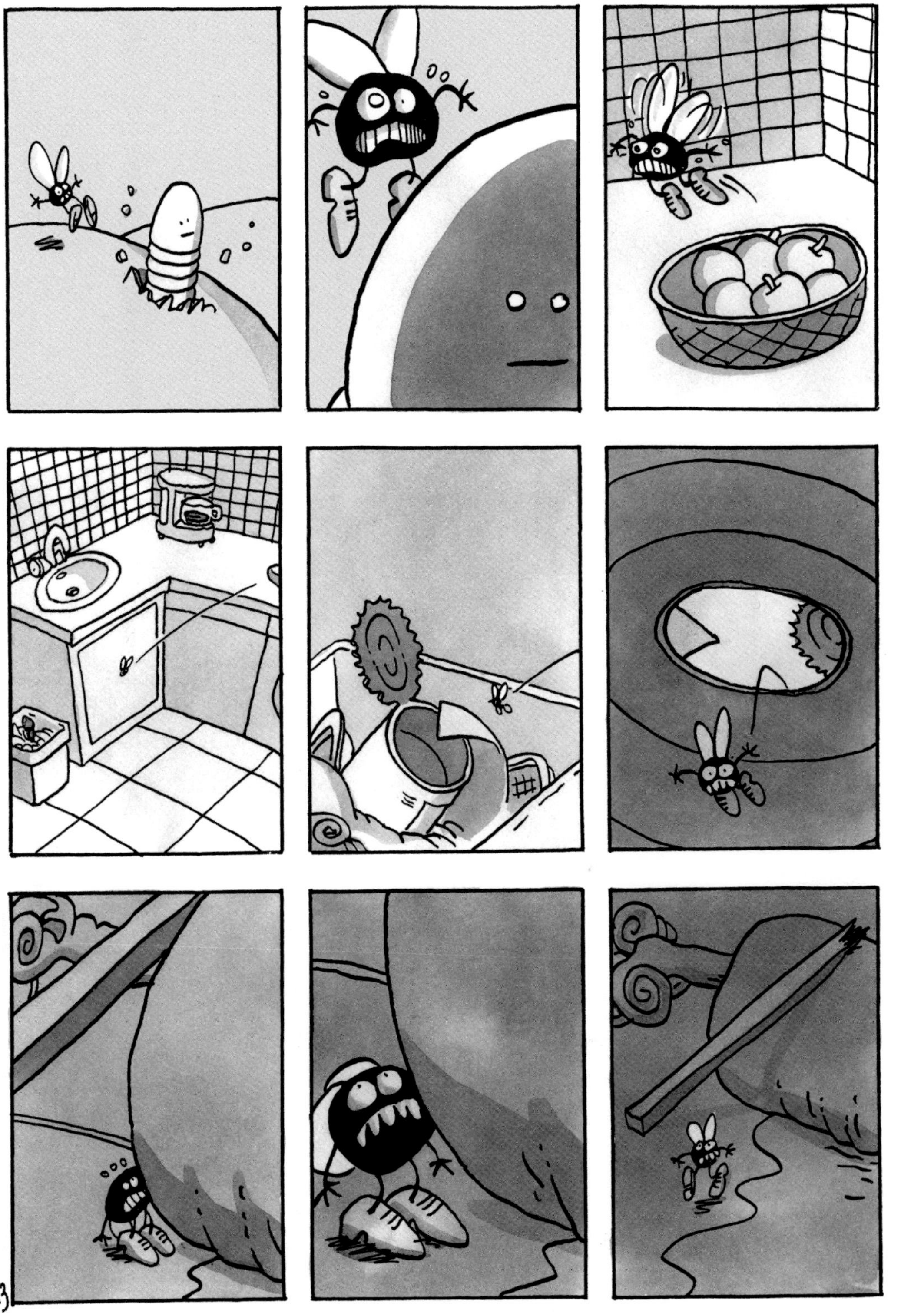

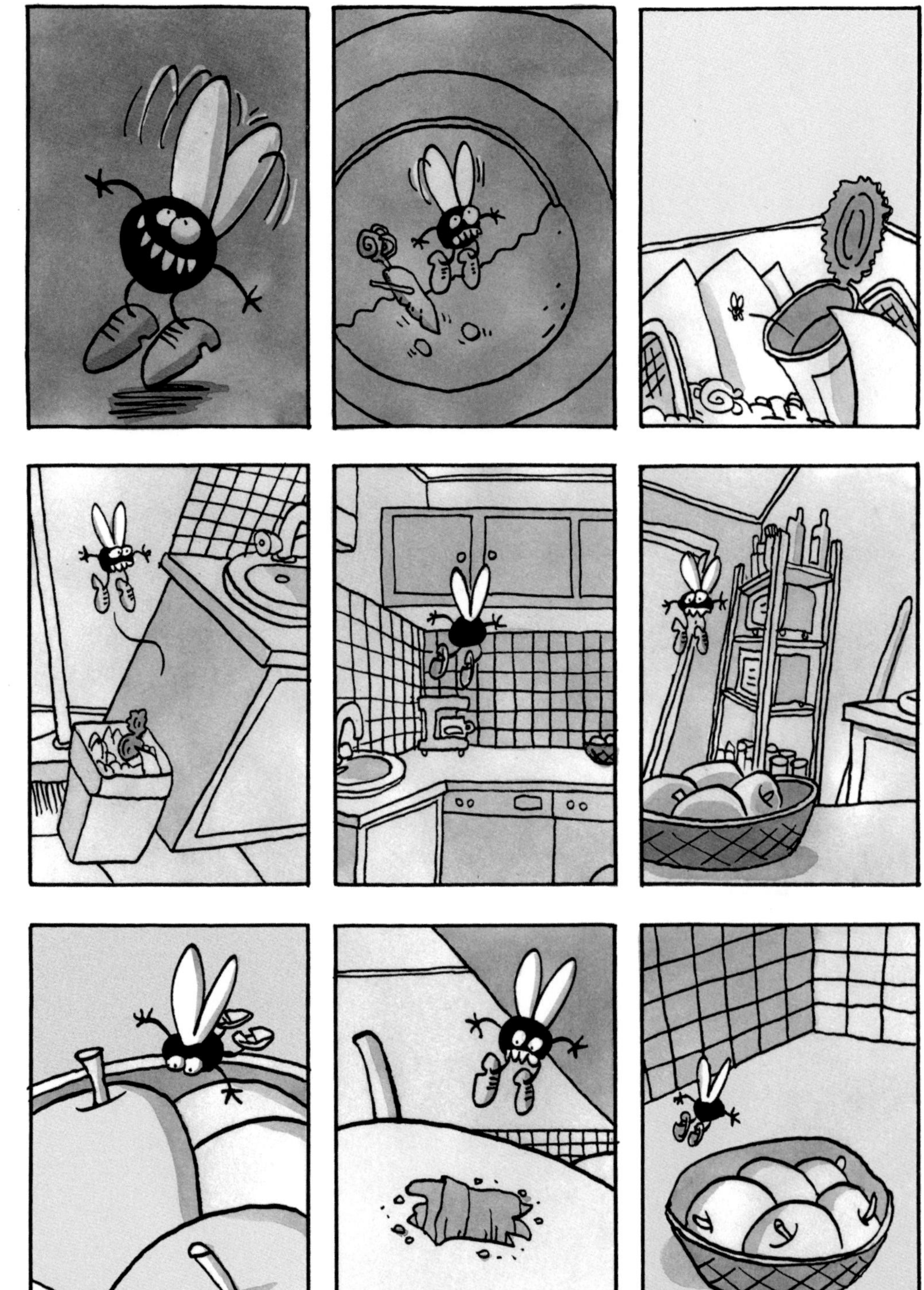
14

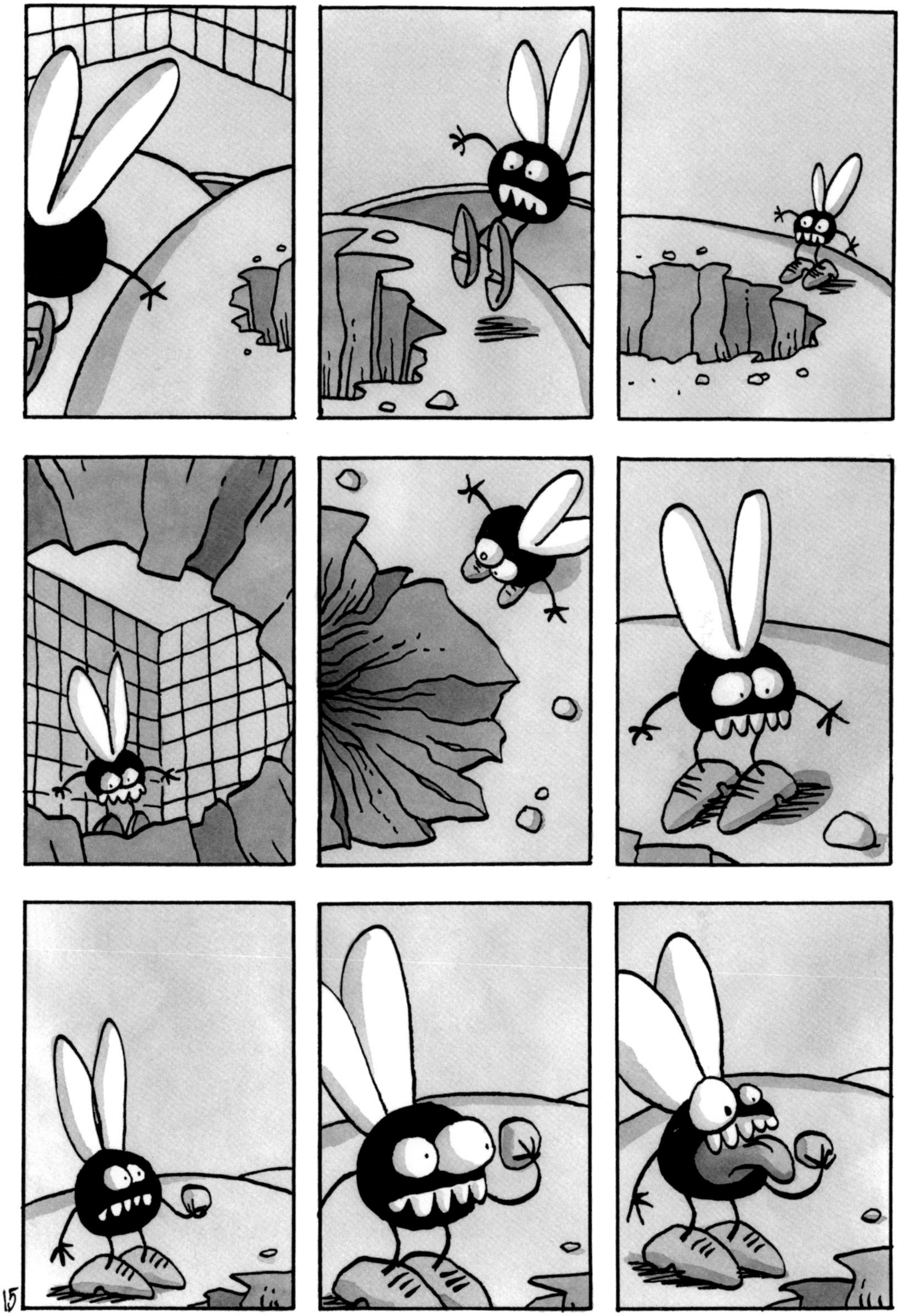

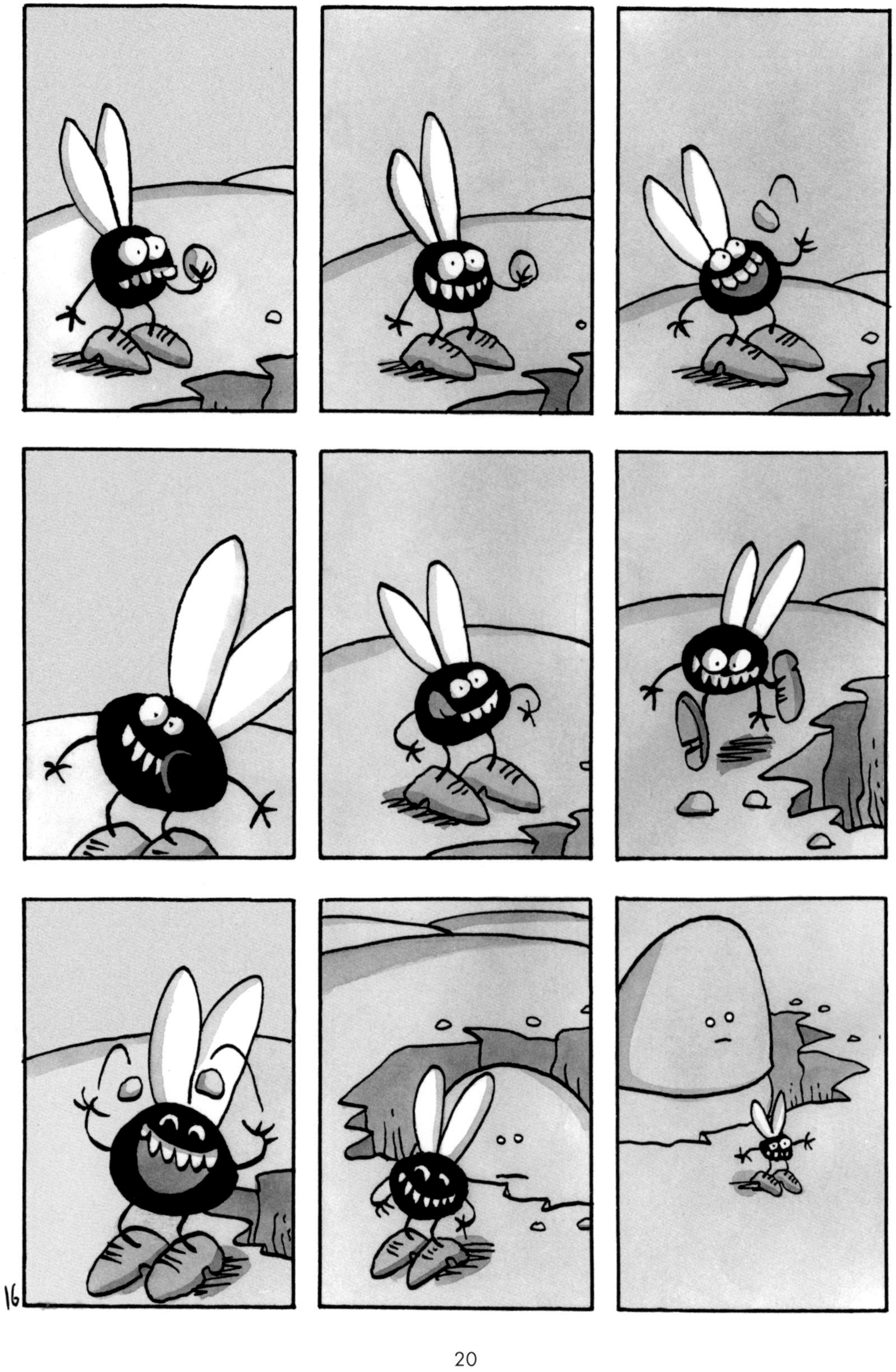
16

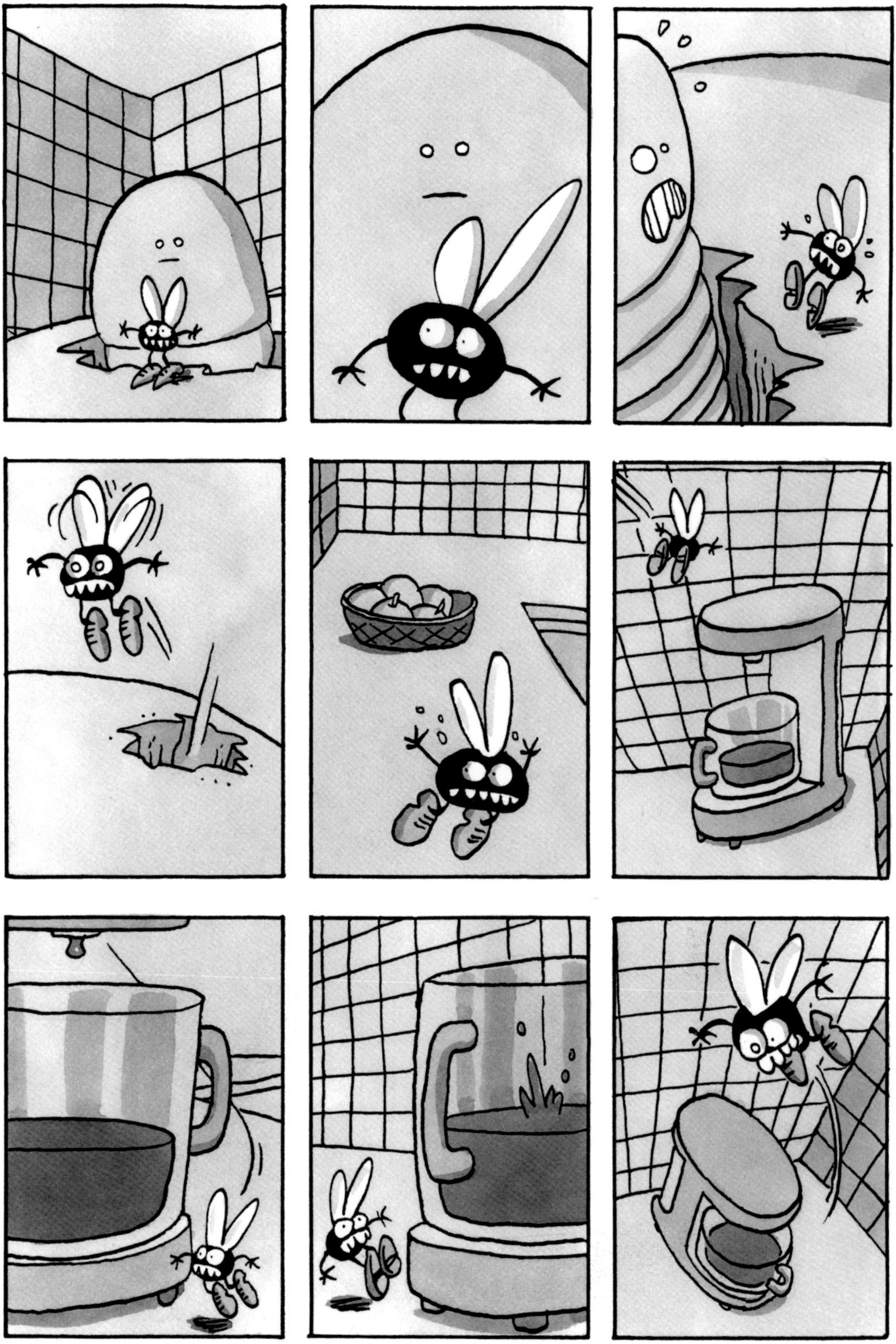

17

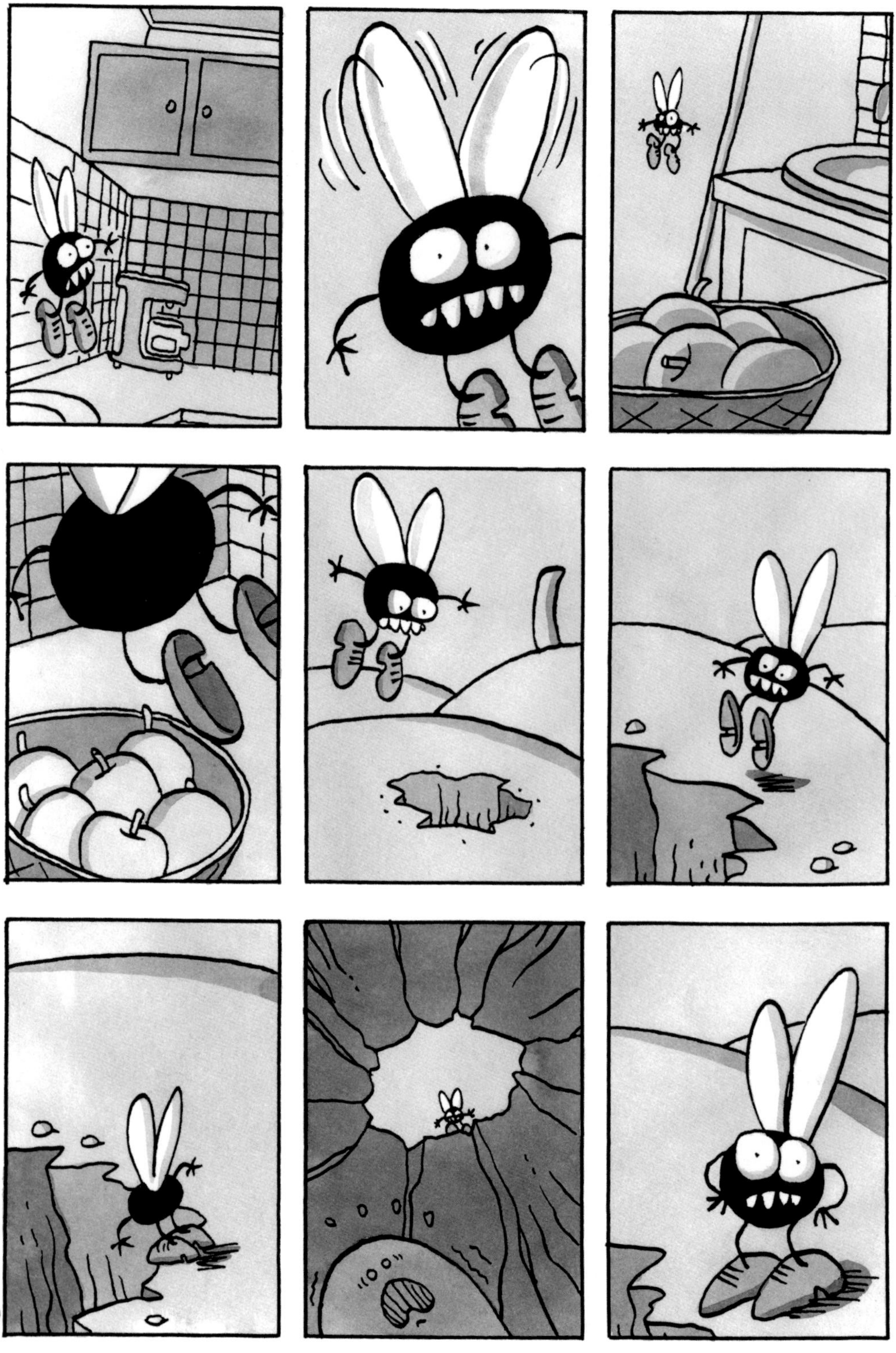

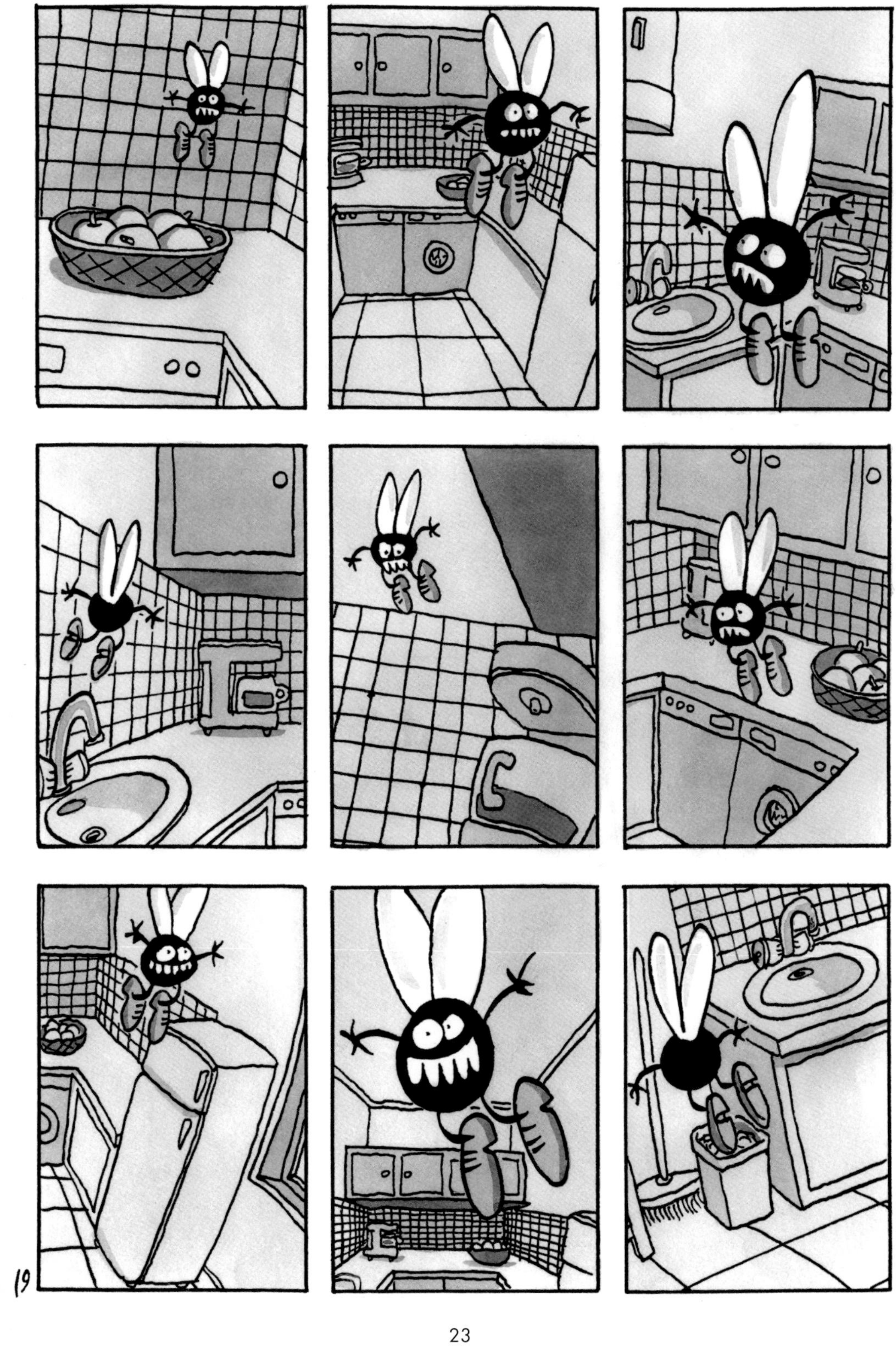

19

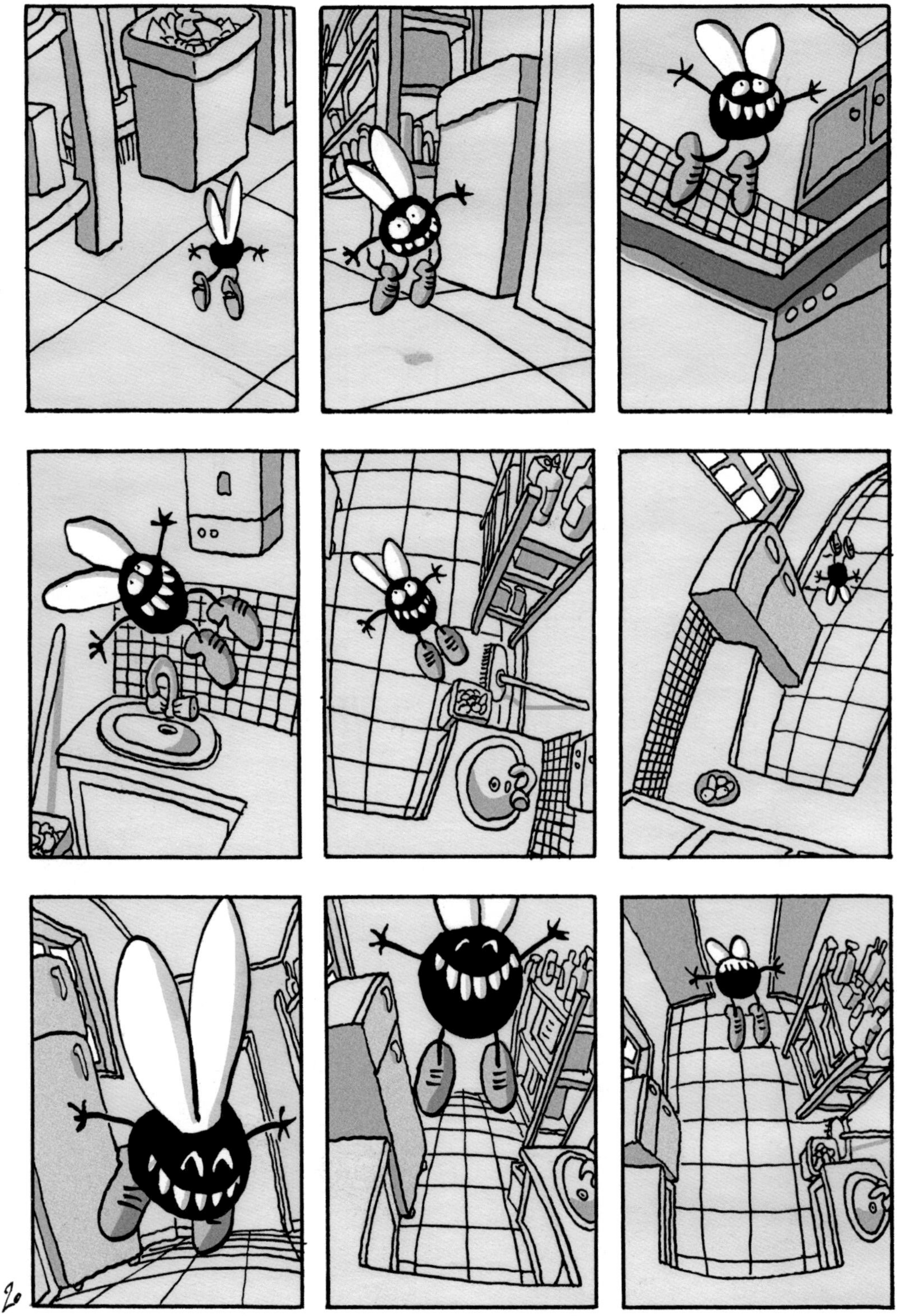

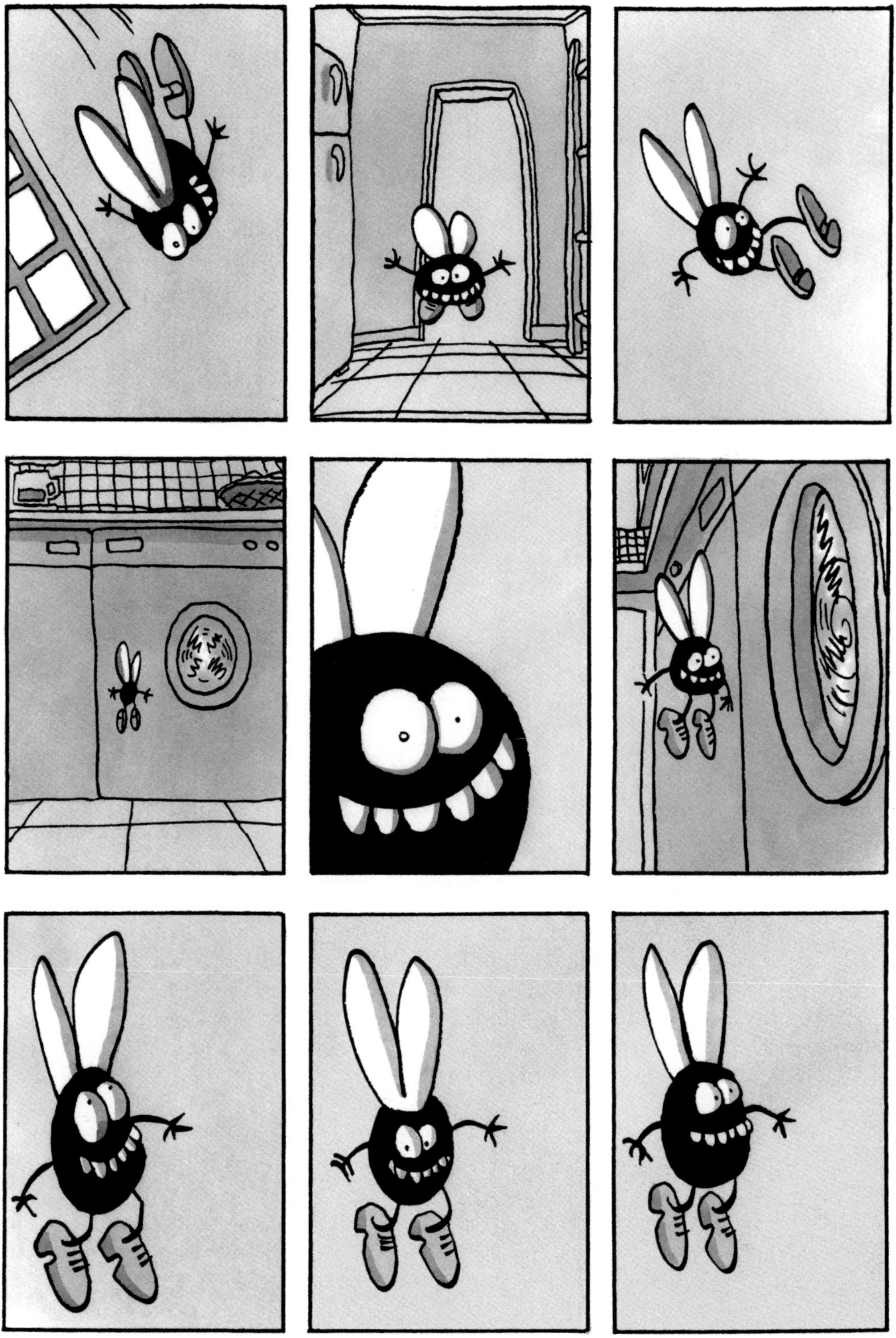

21

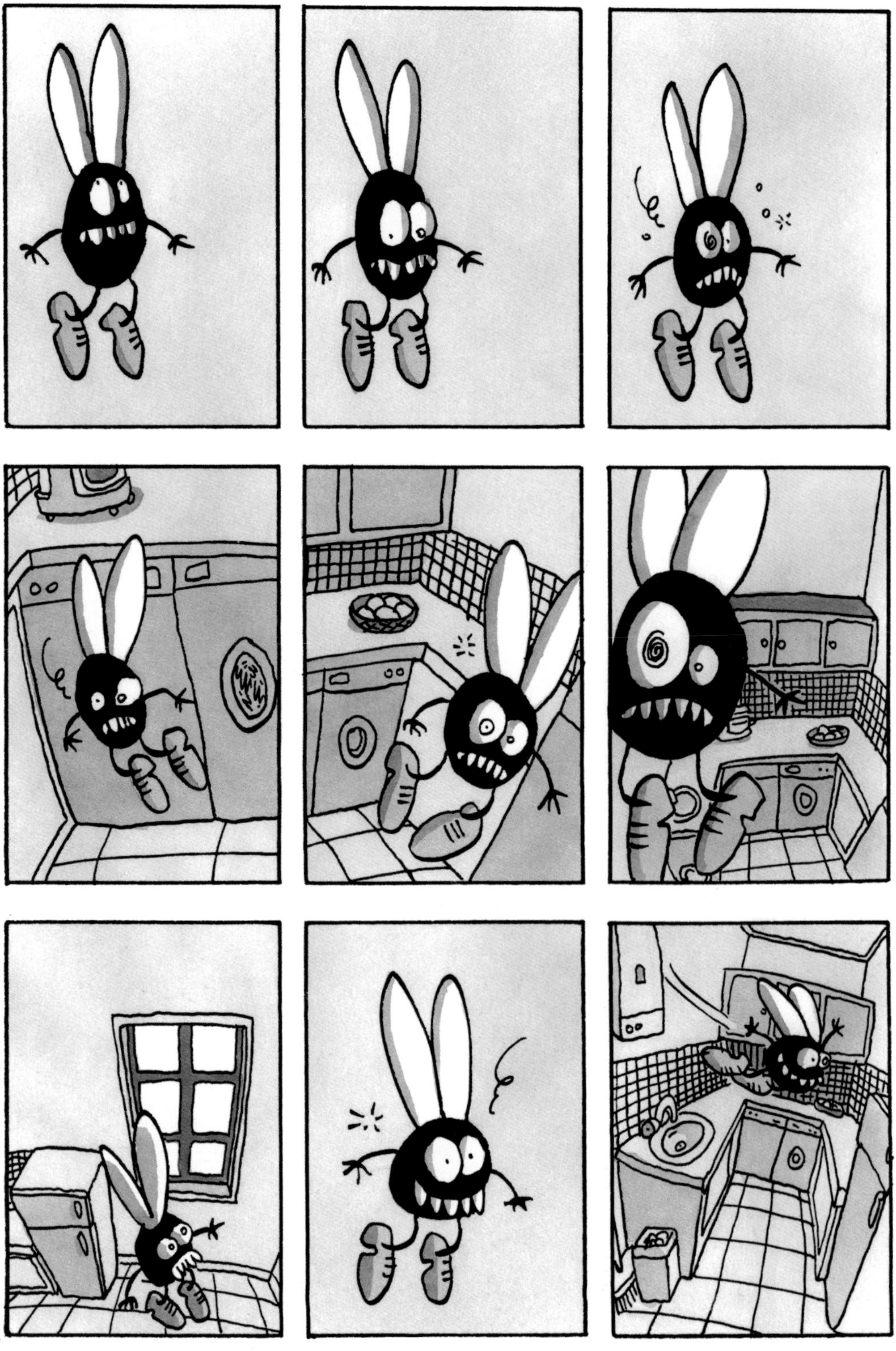

22

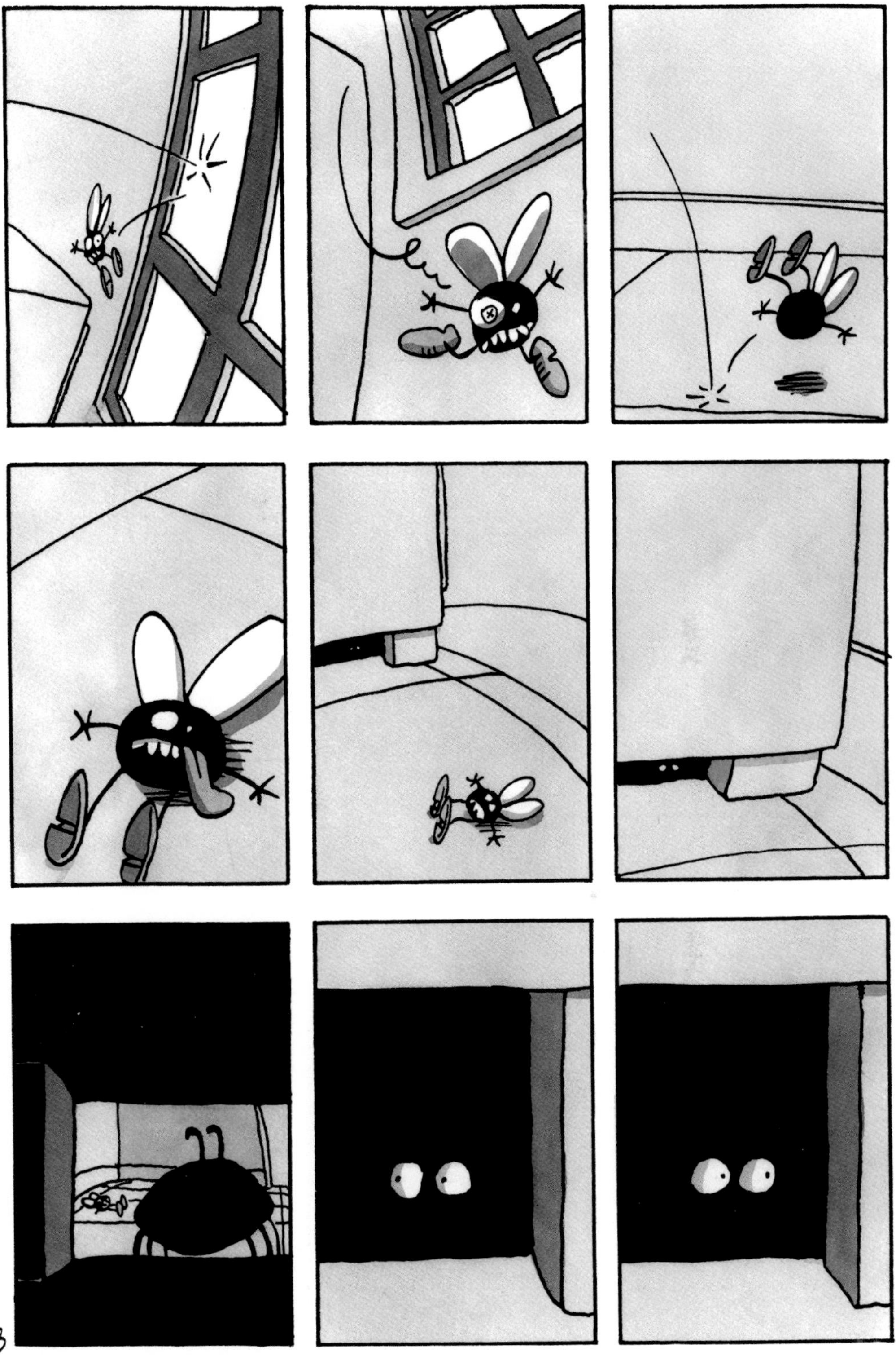

23

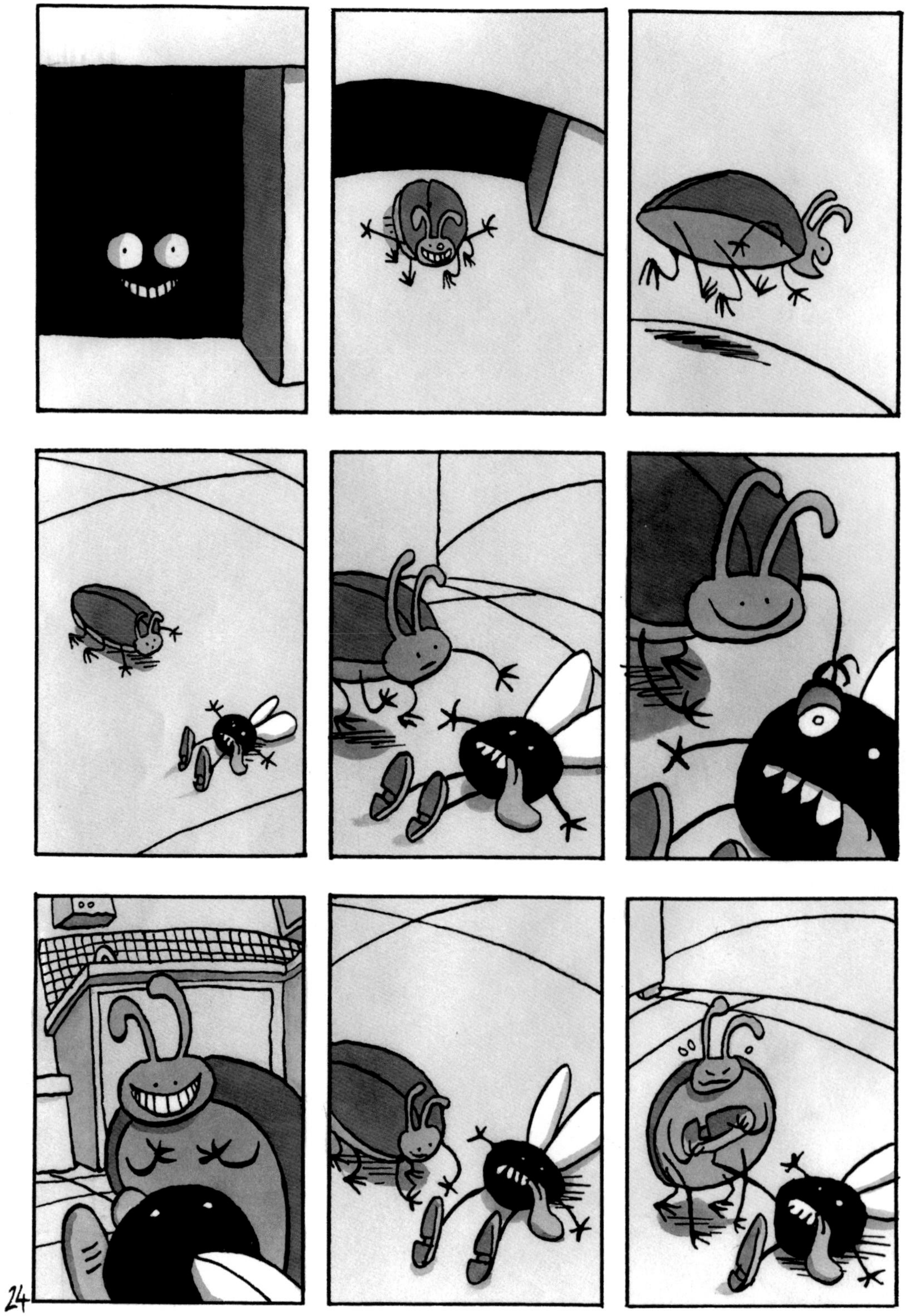
24

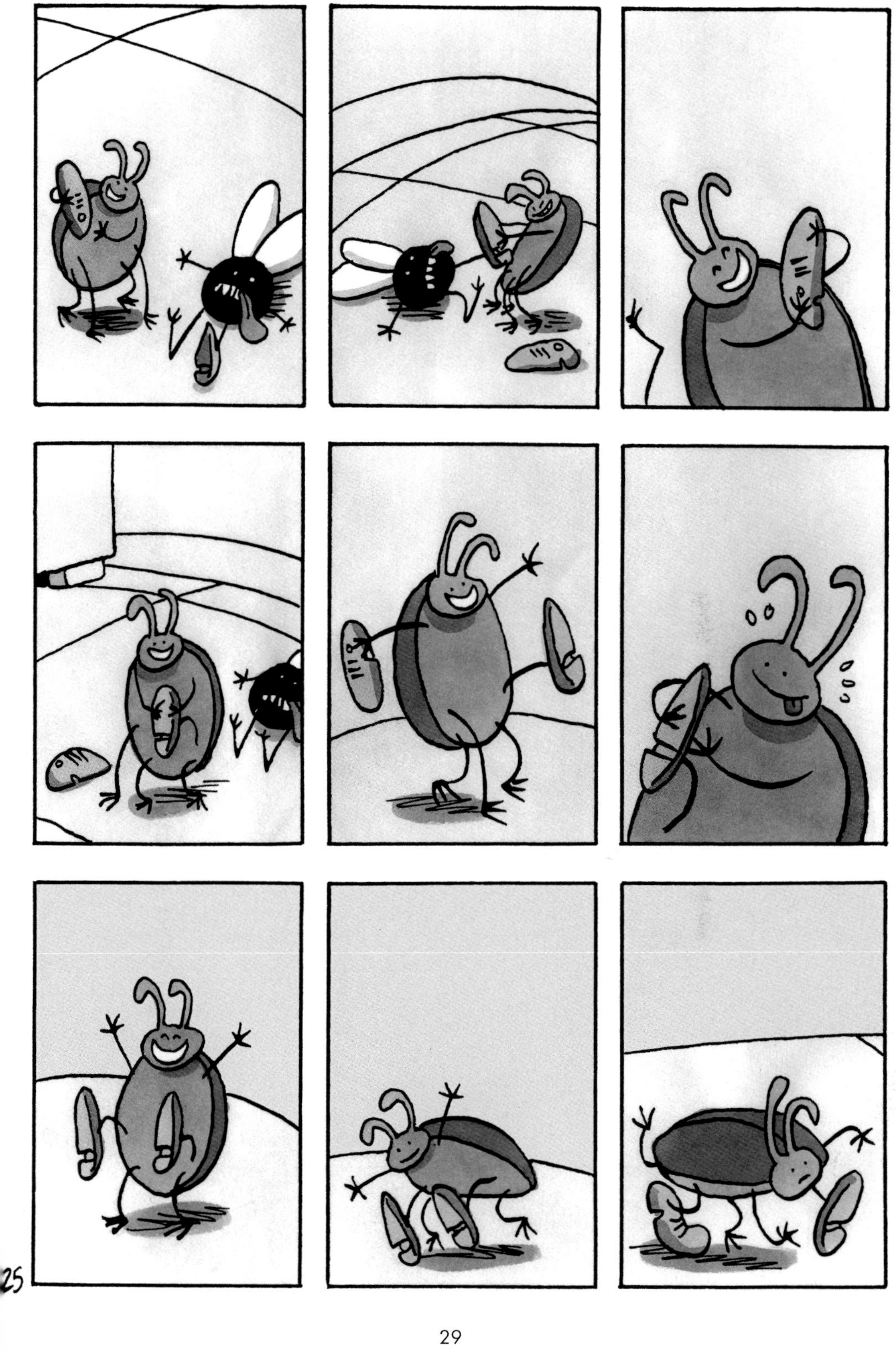

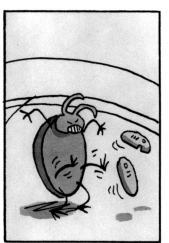

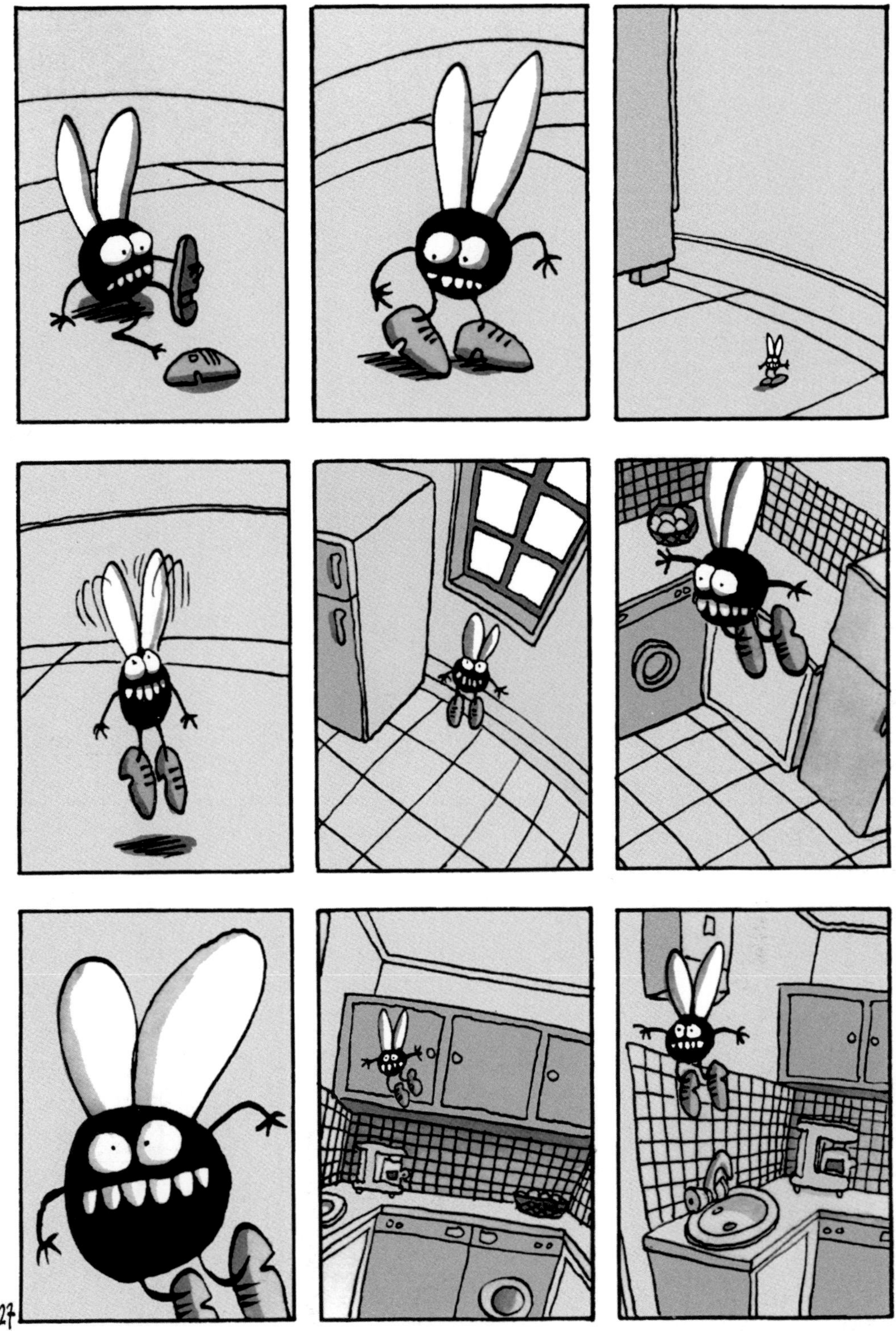
27

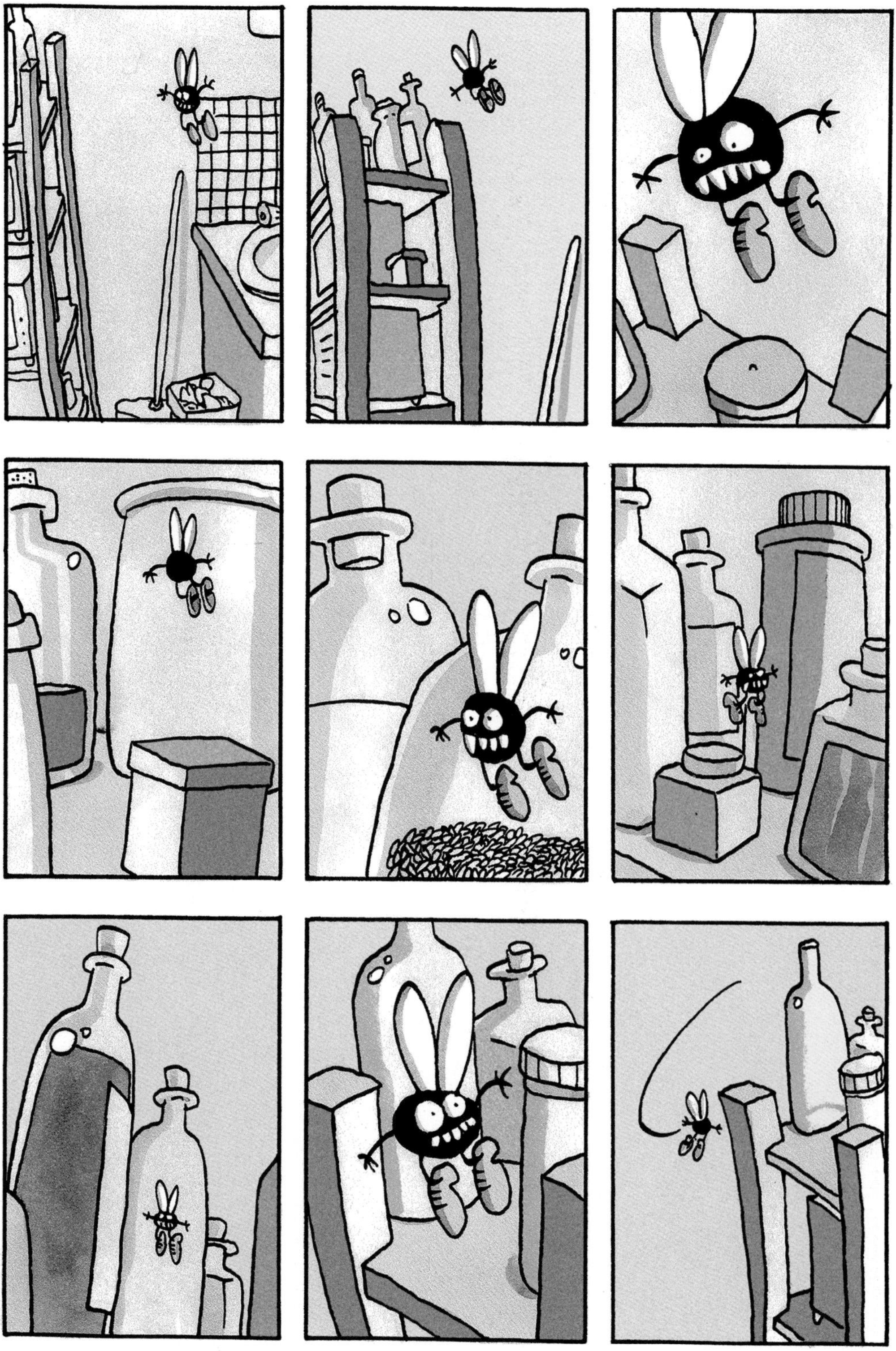

28

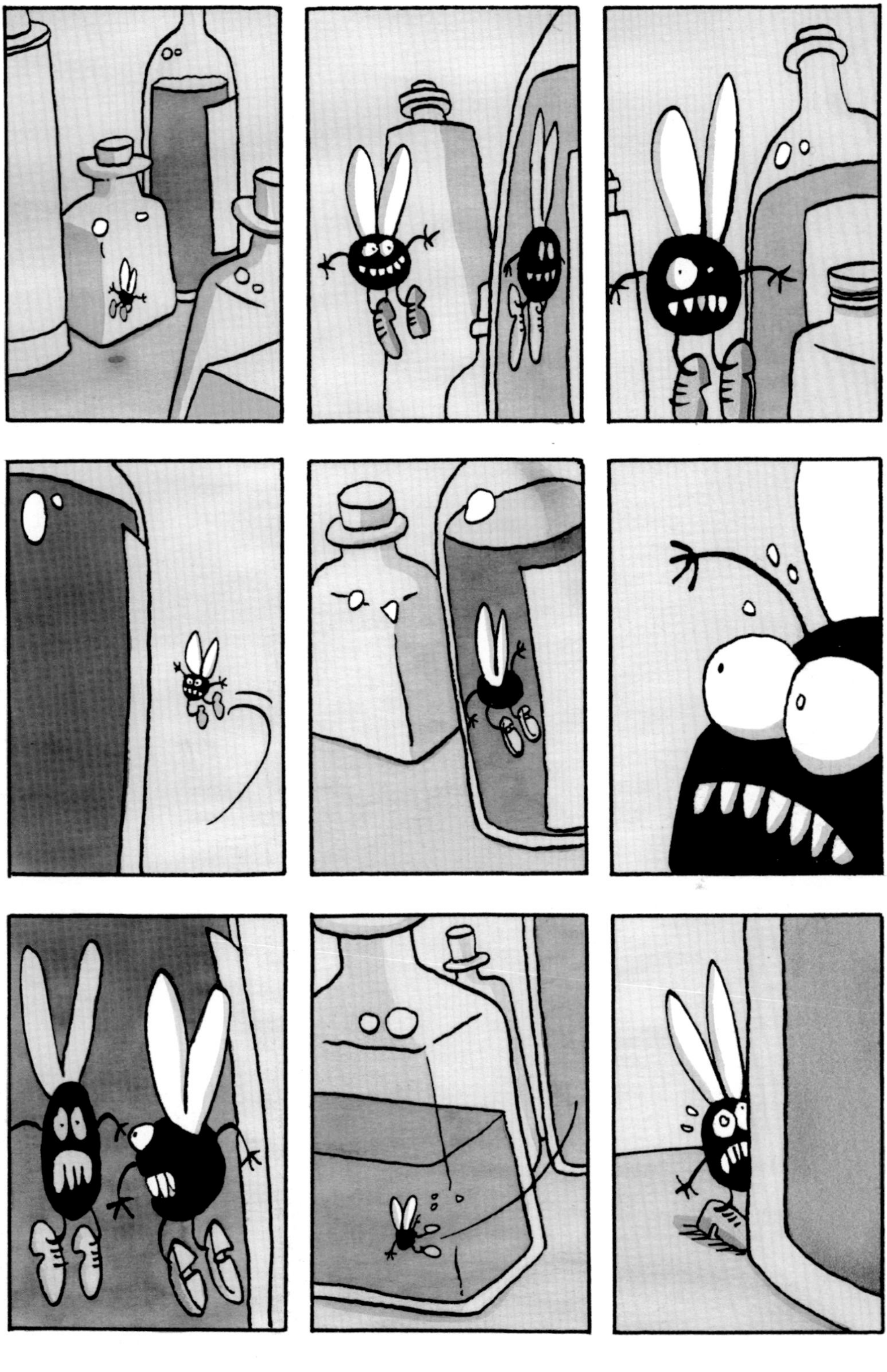

29

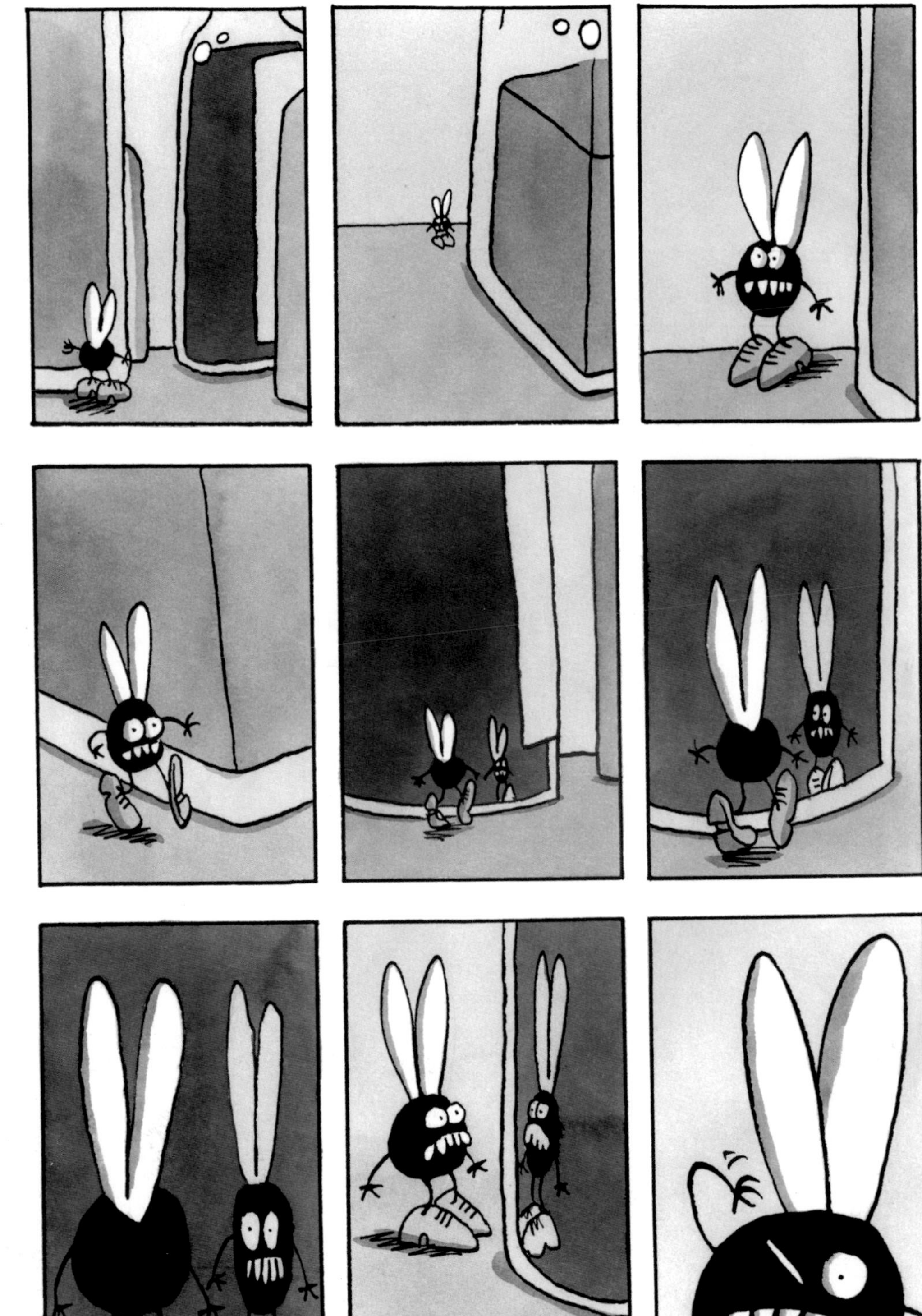
30

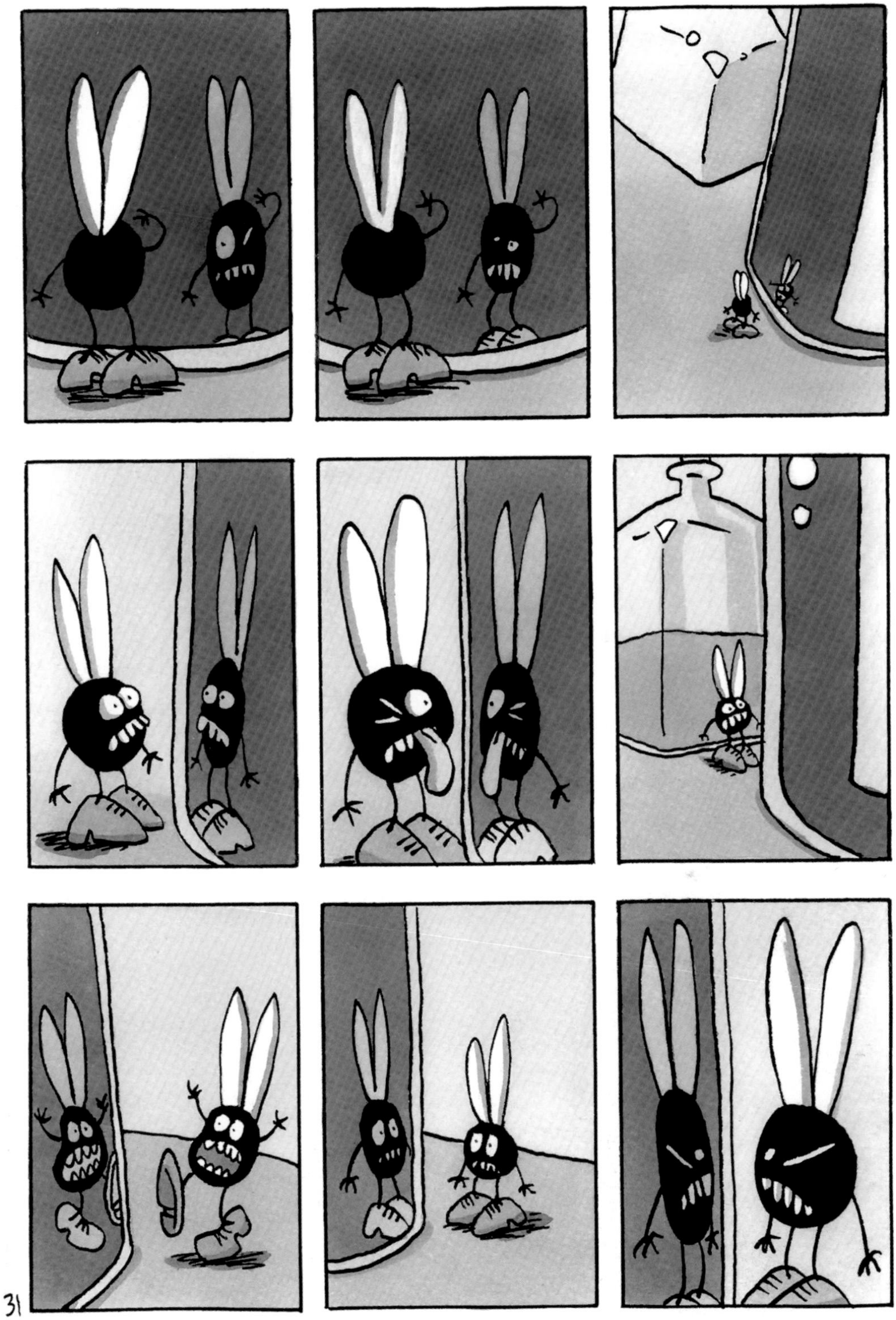

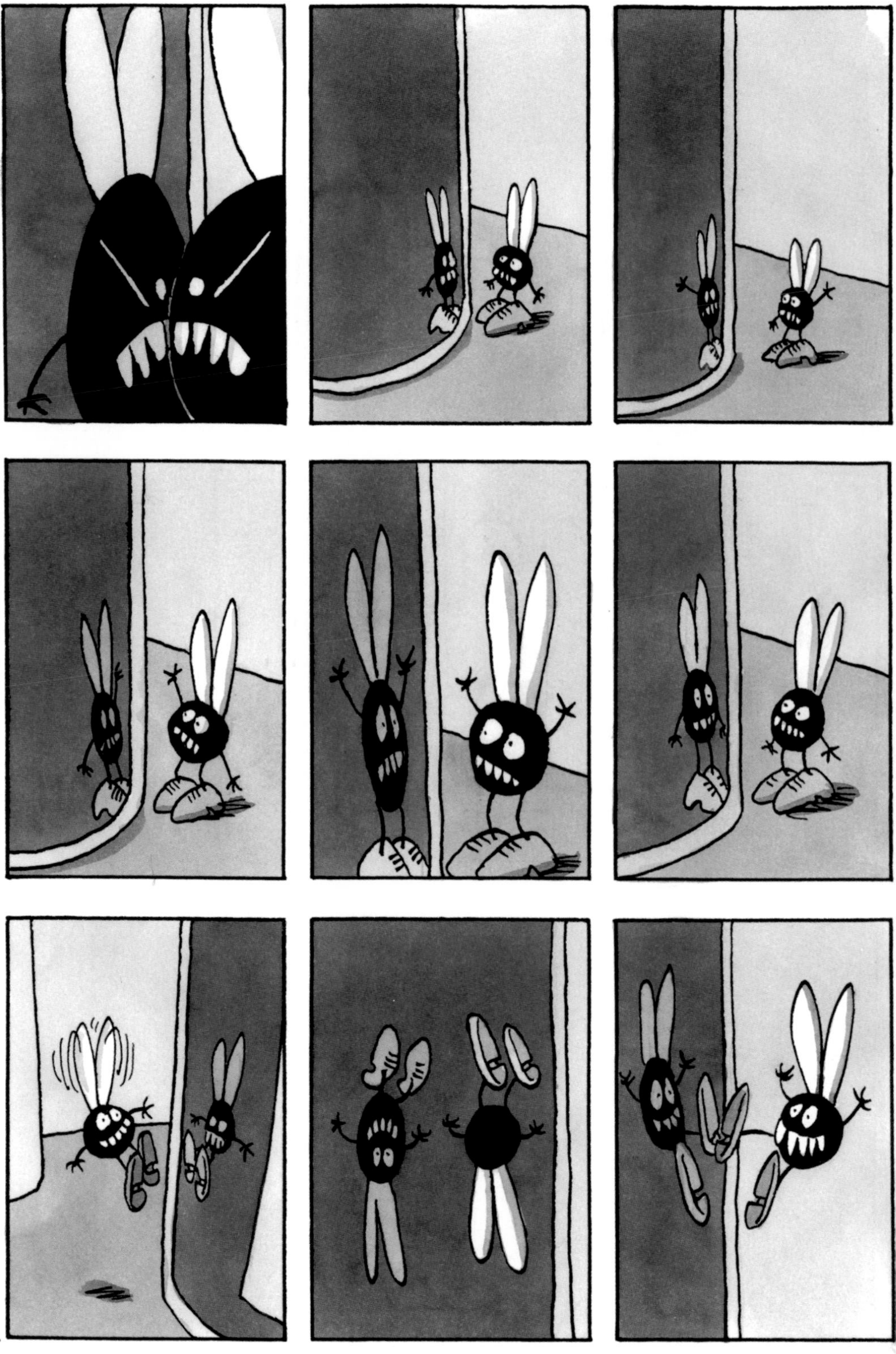
32

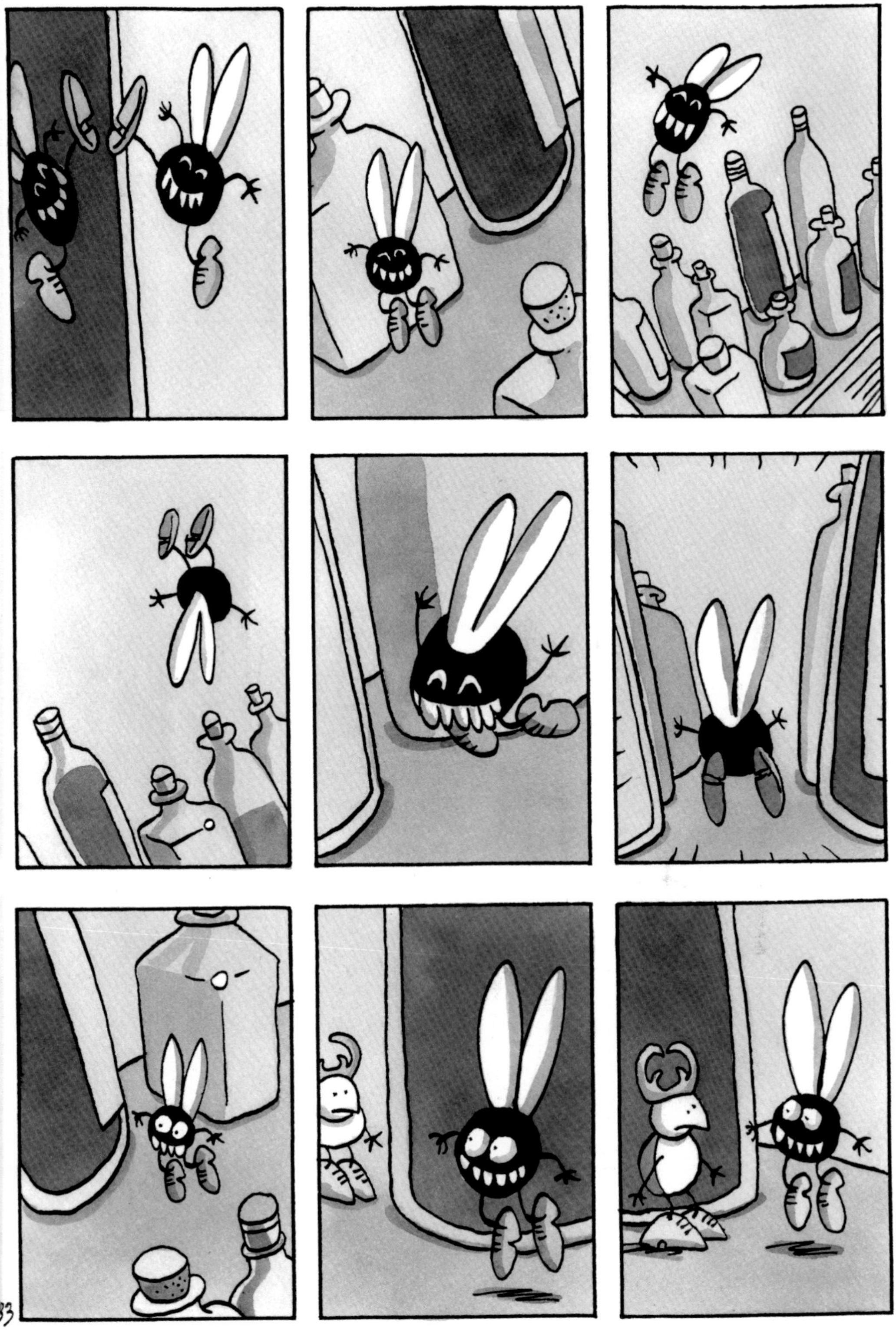

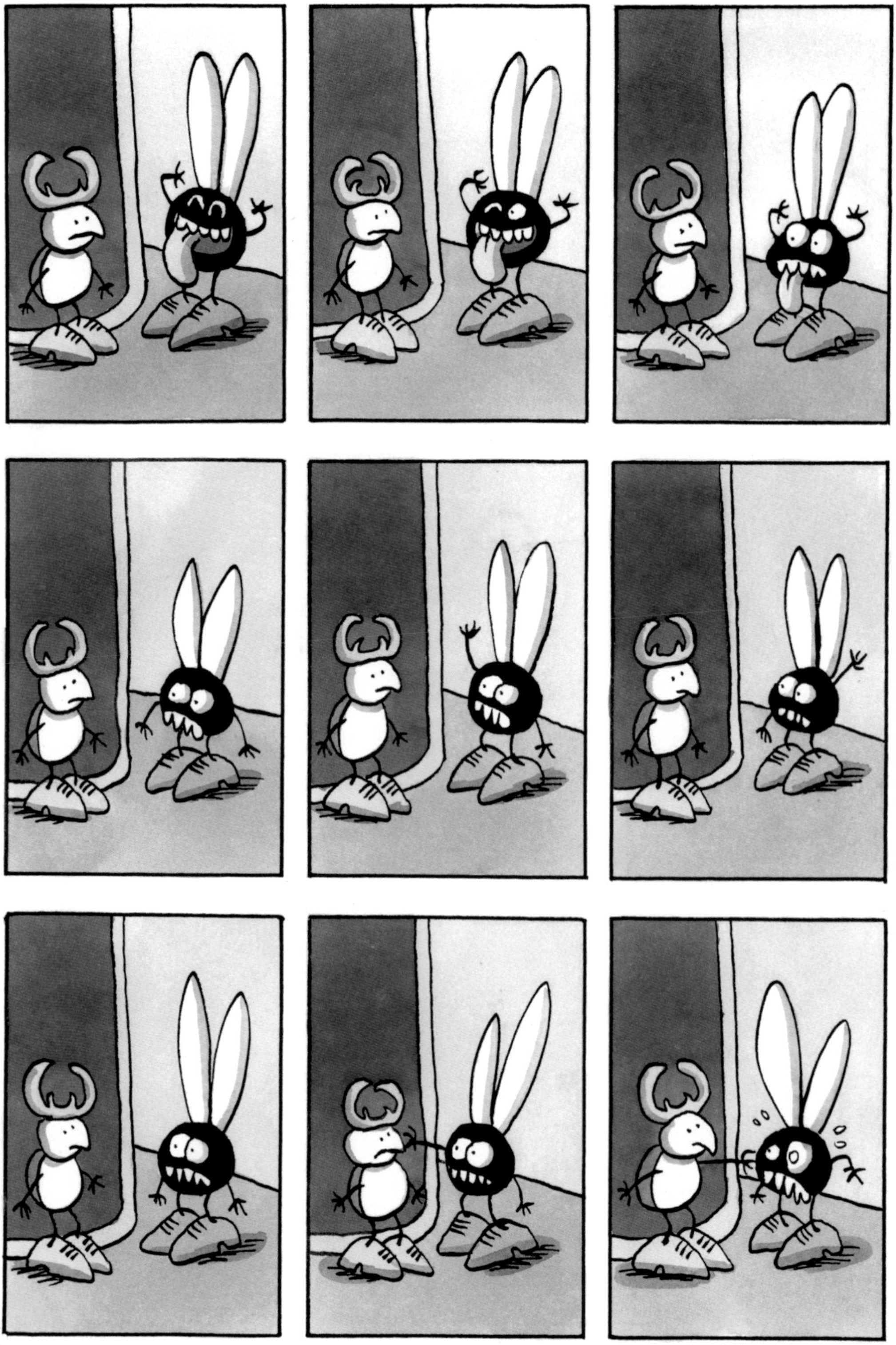

34

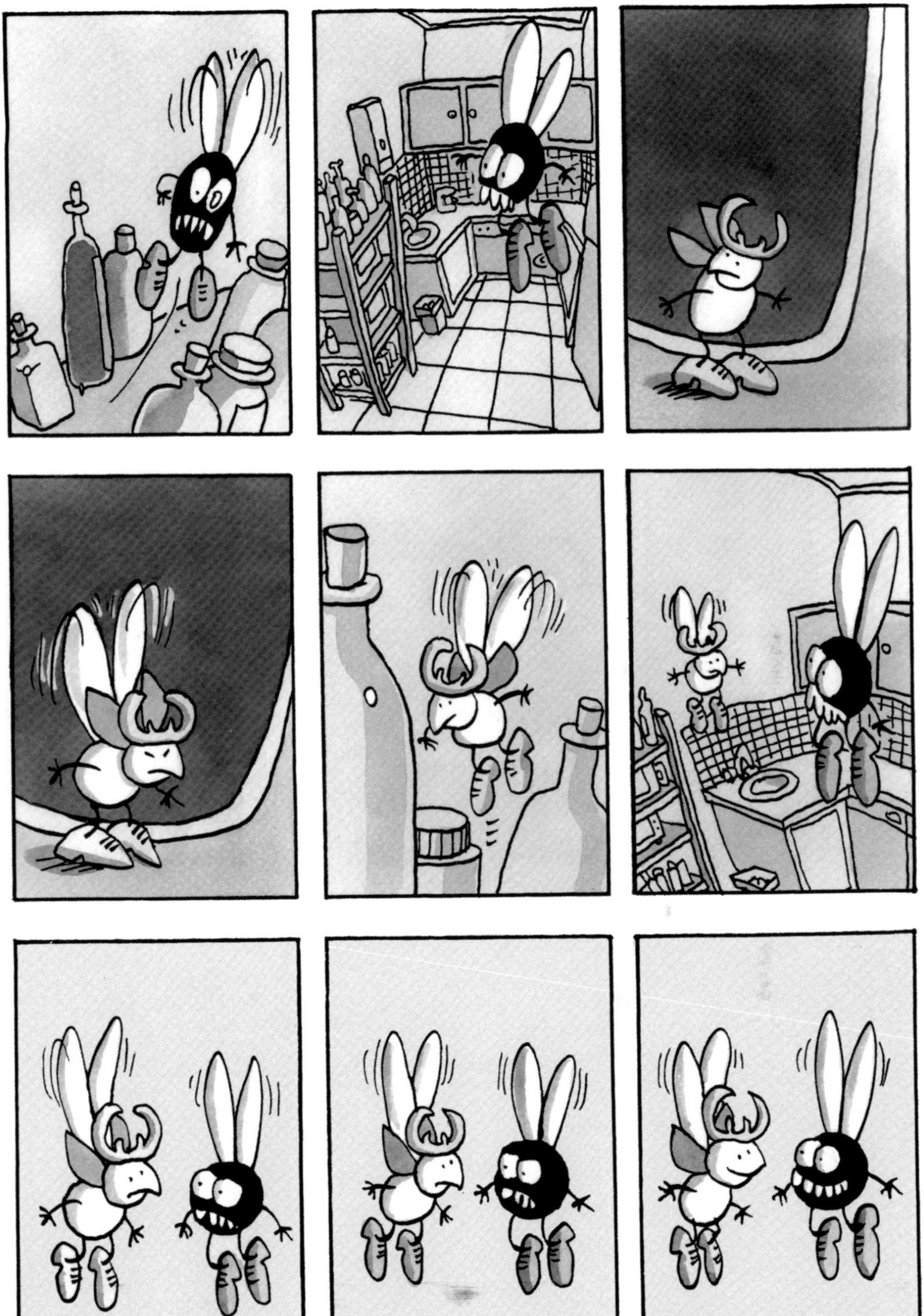

35

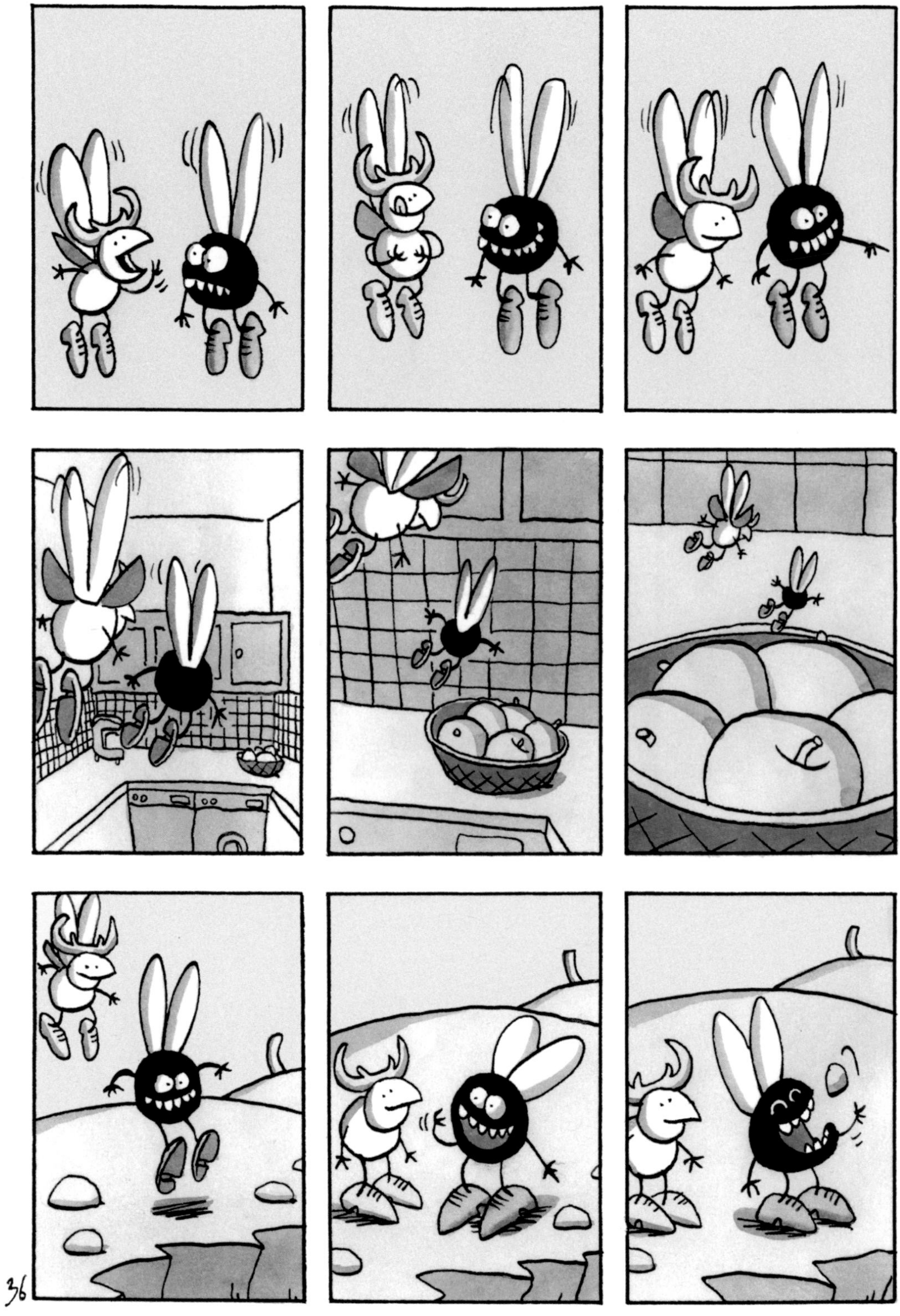
36

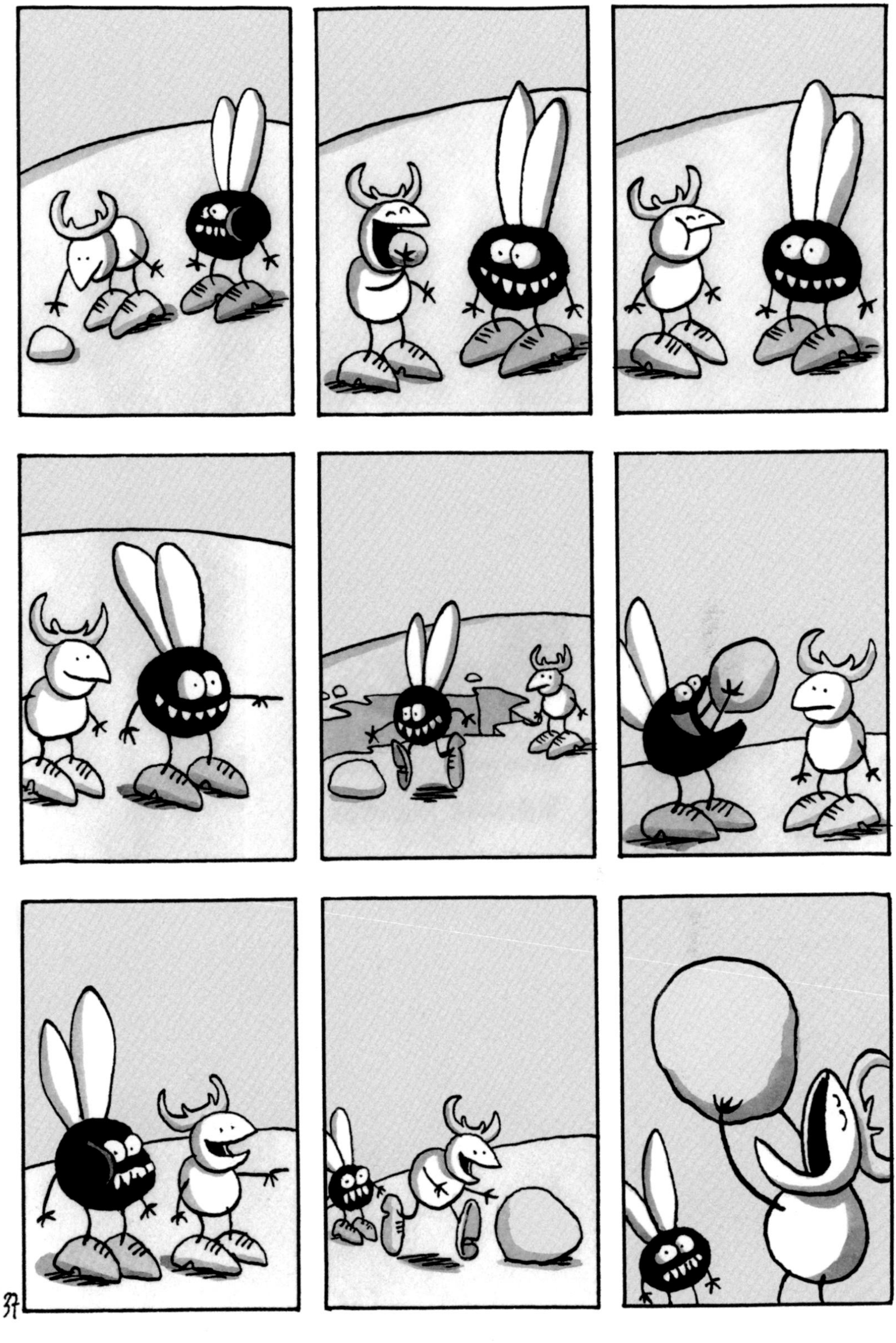

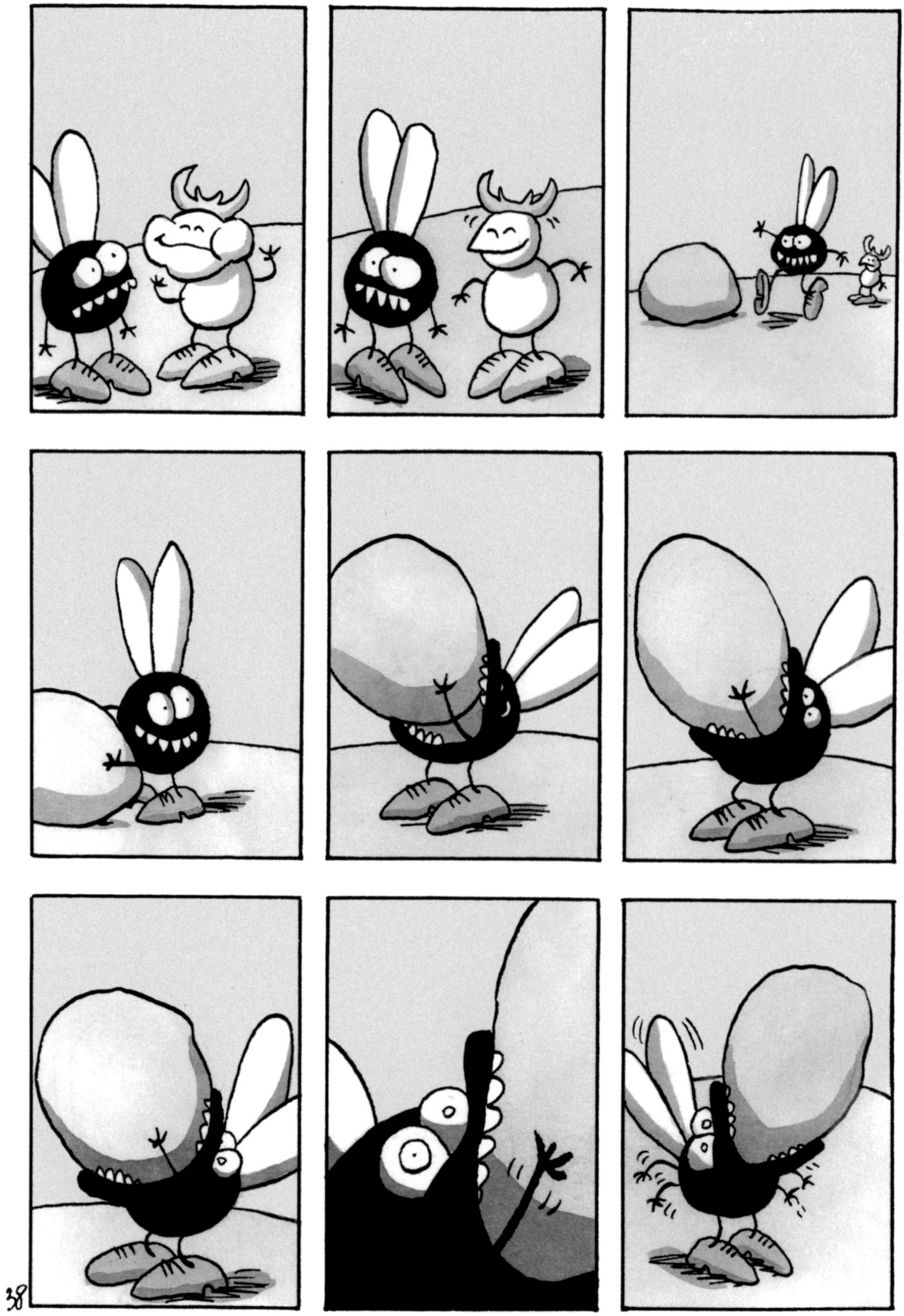
38

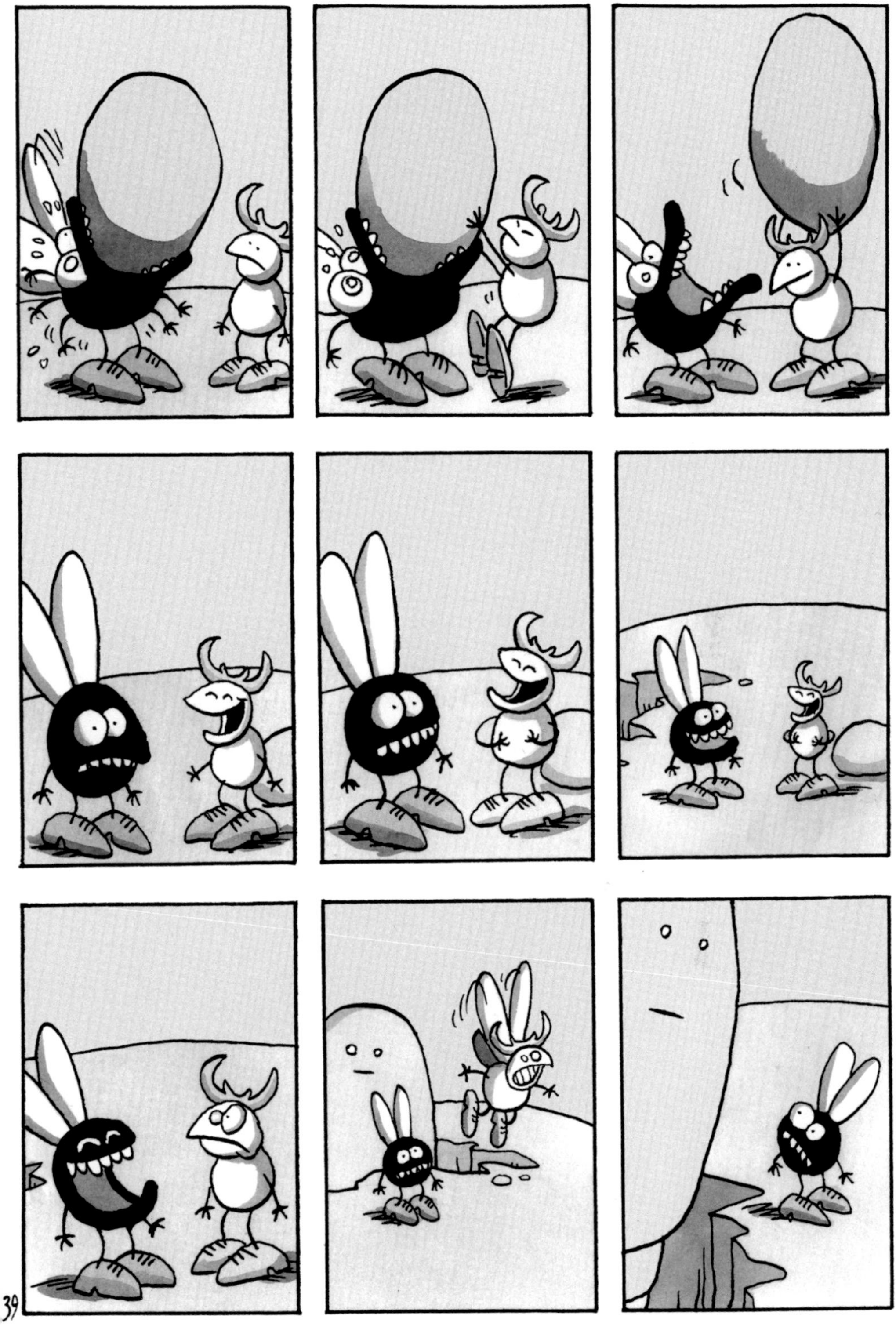

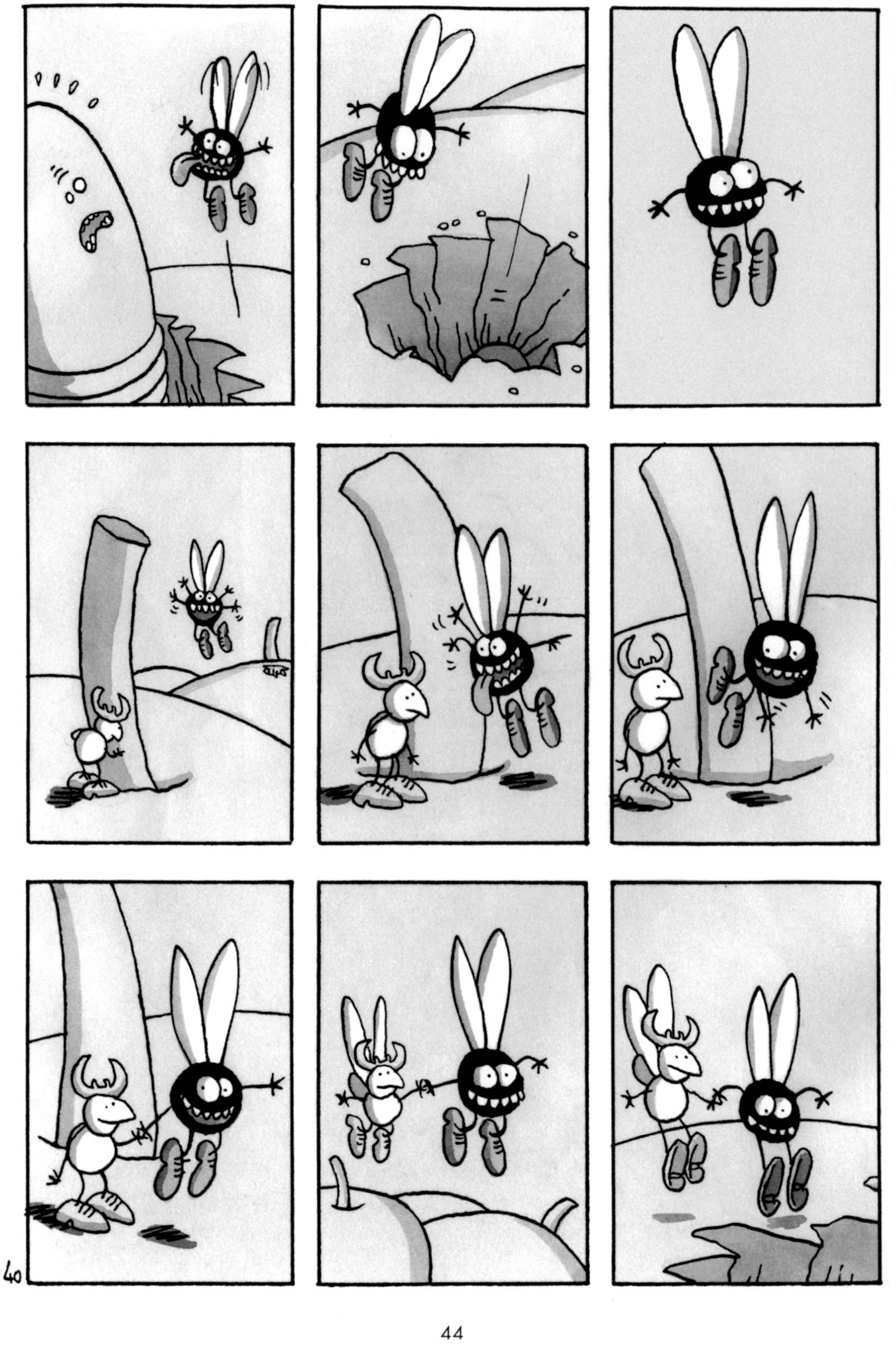
40

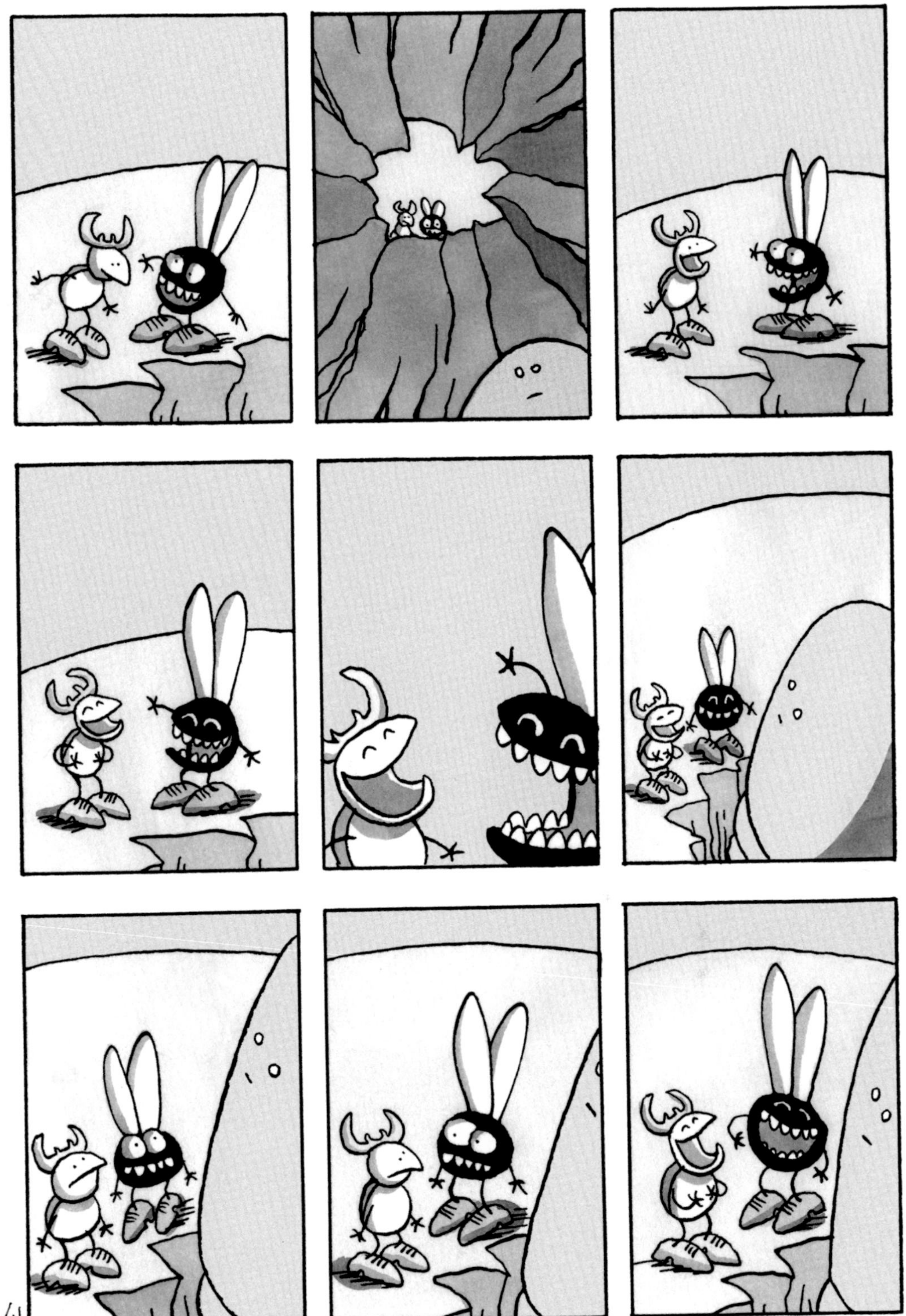
41

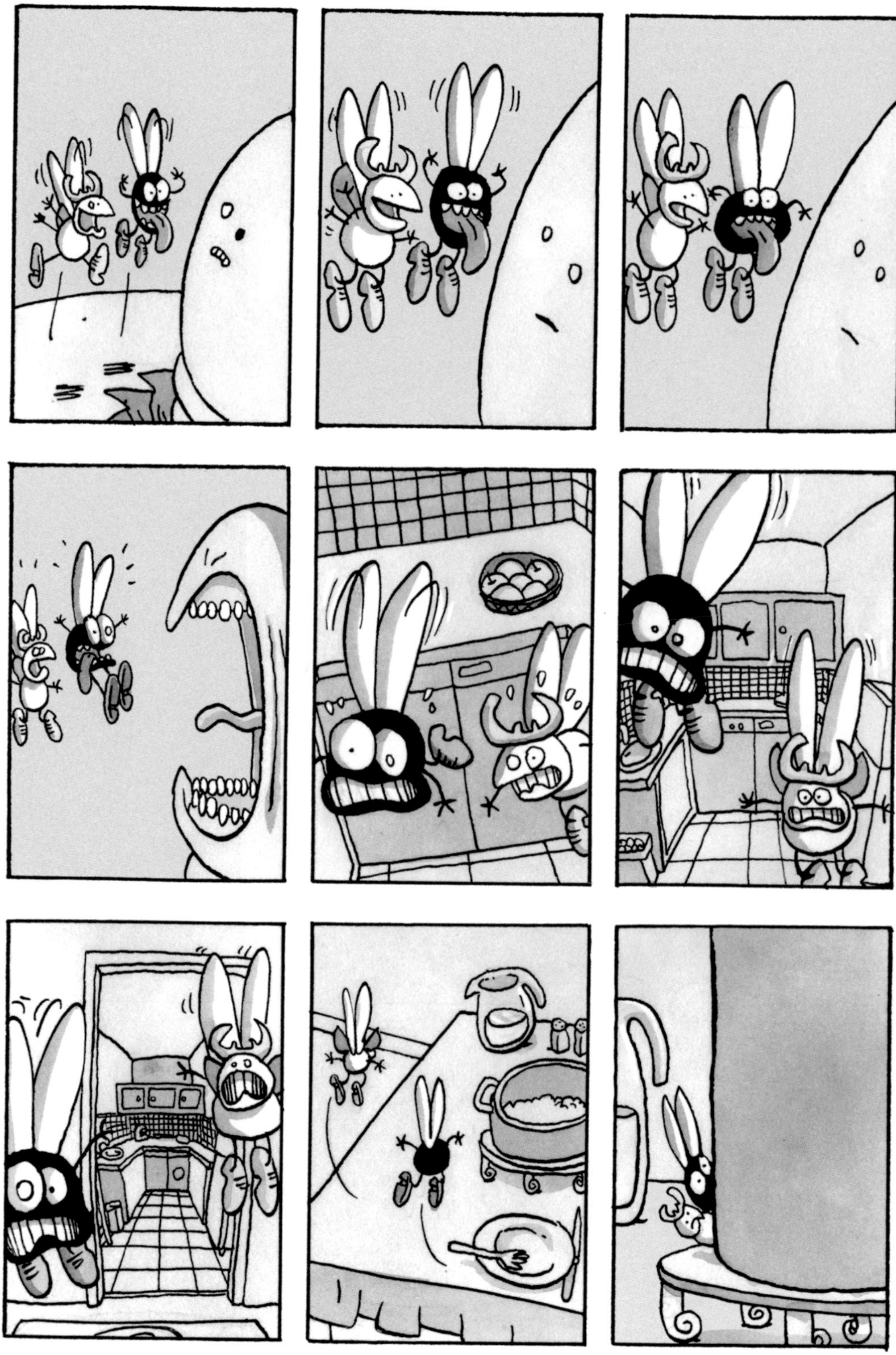

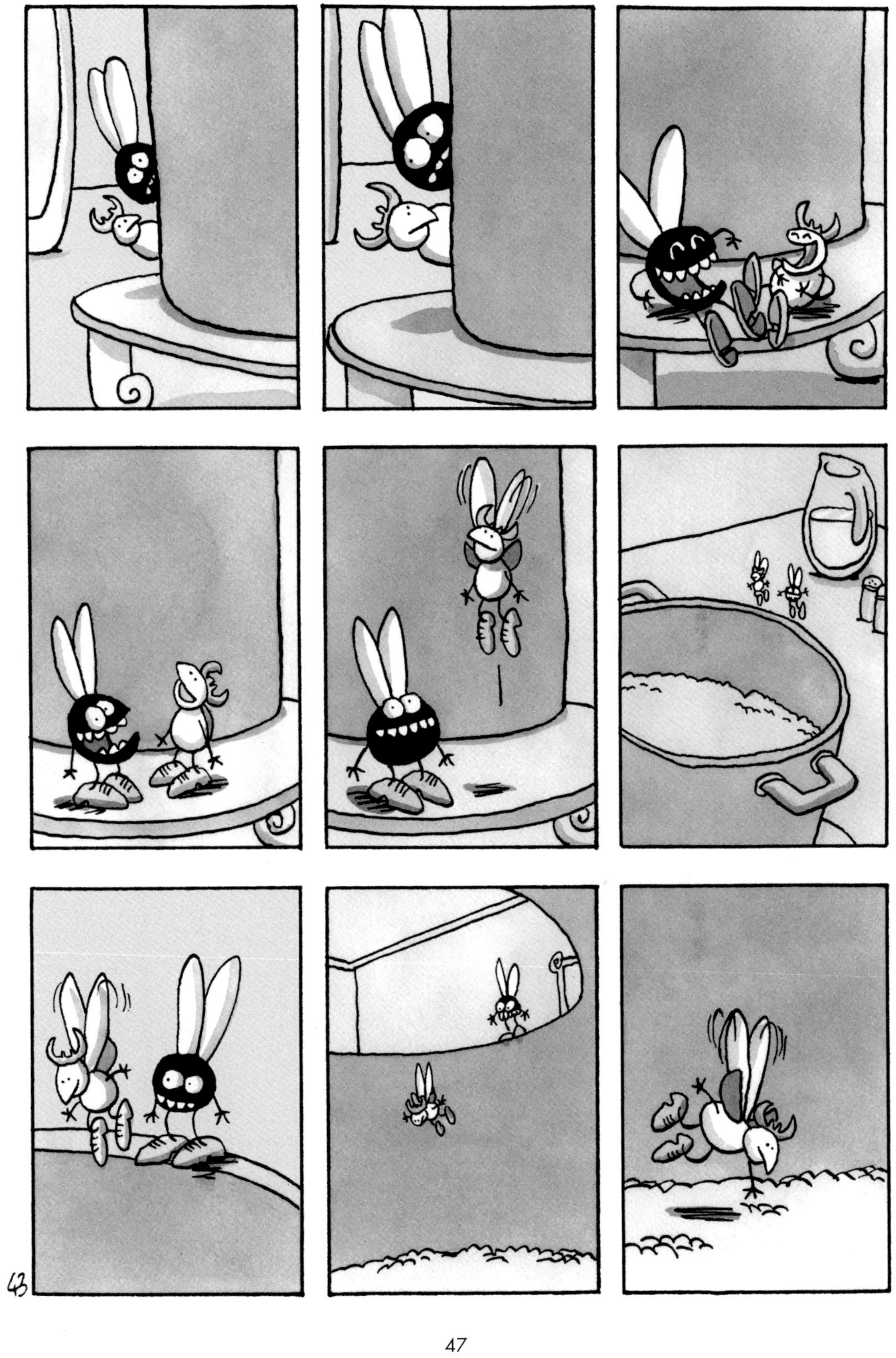

43

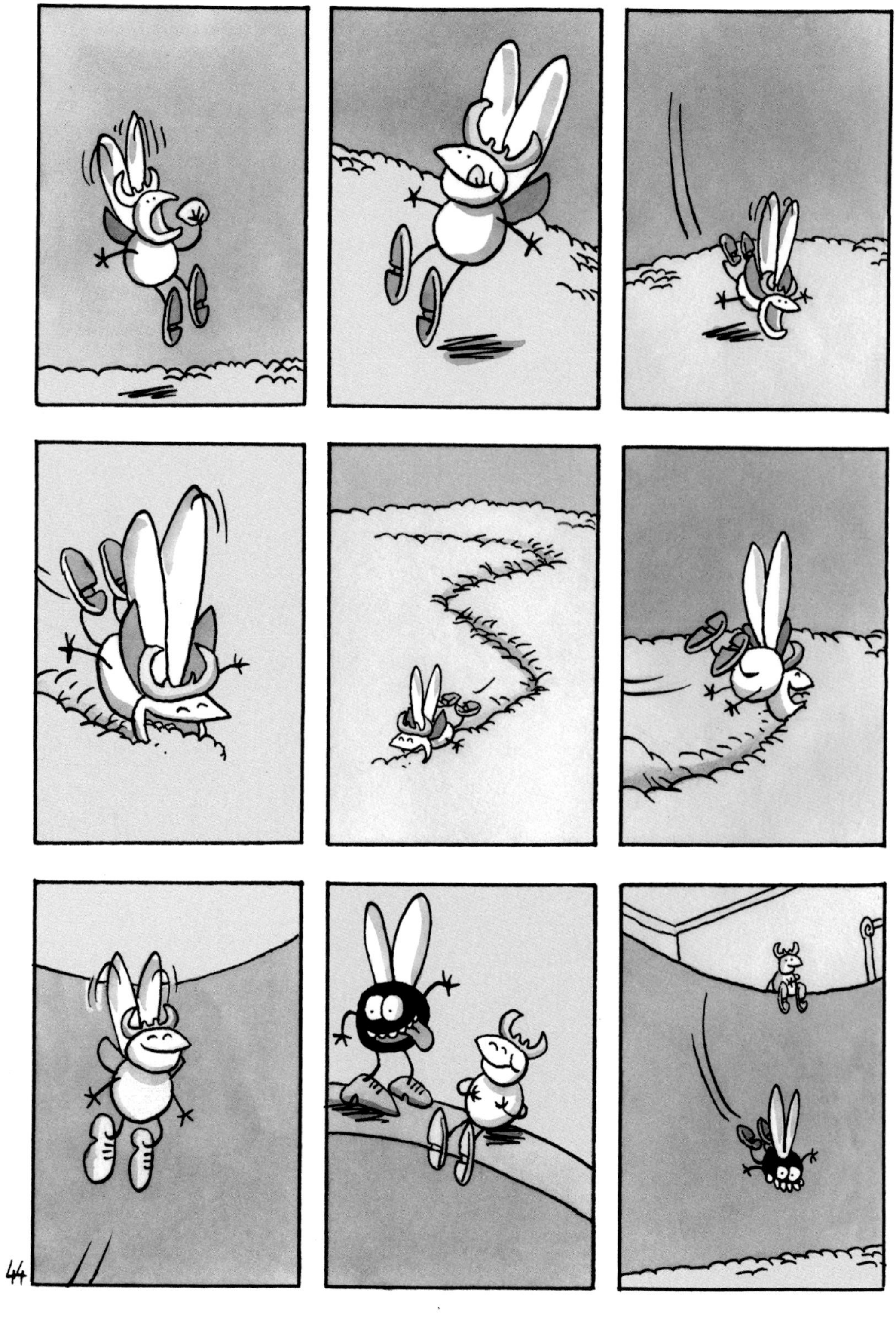
44

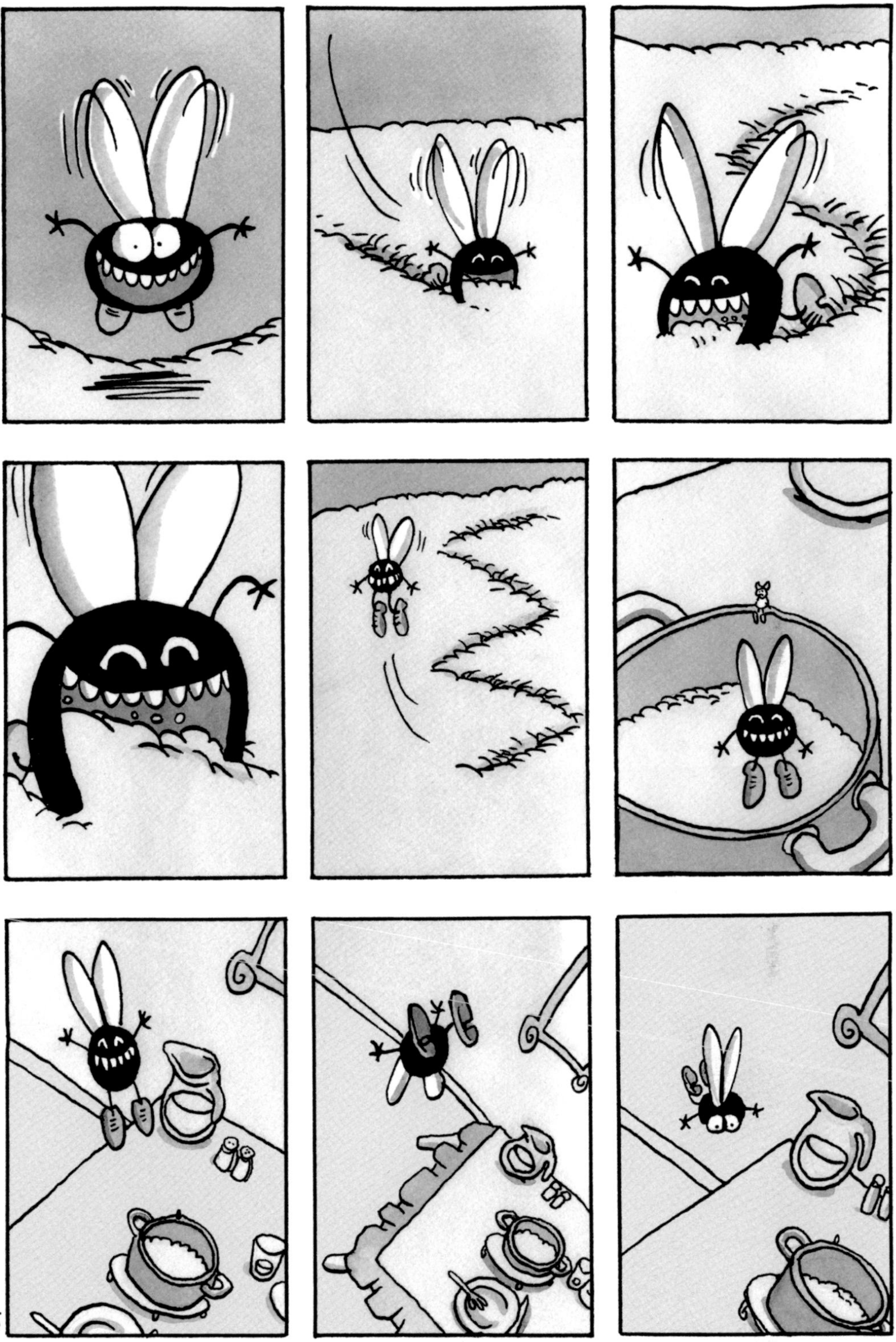

45

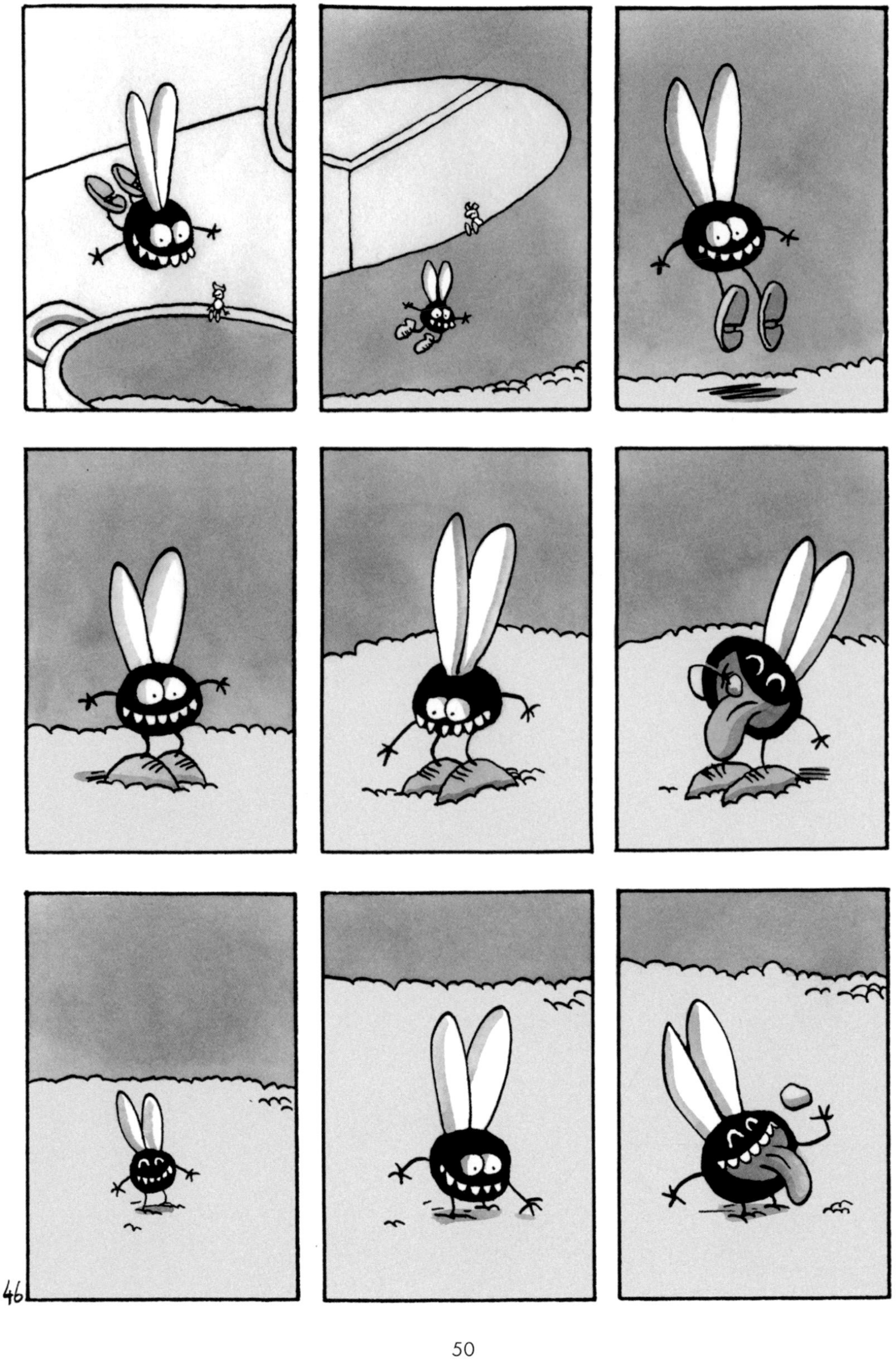

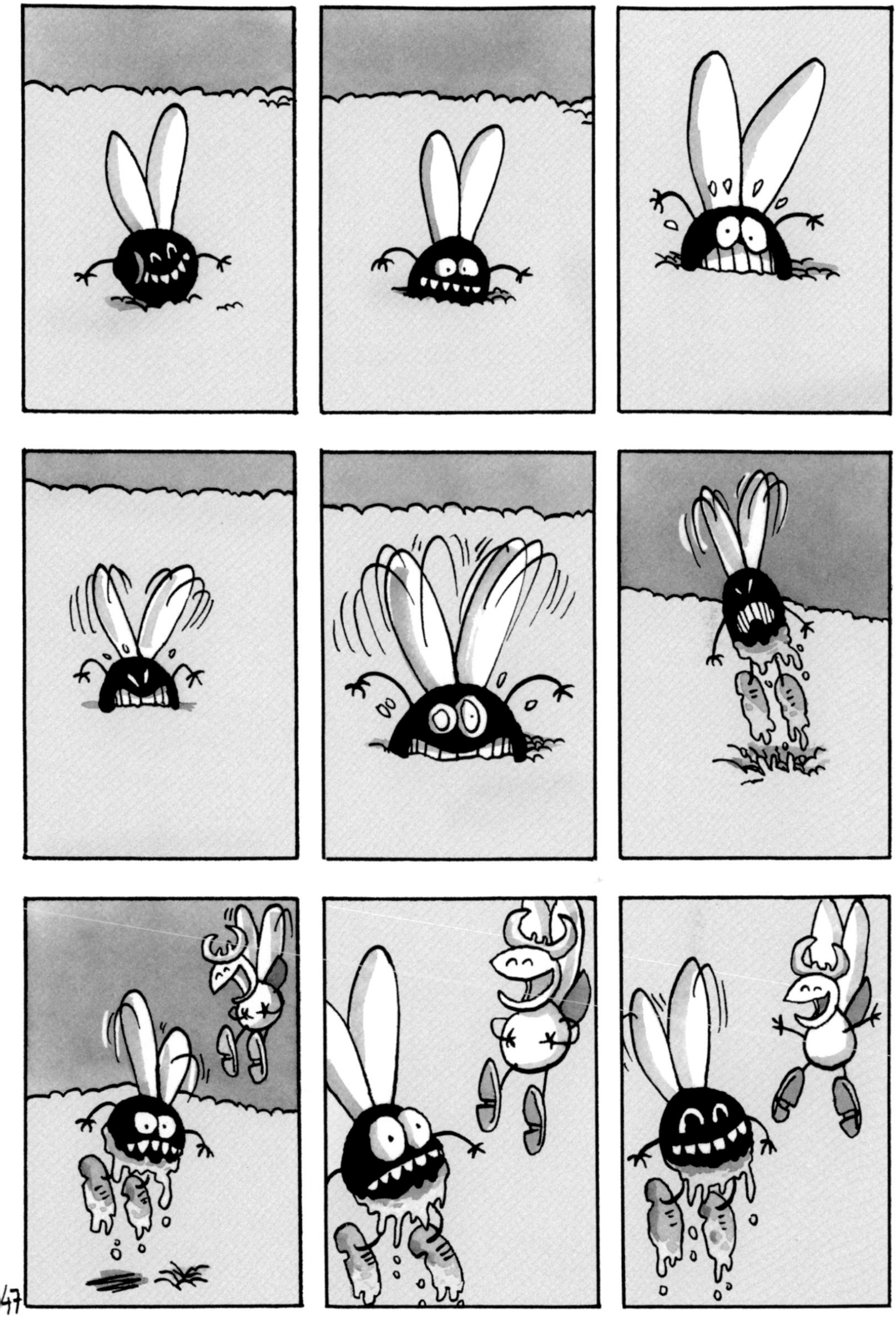
47

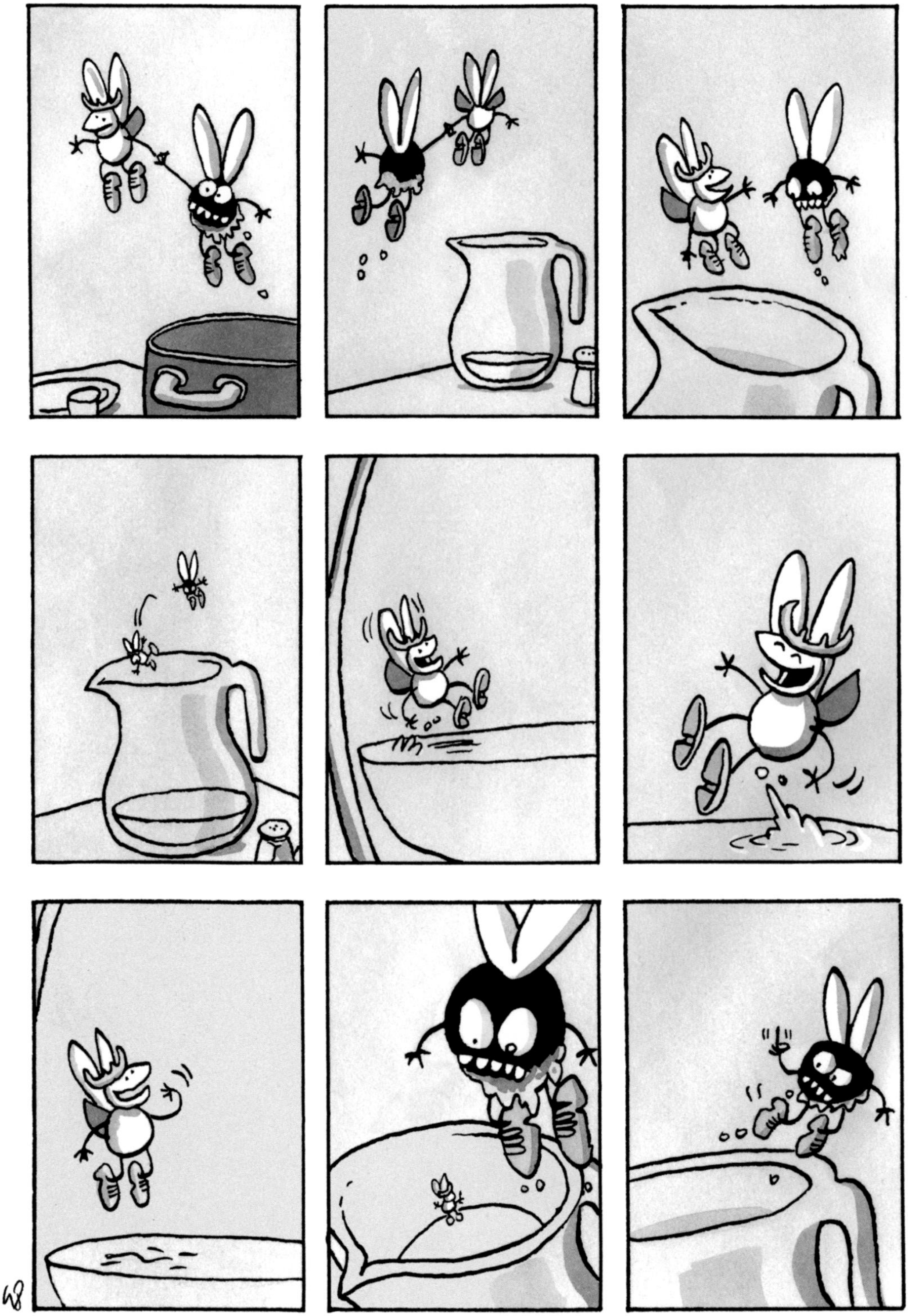

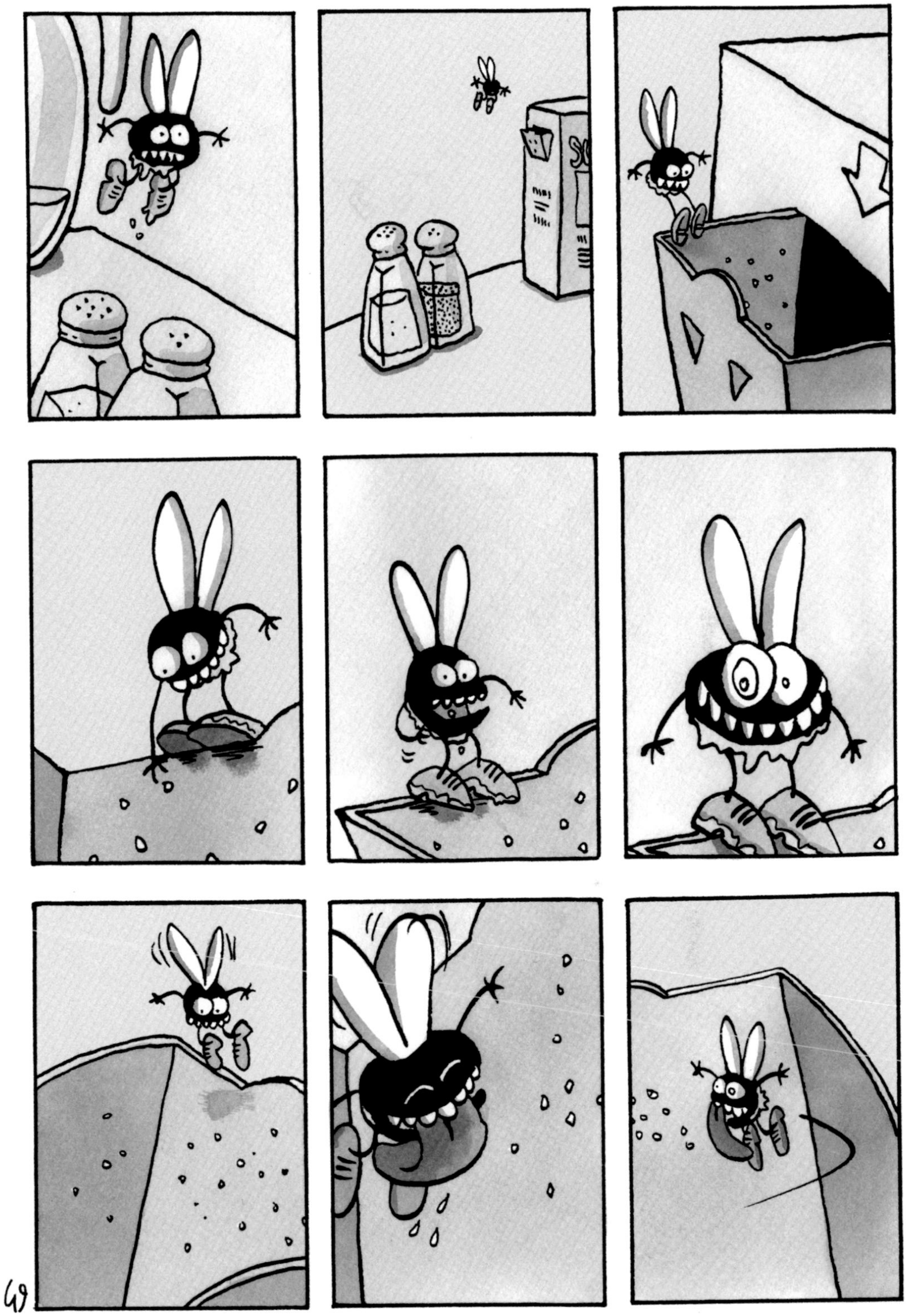

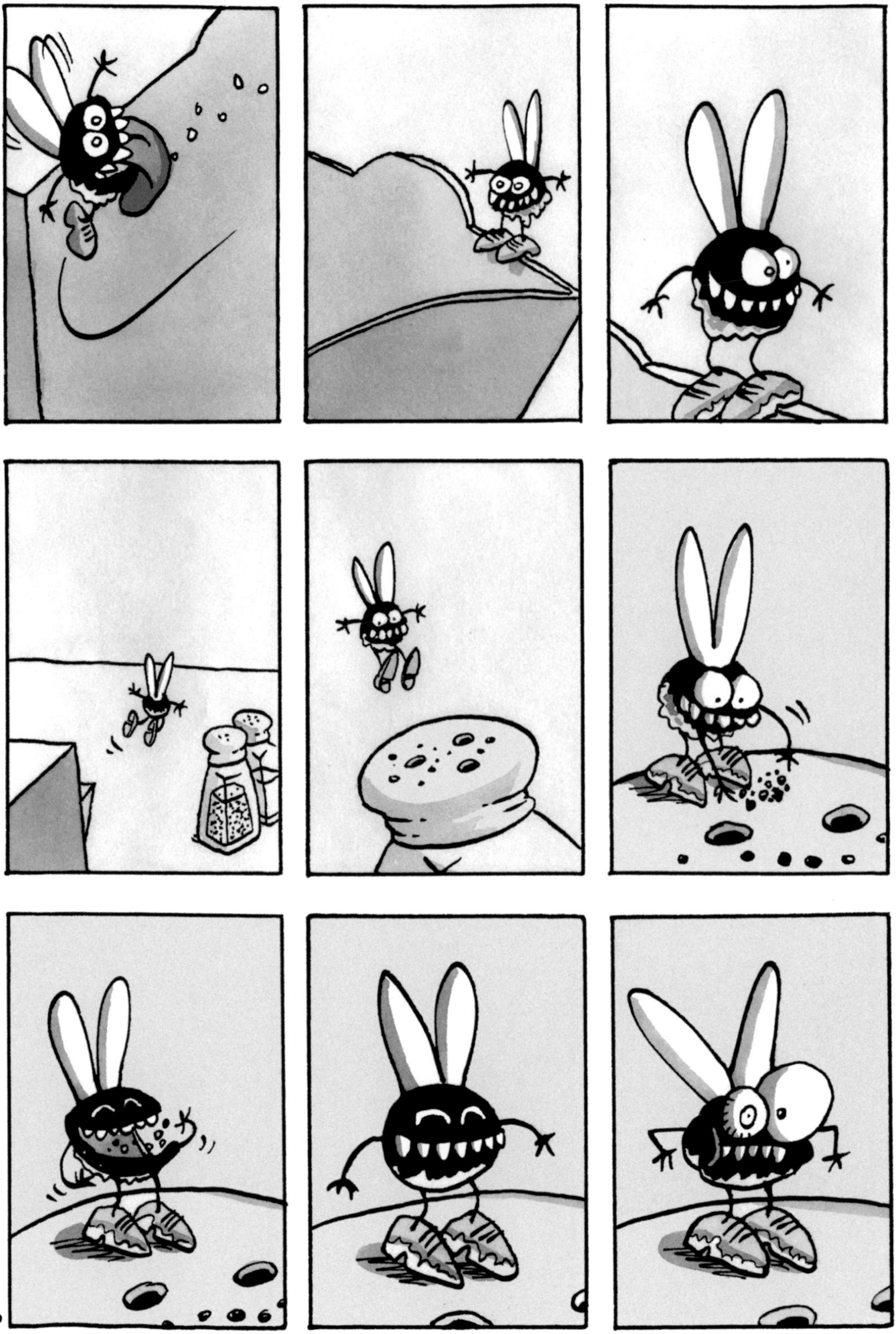

50

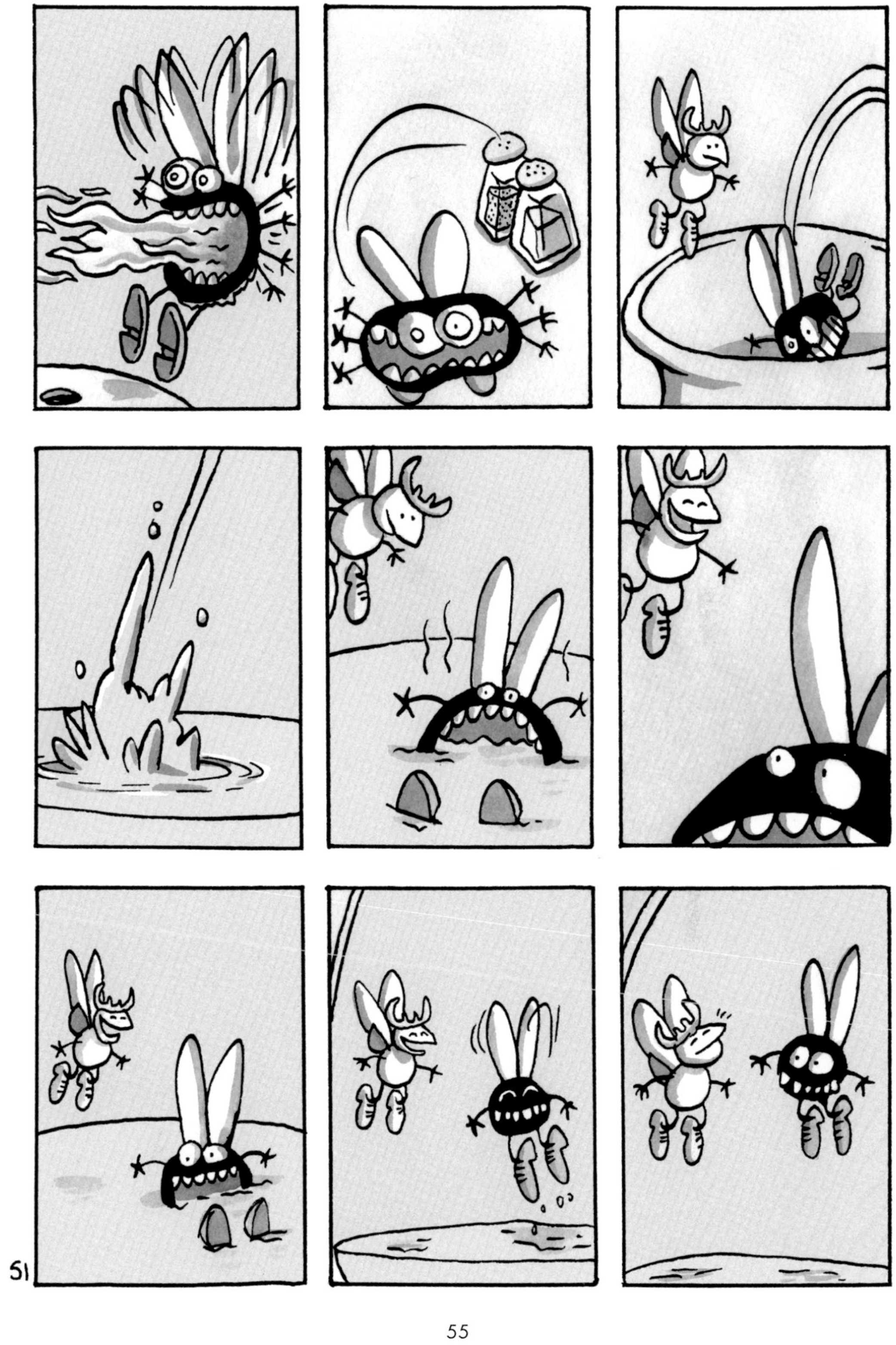

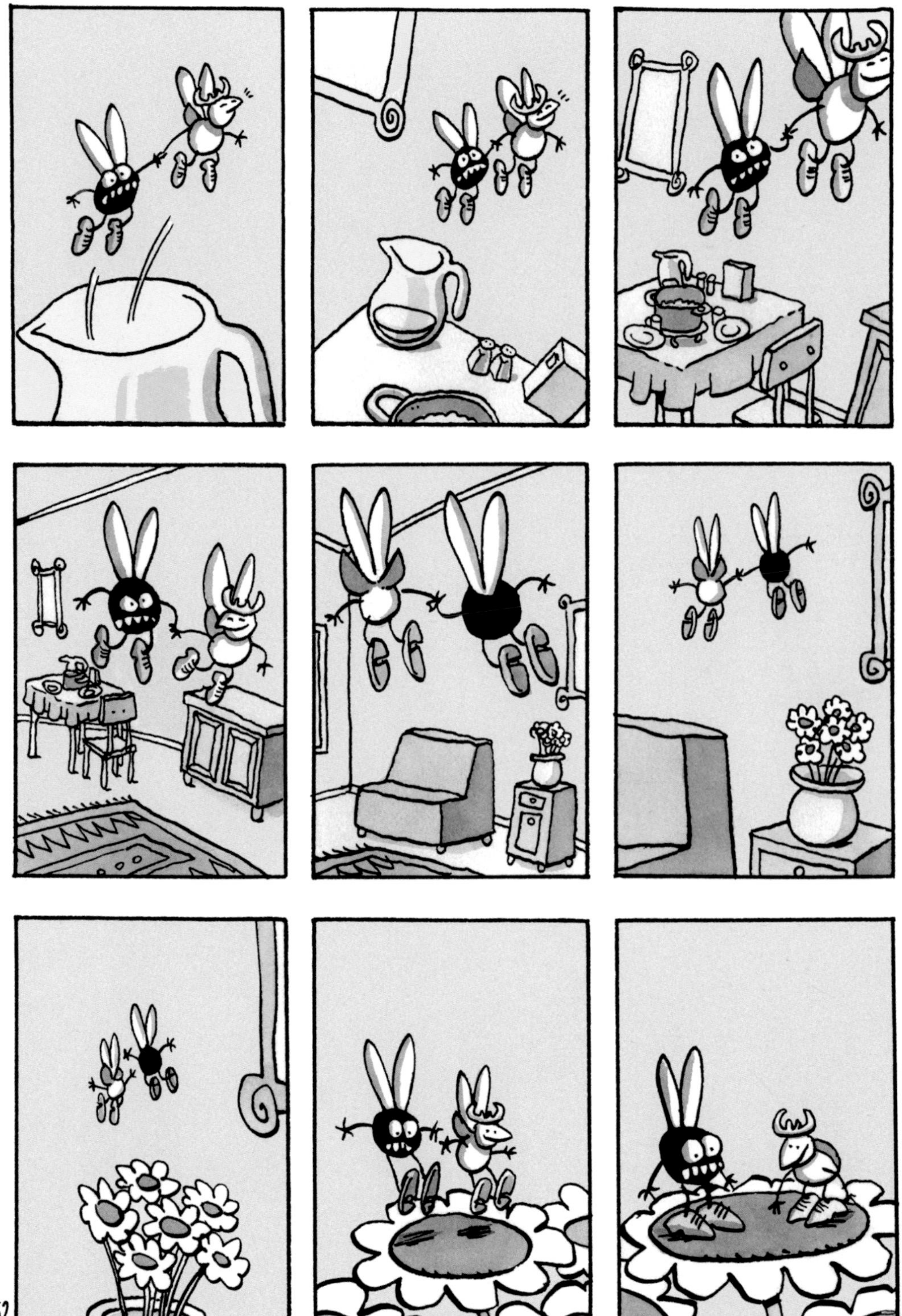

52

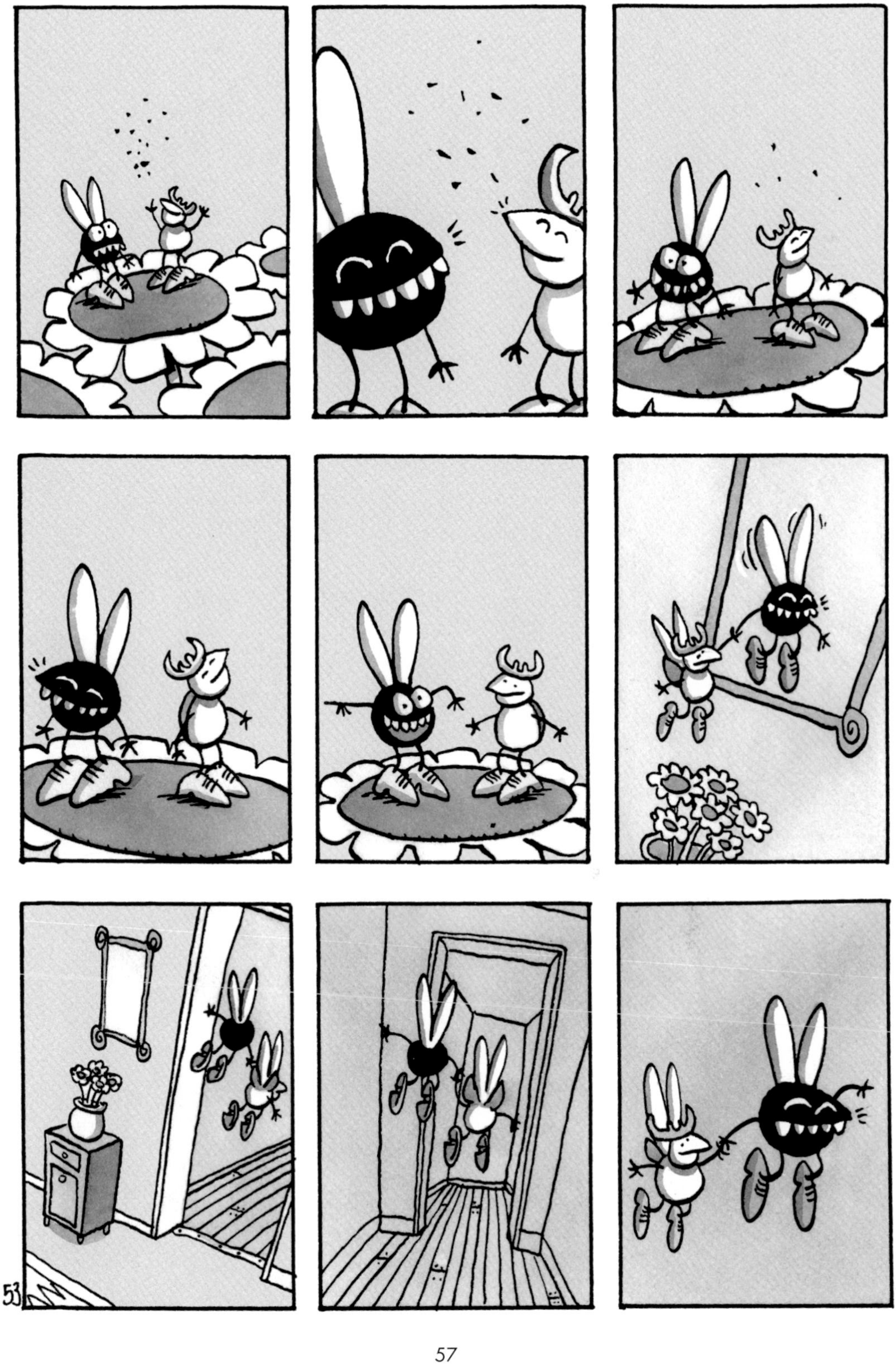
53

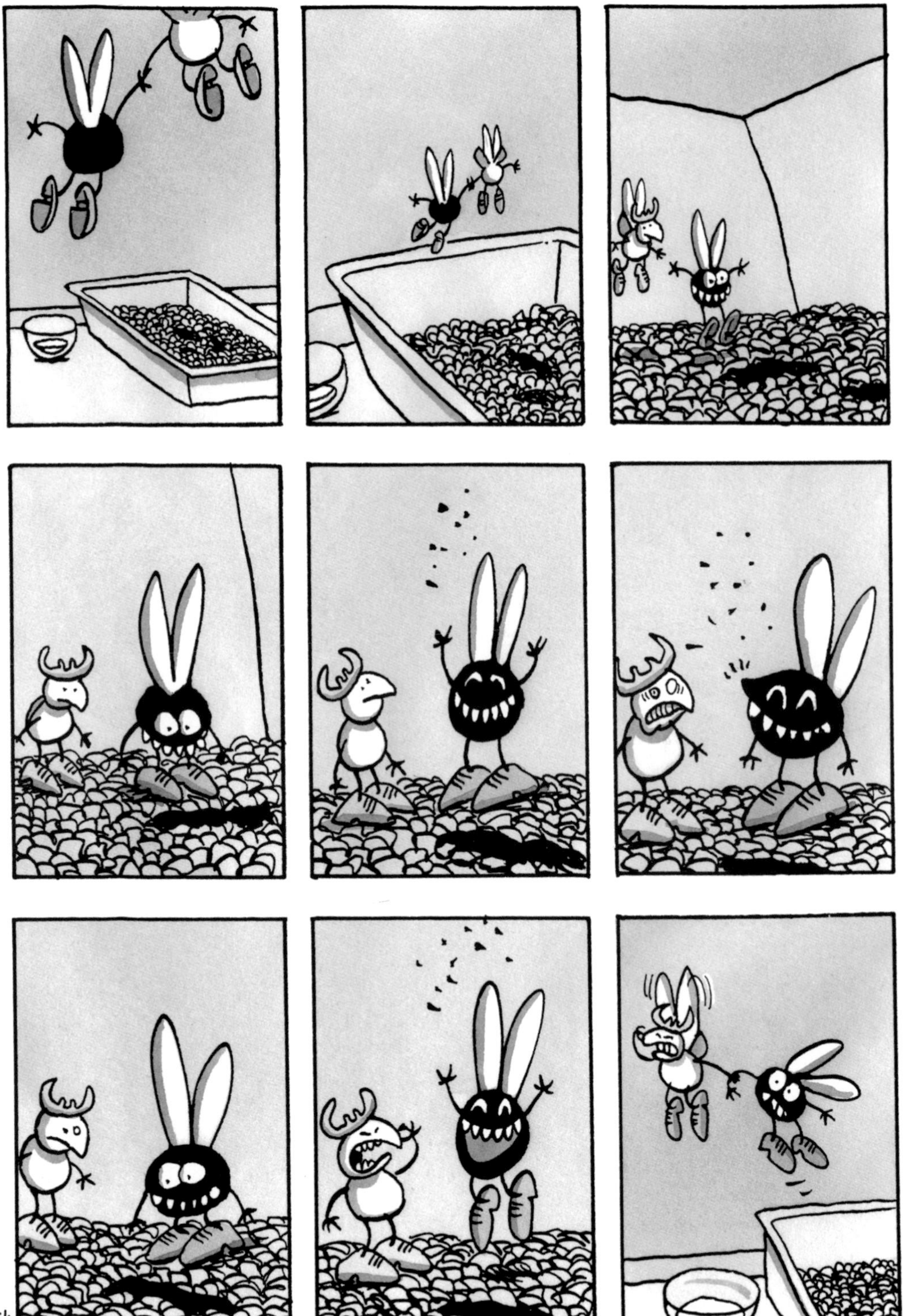

54

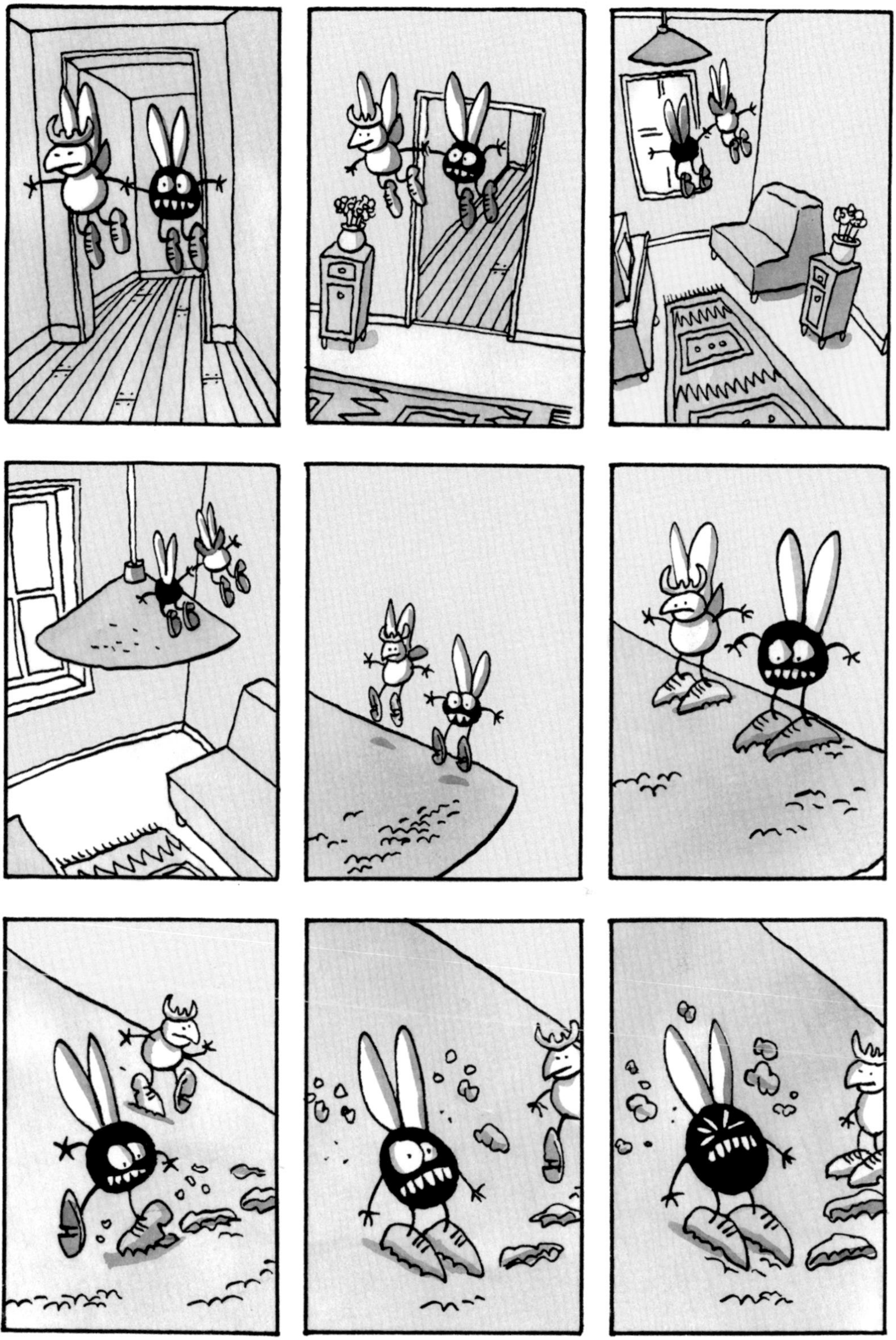

55

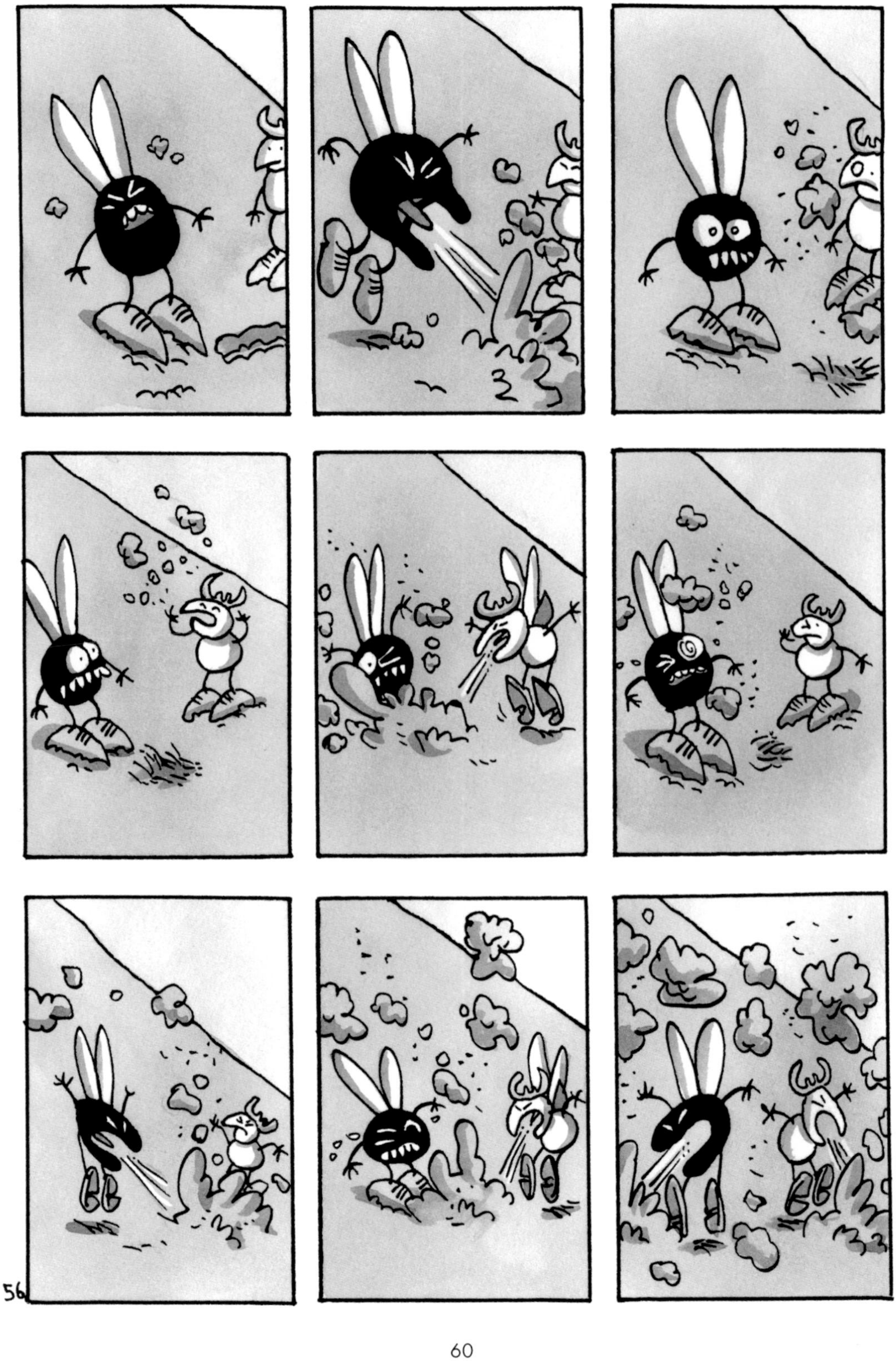
56

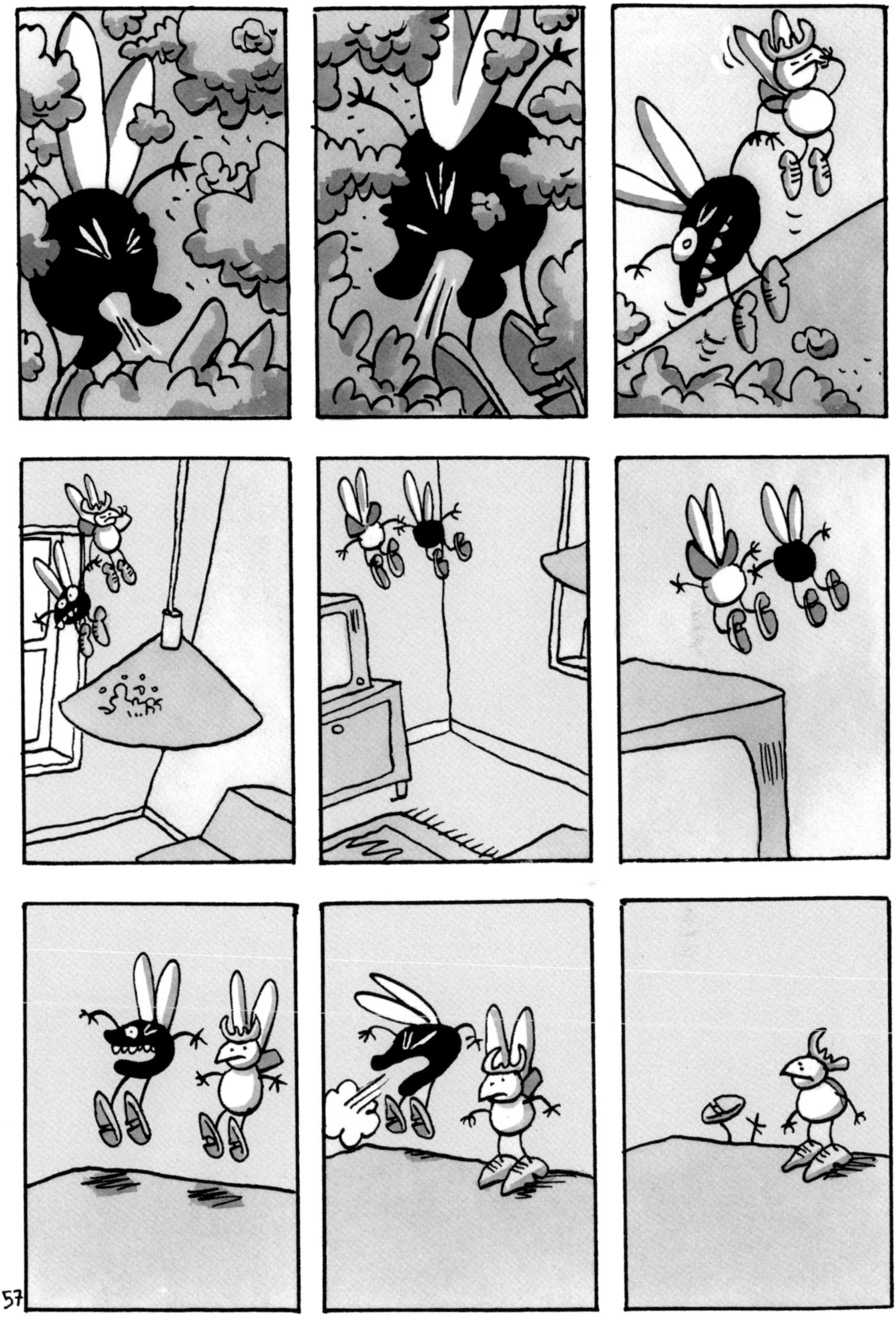
57

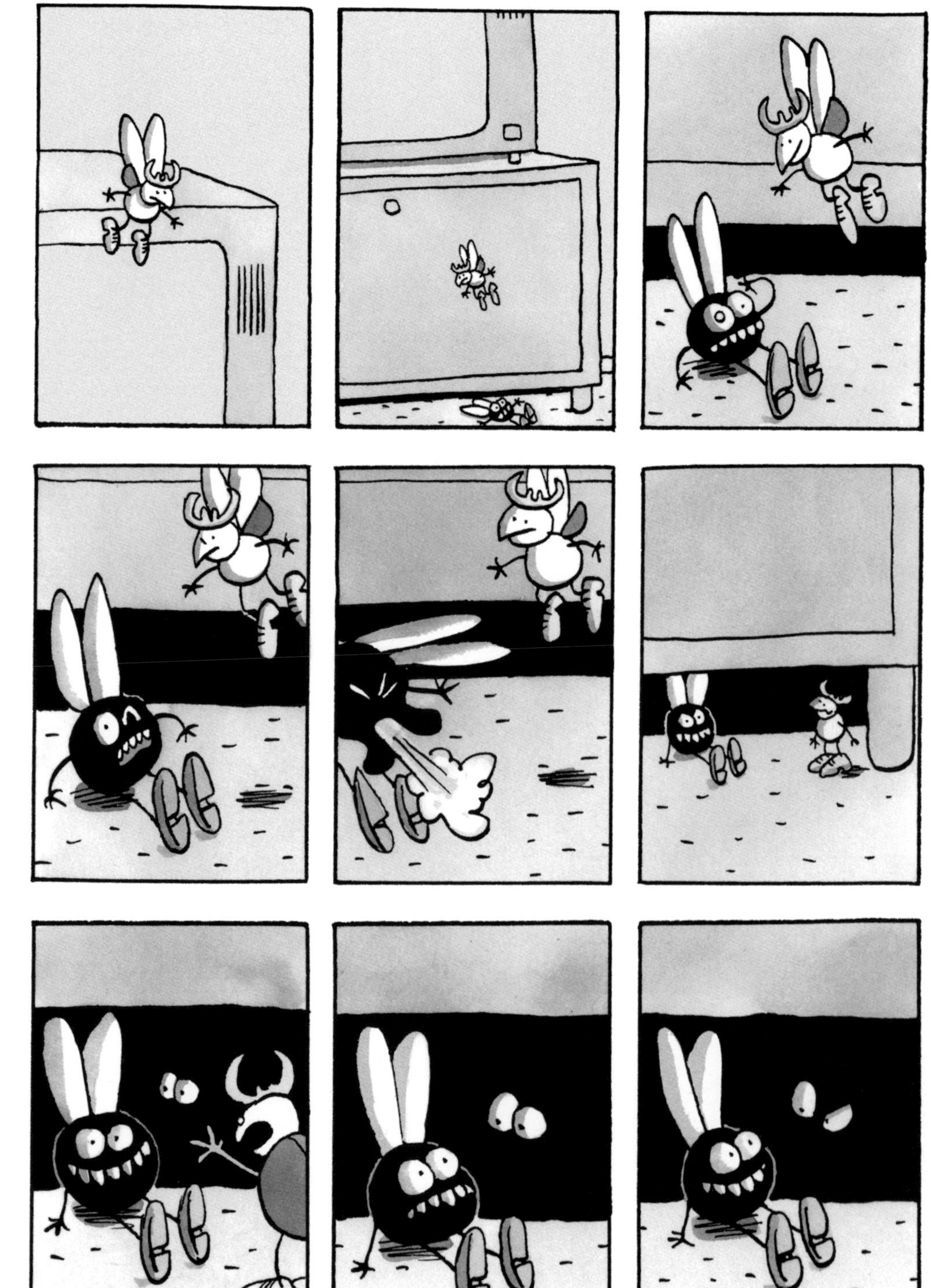
58

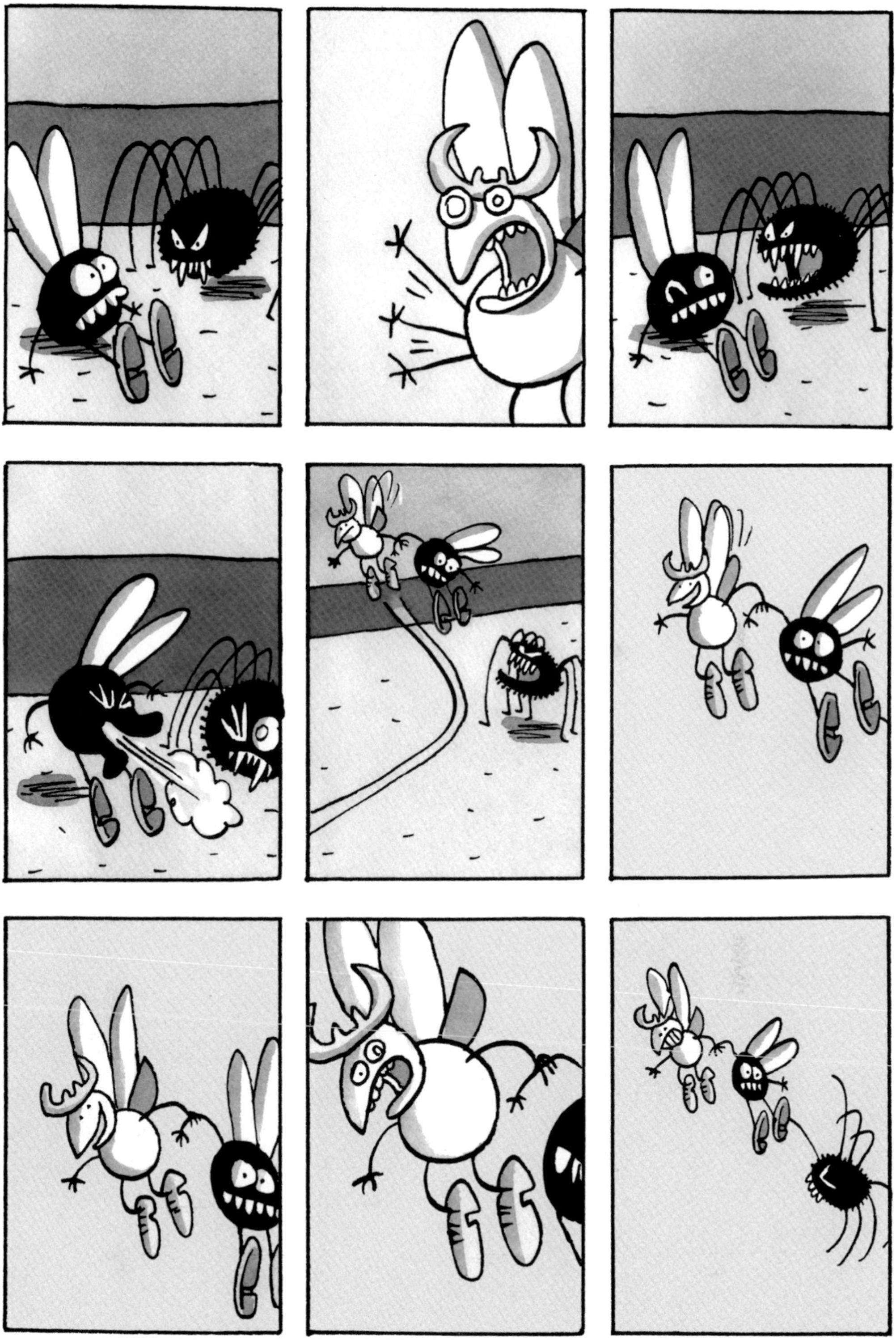

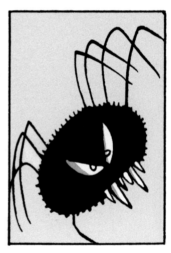
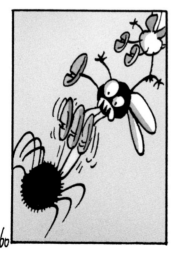

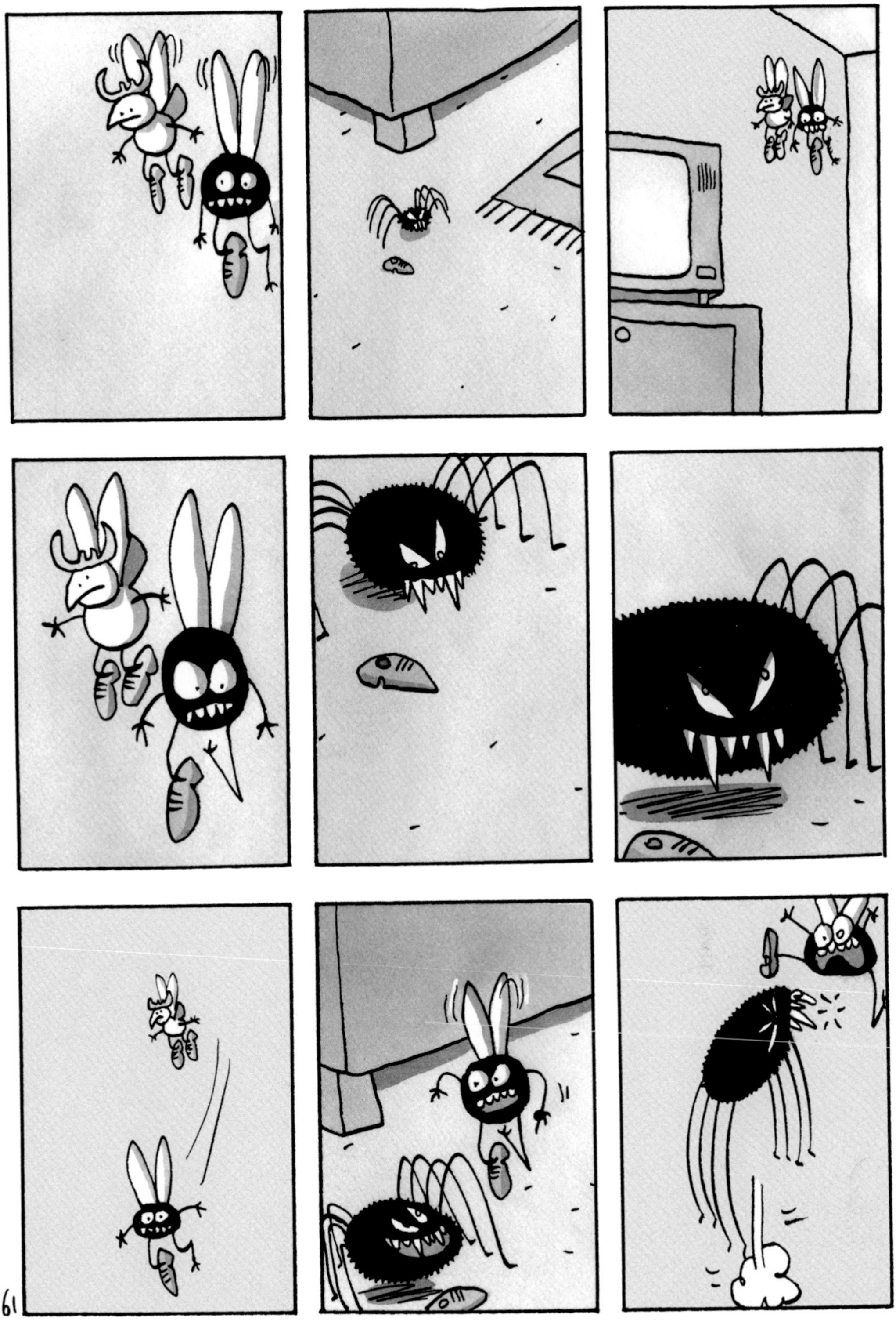
61

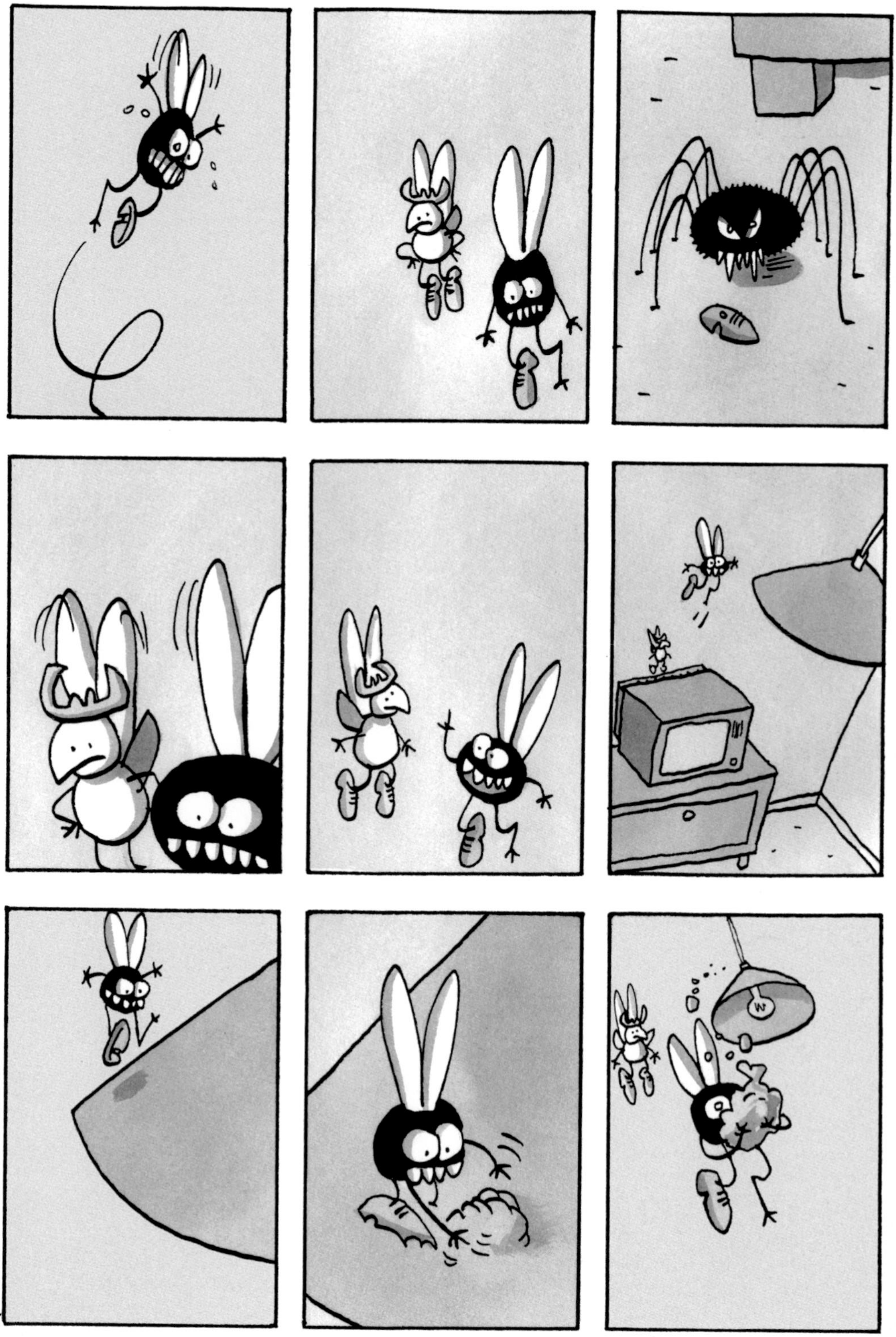

62

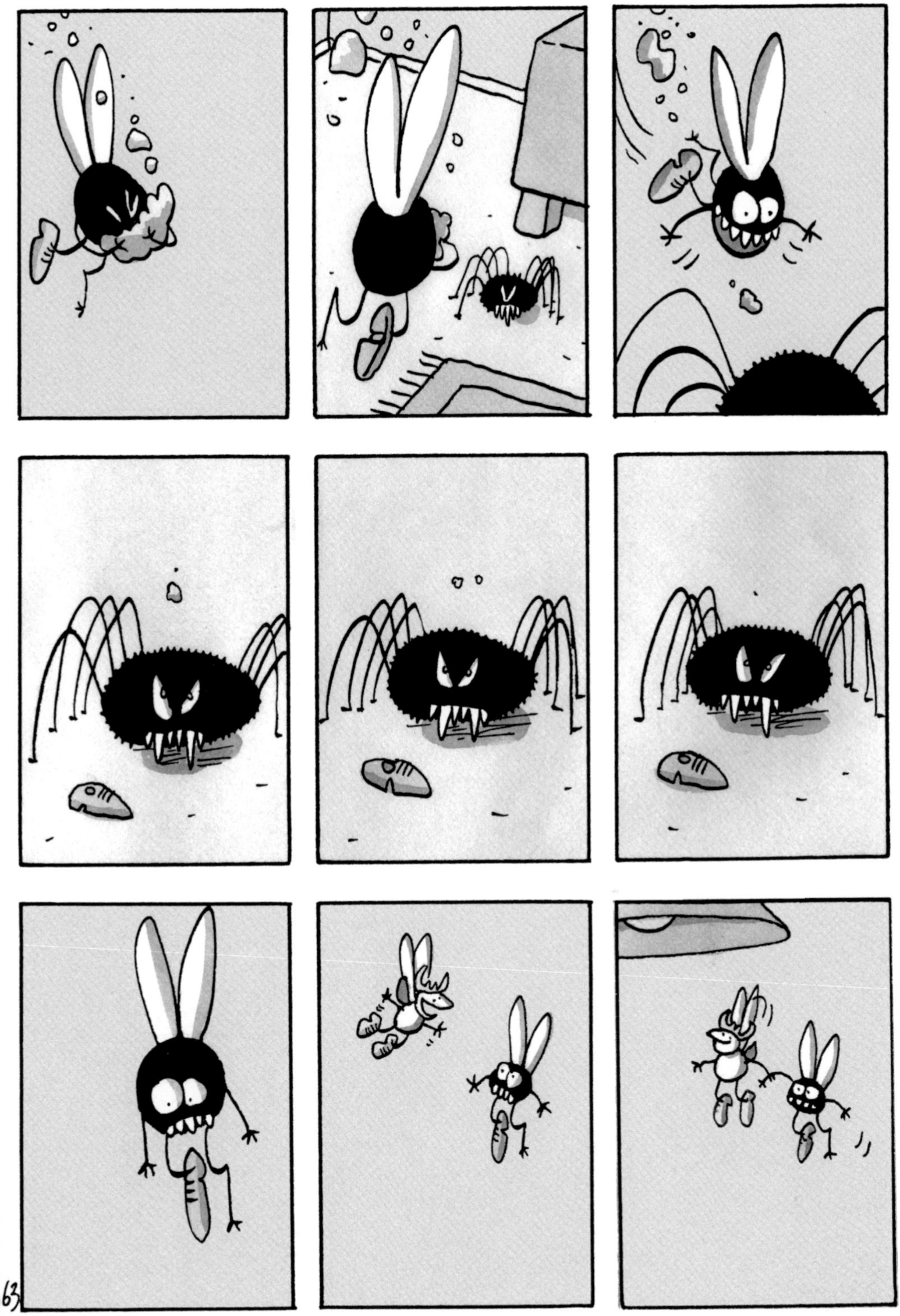
63

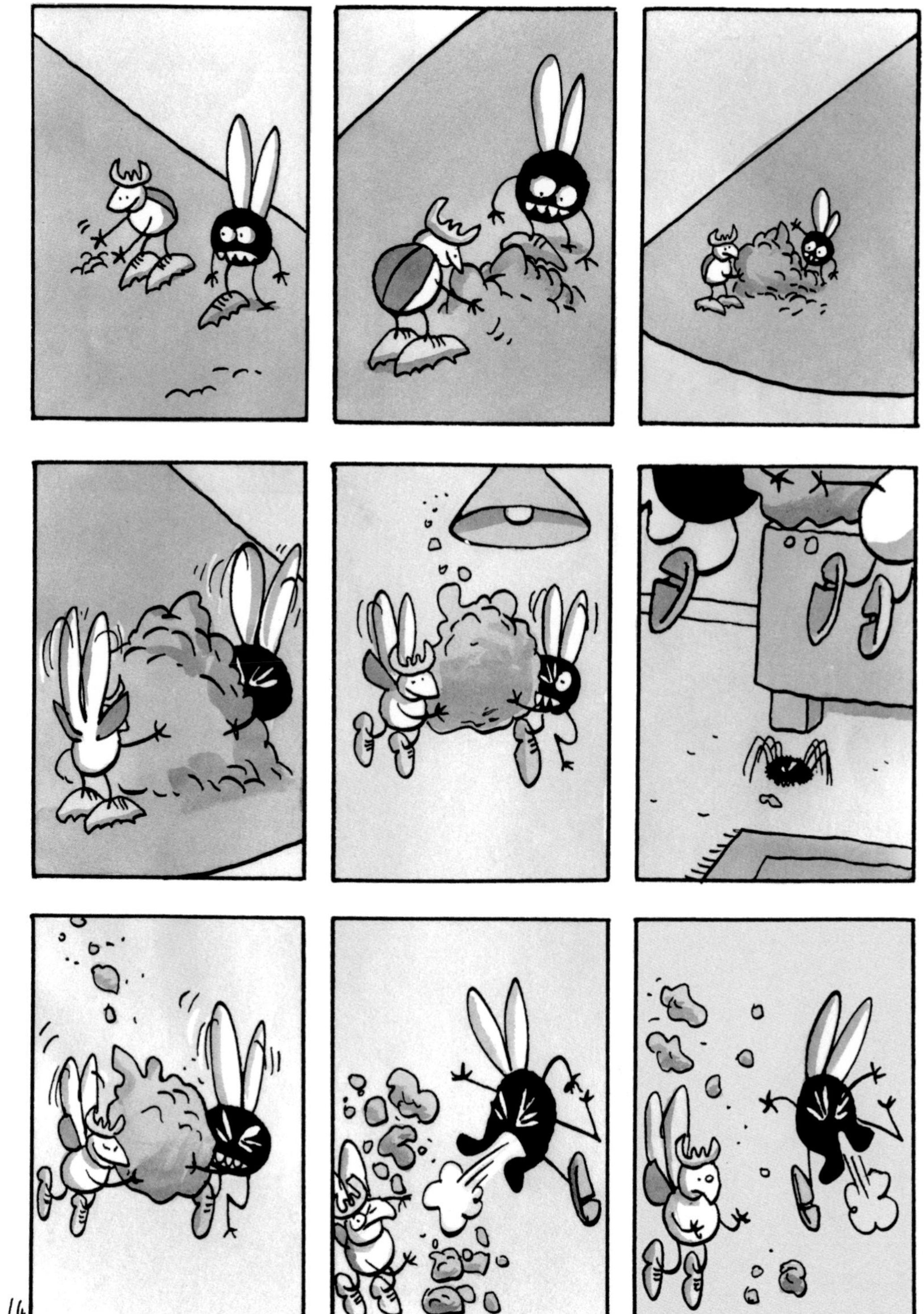

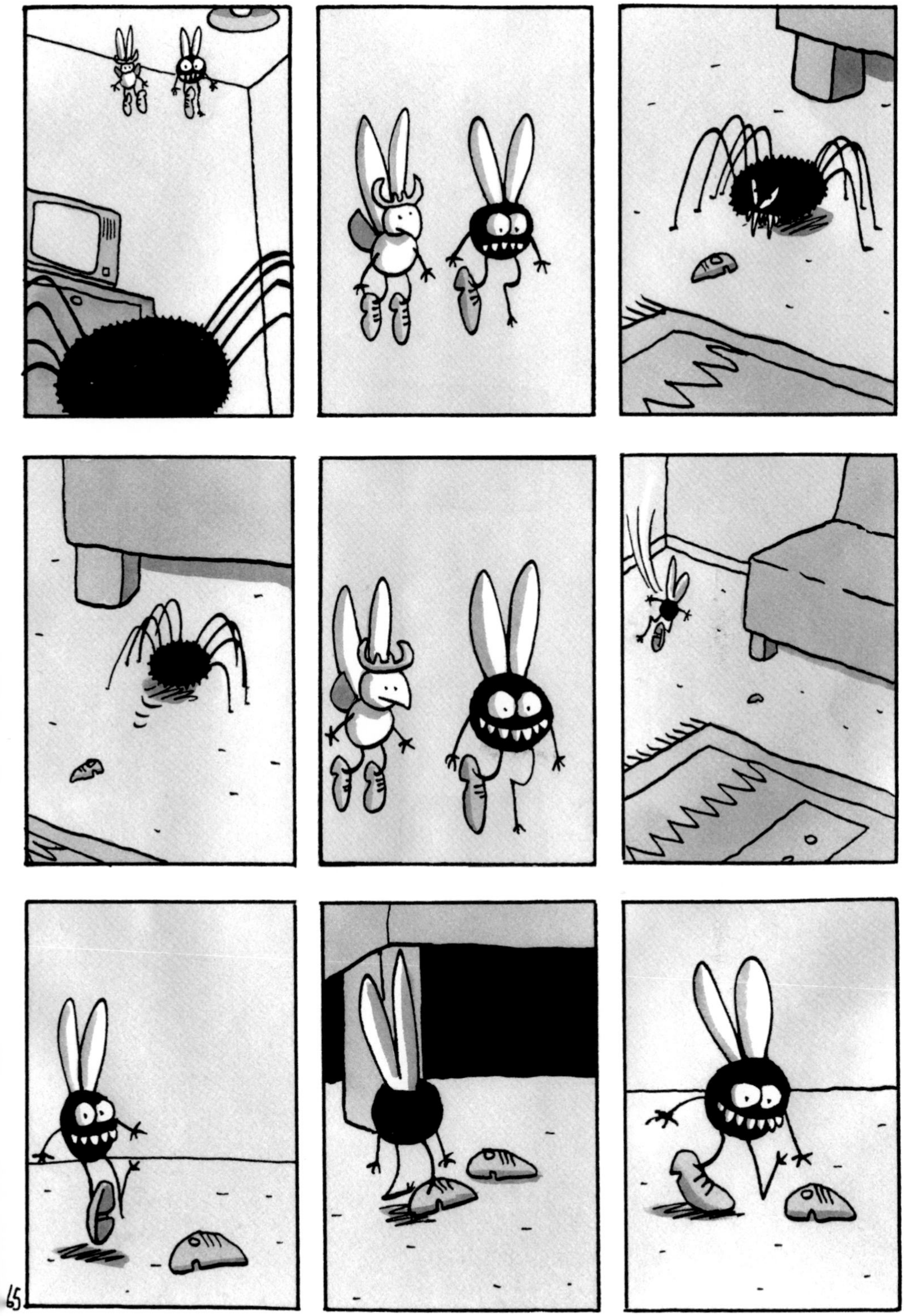

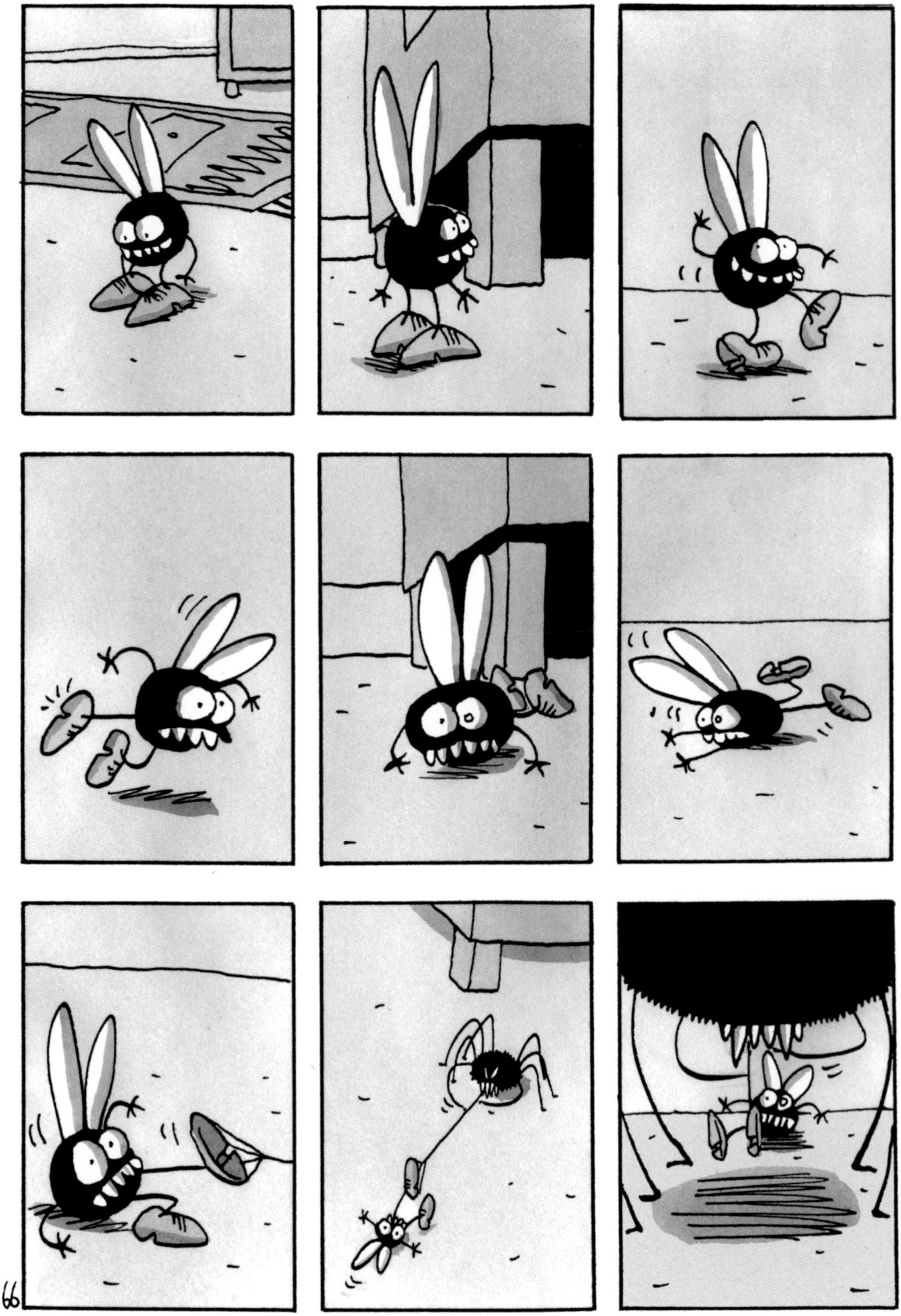

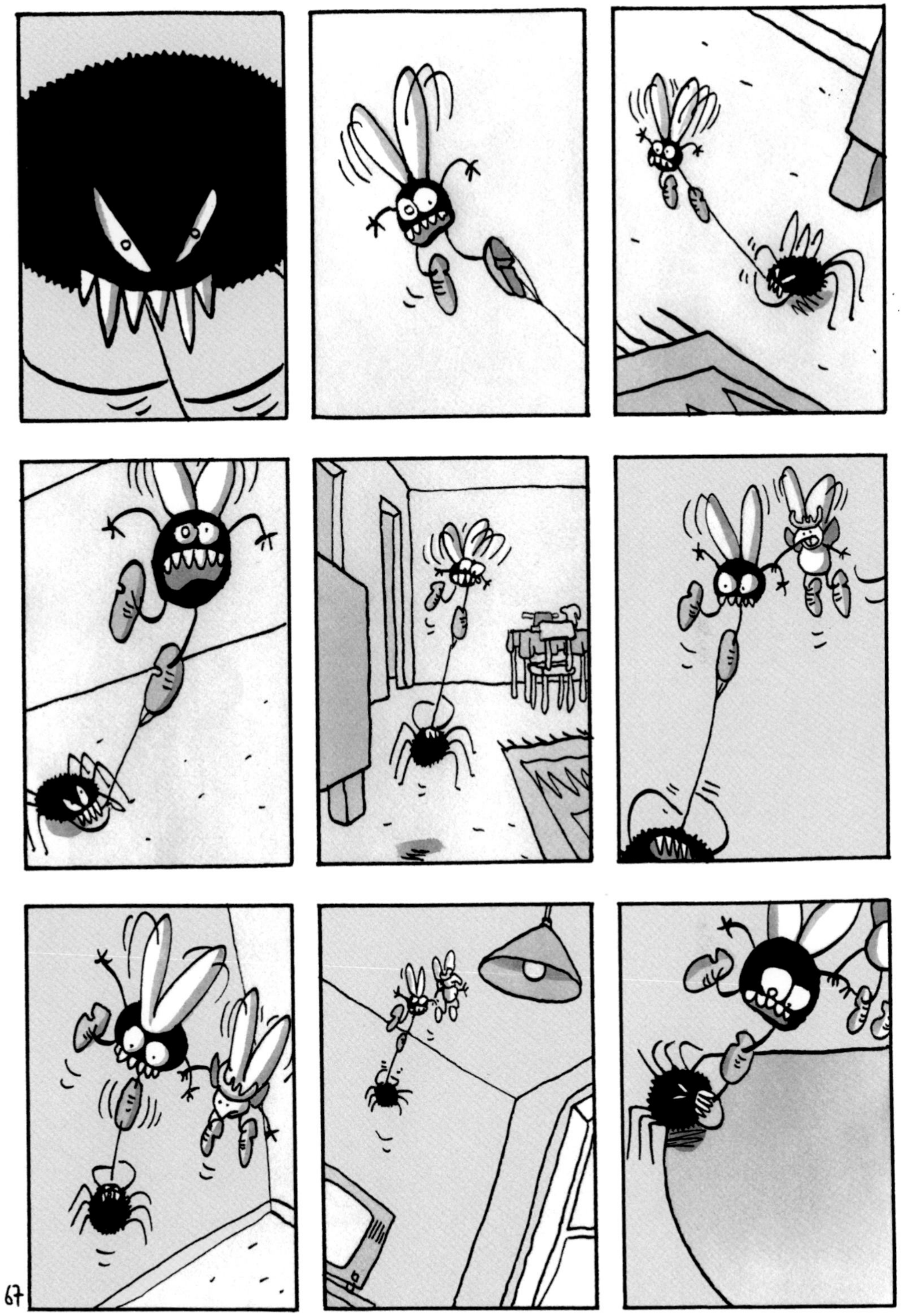
67

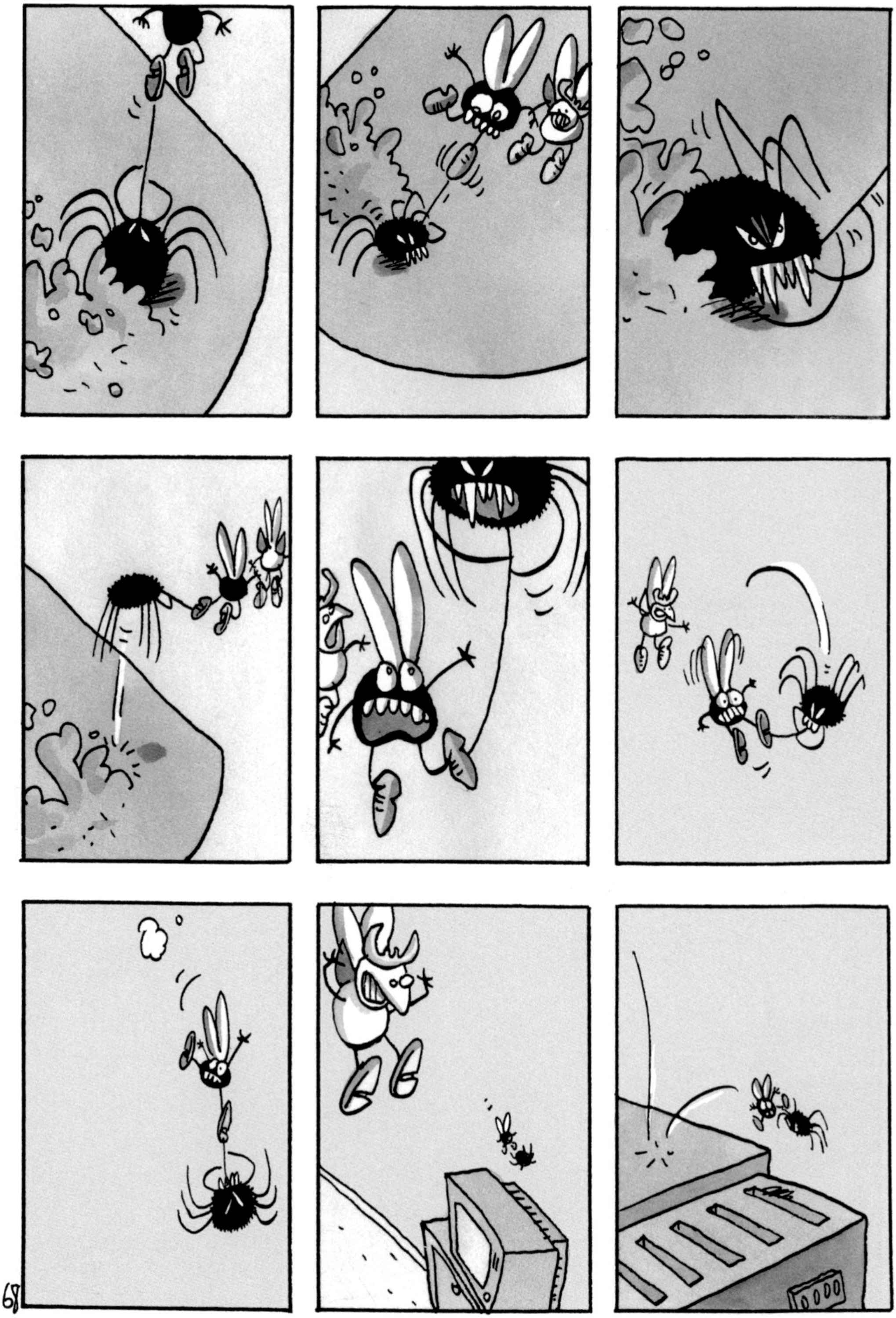

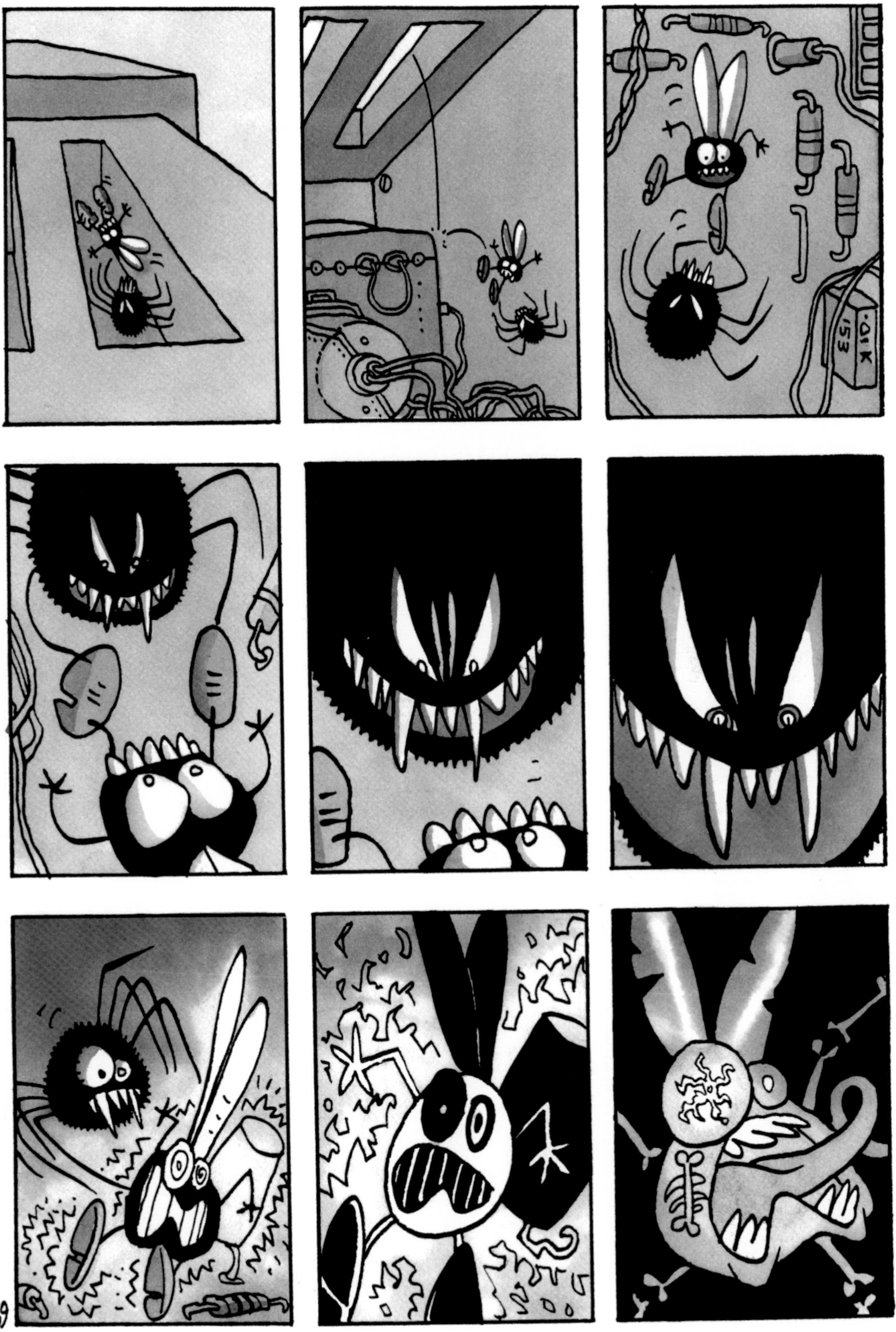
.01K
153

69

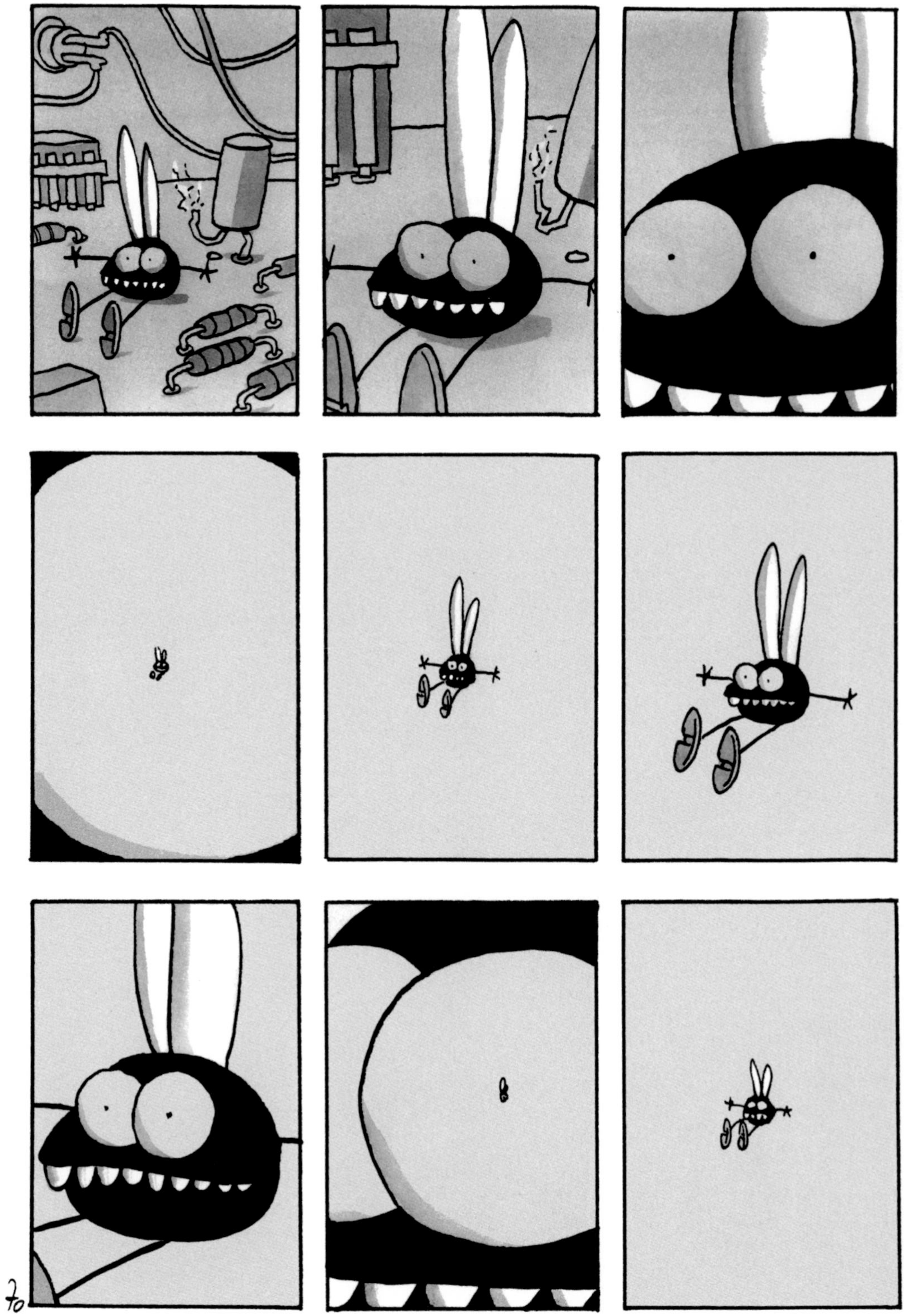

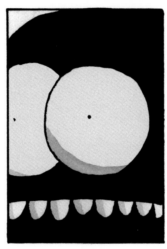

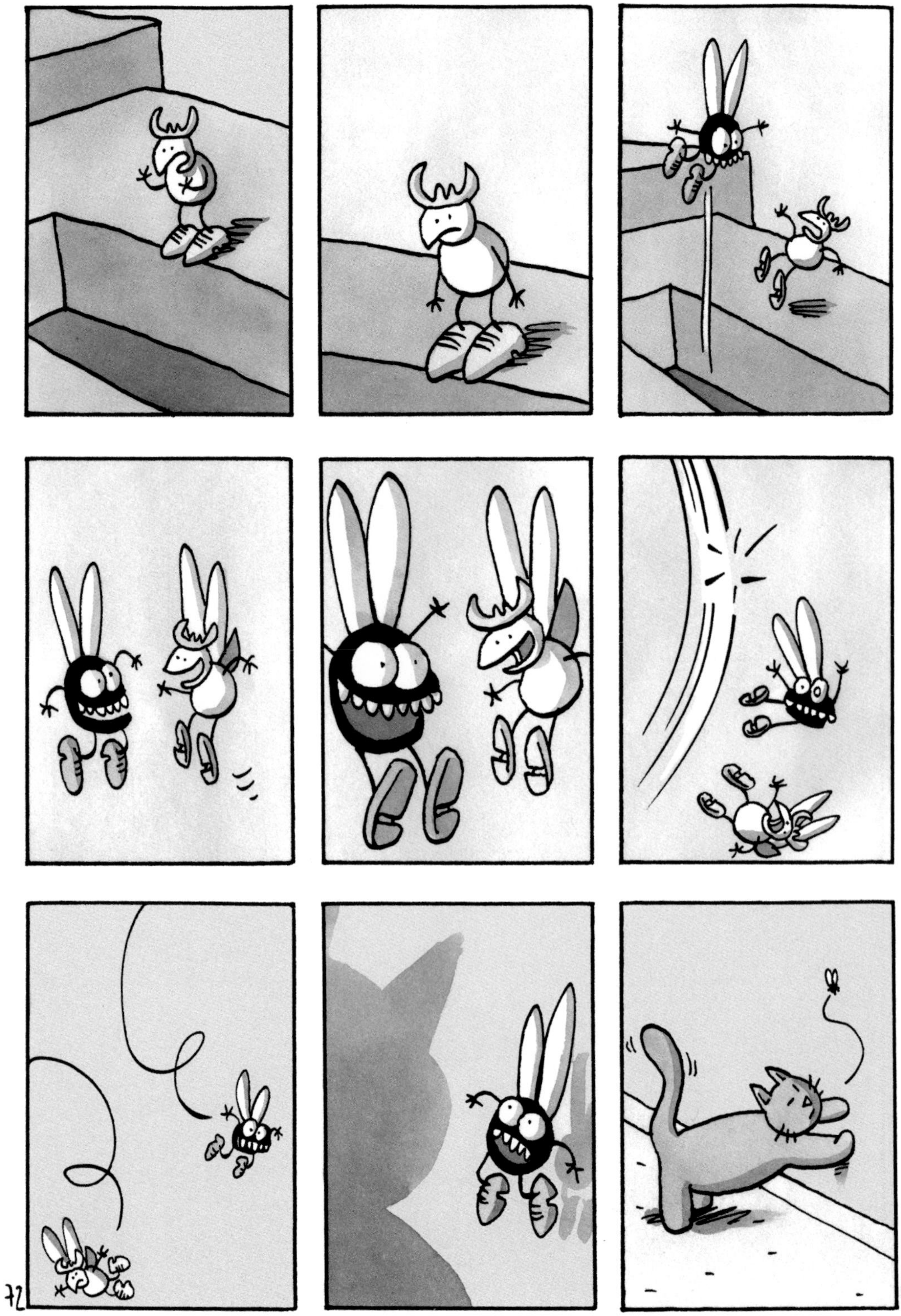
72

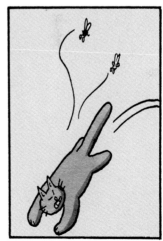

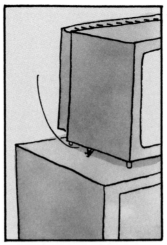

74

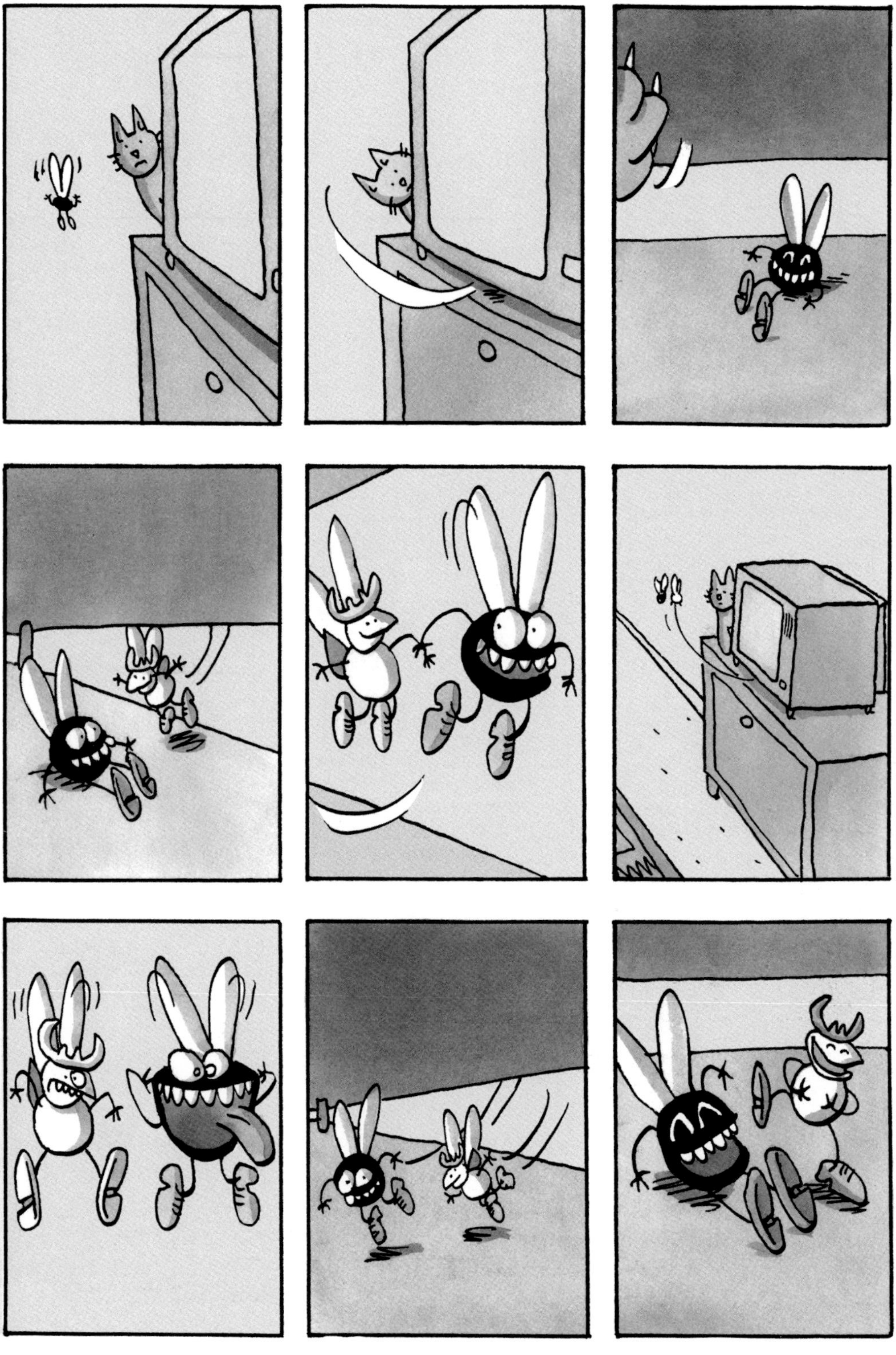

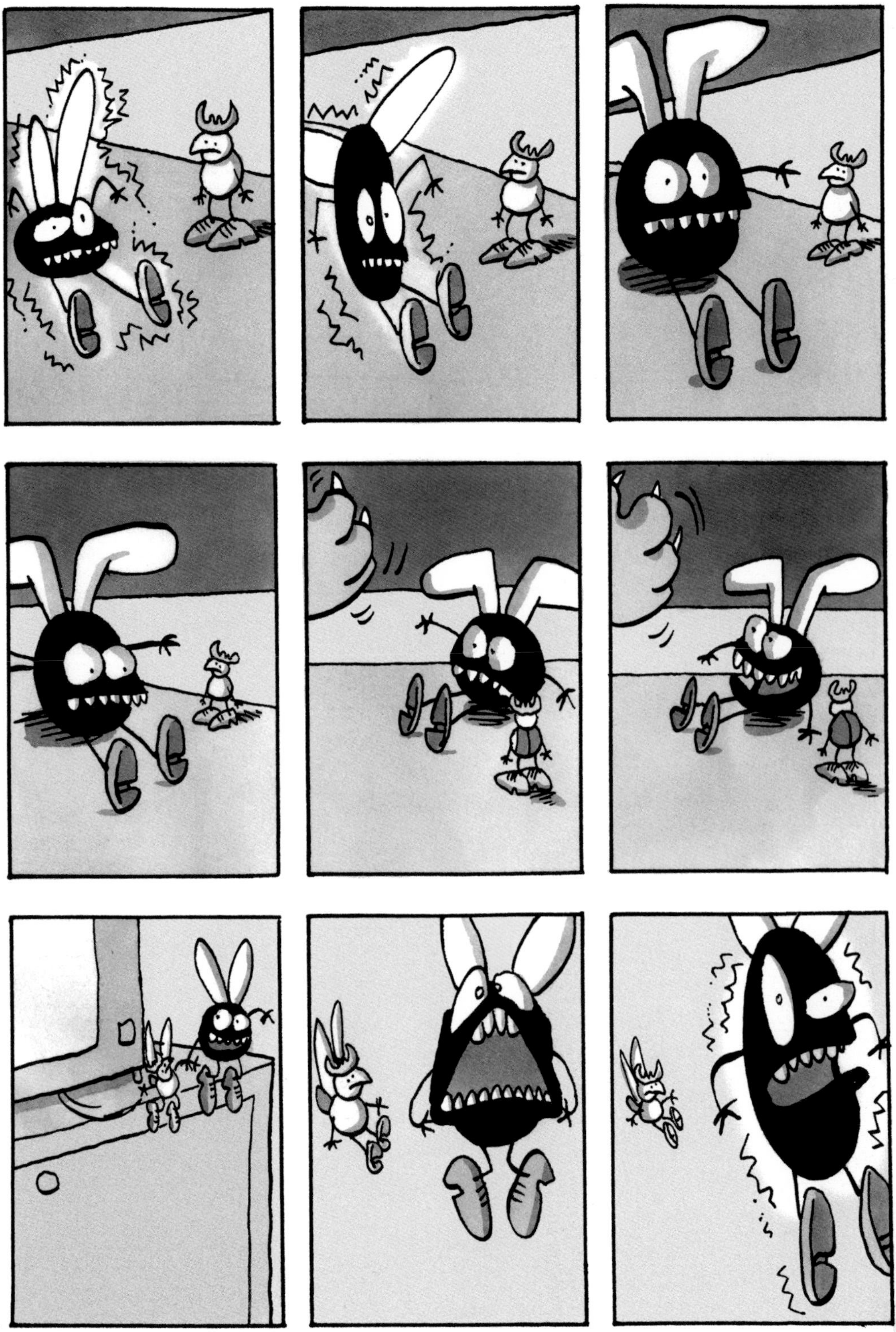

76

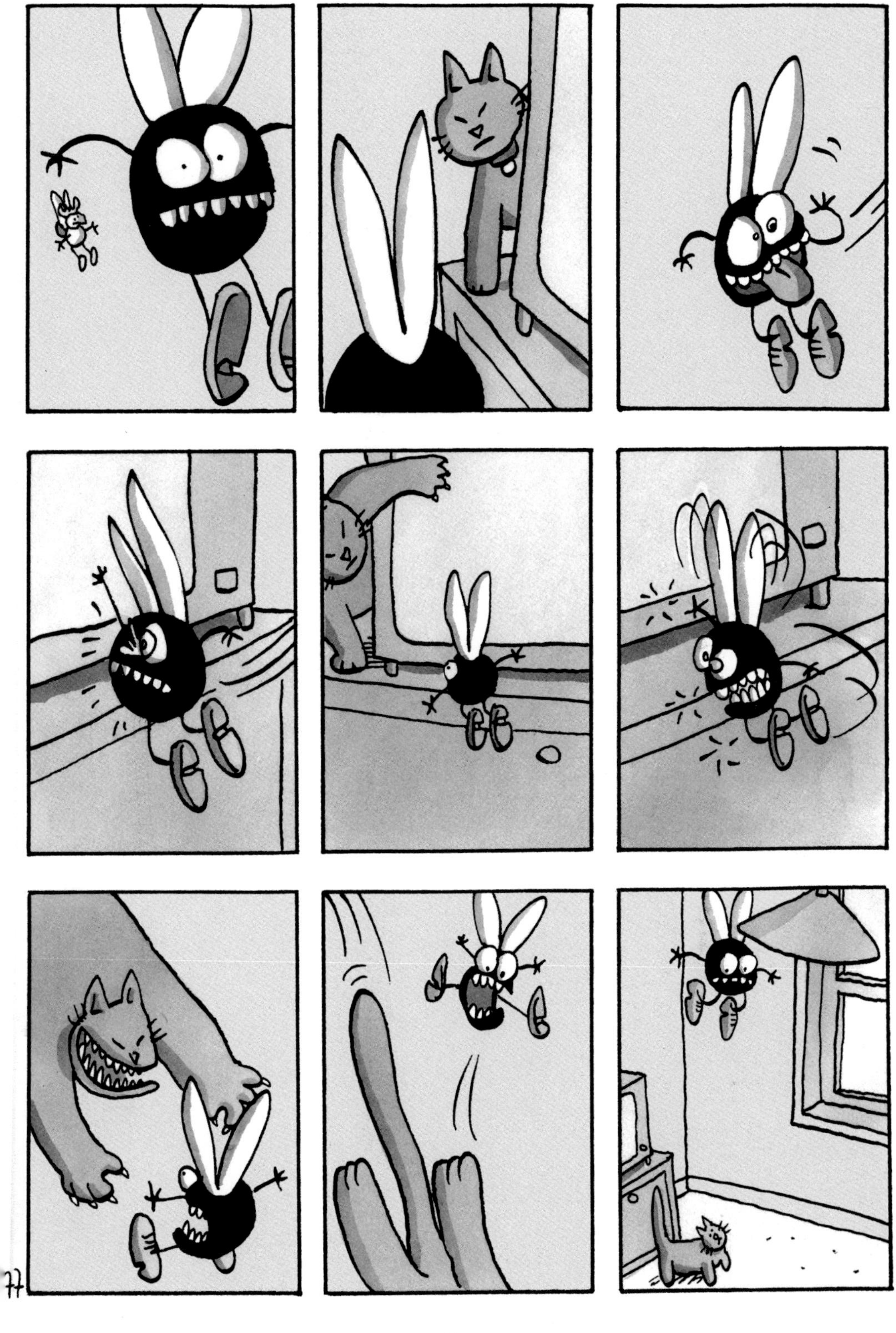

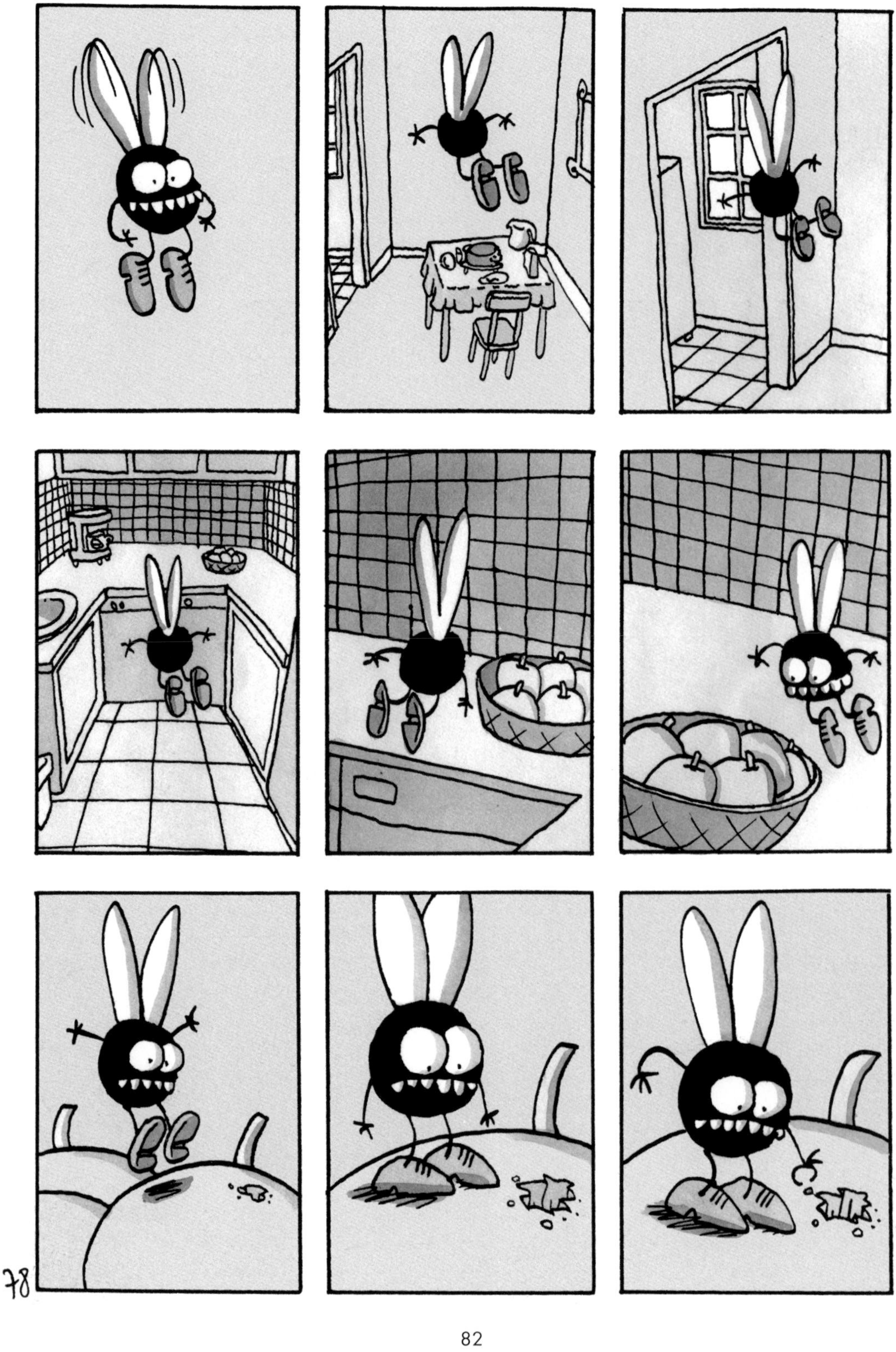

78

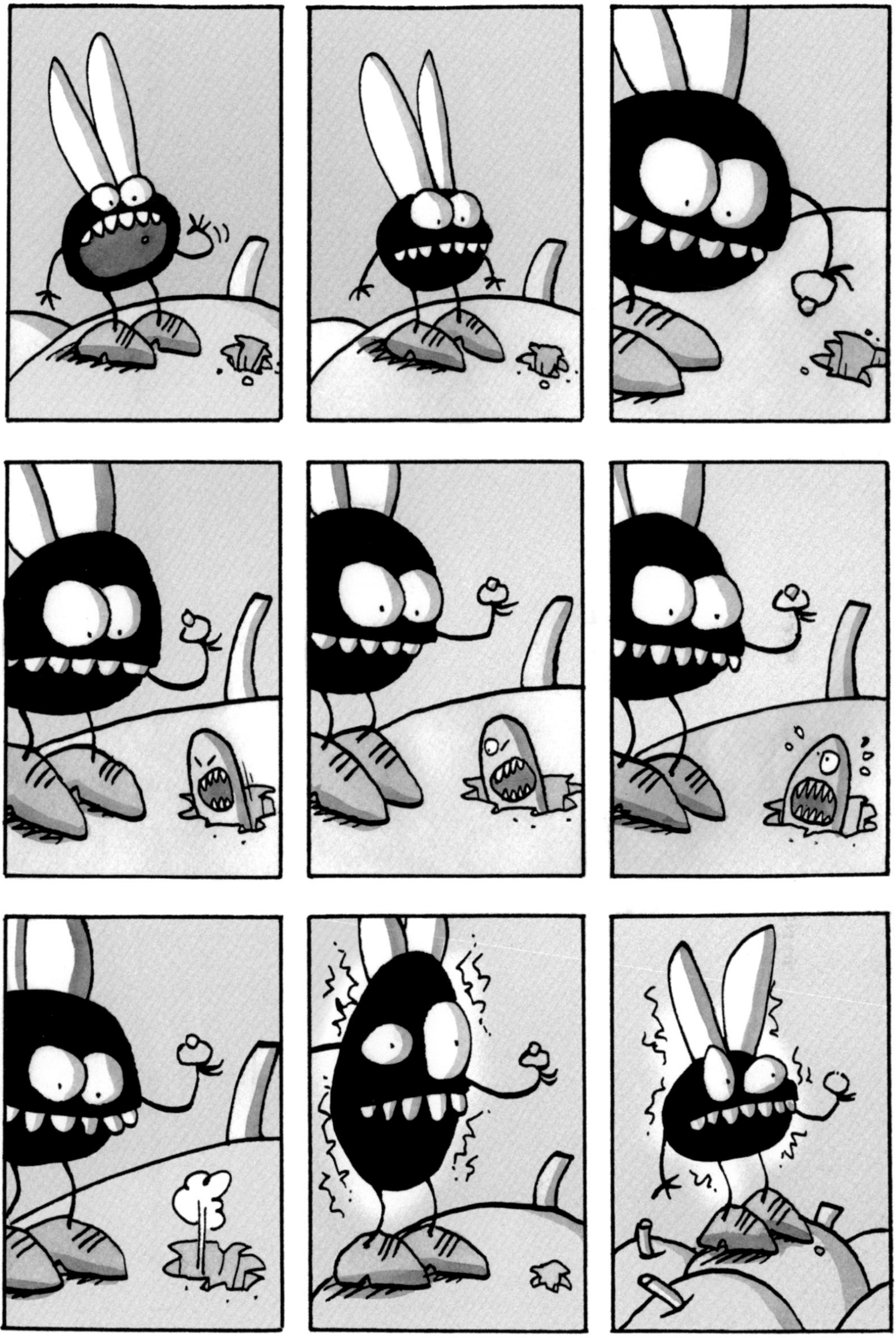

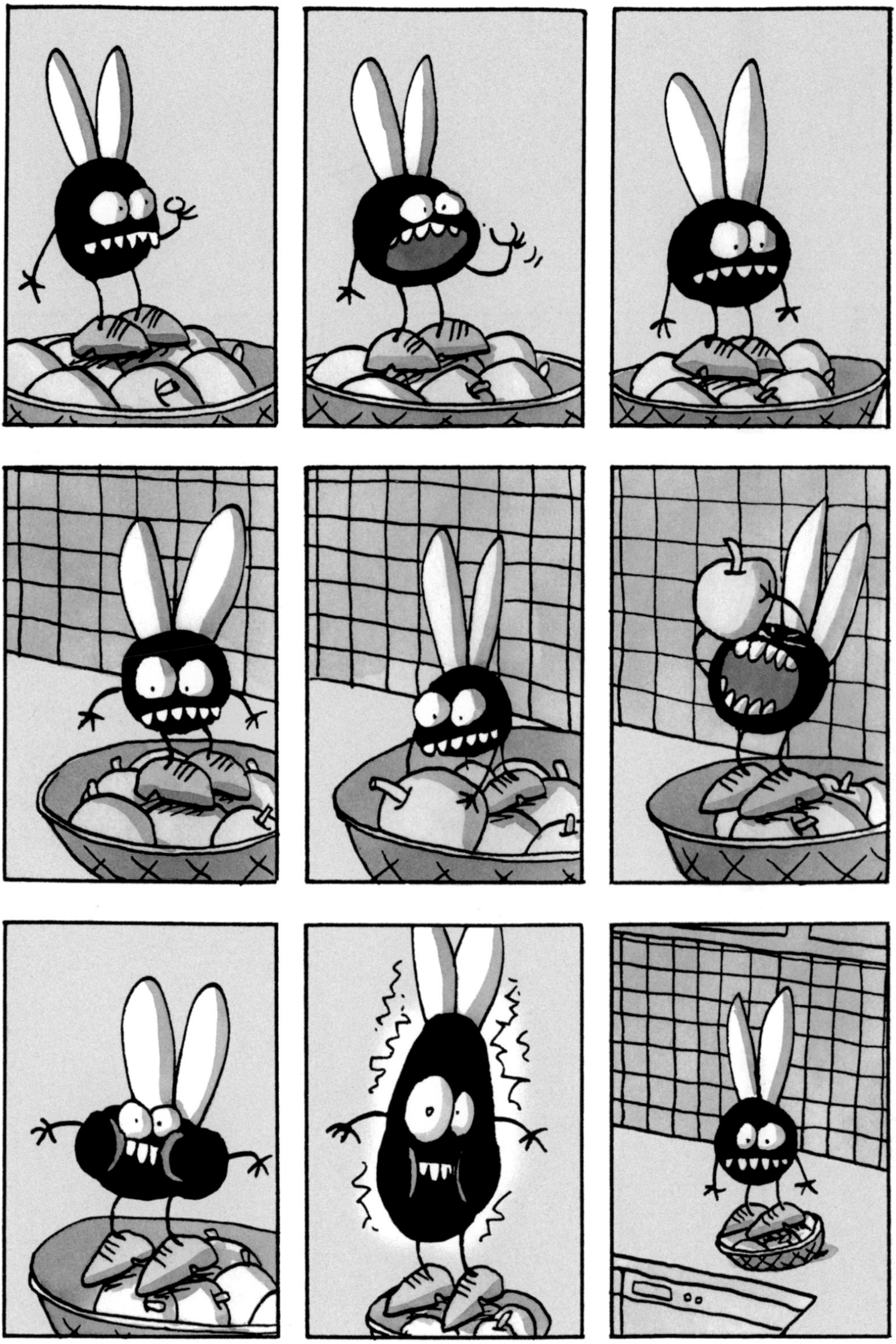

80

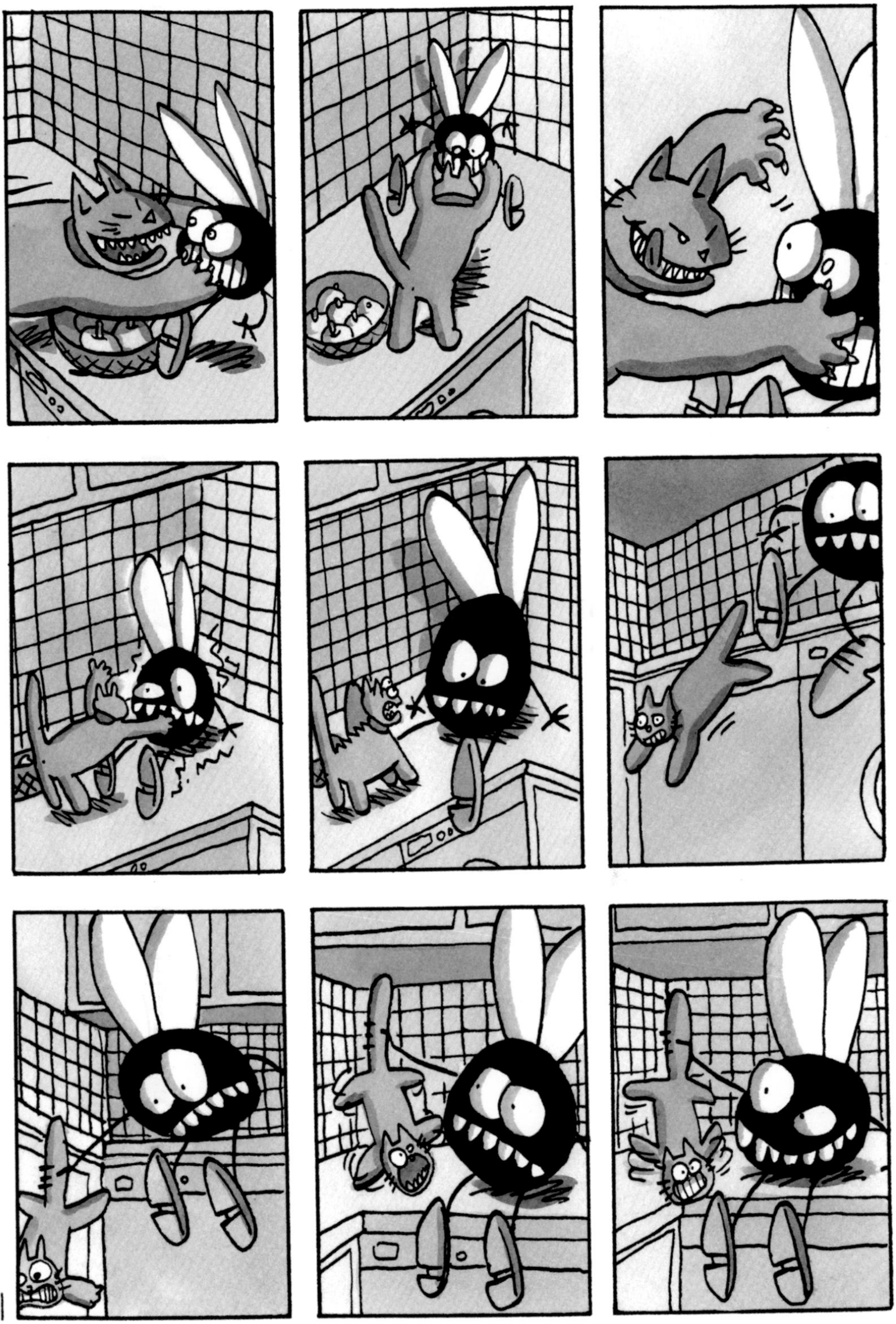

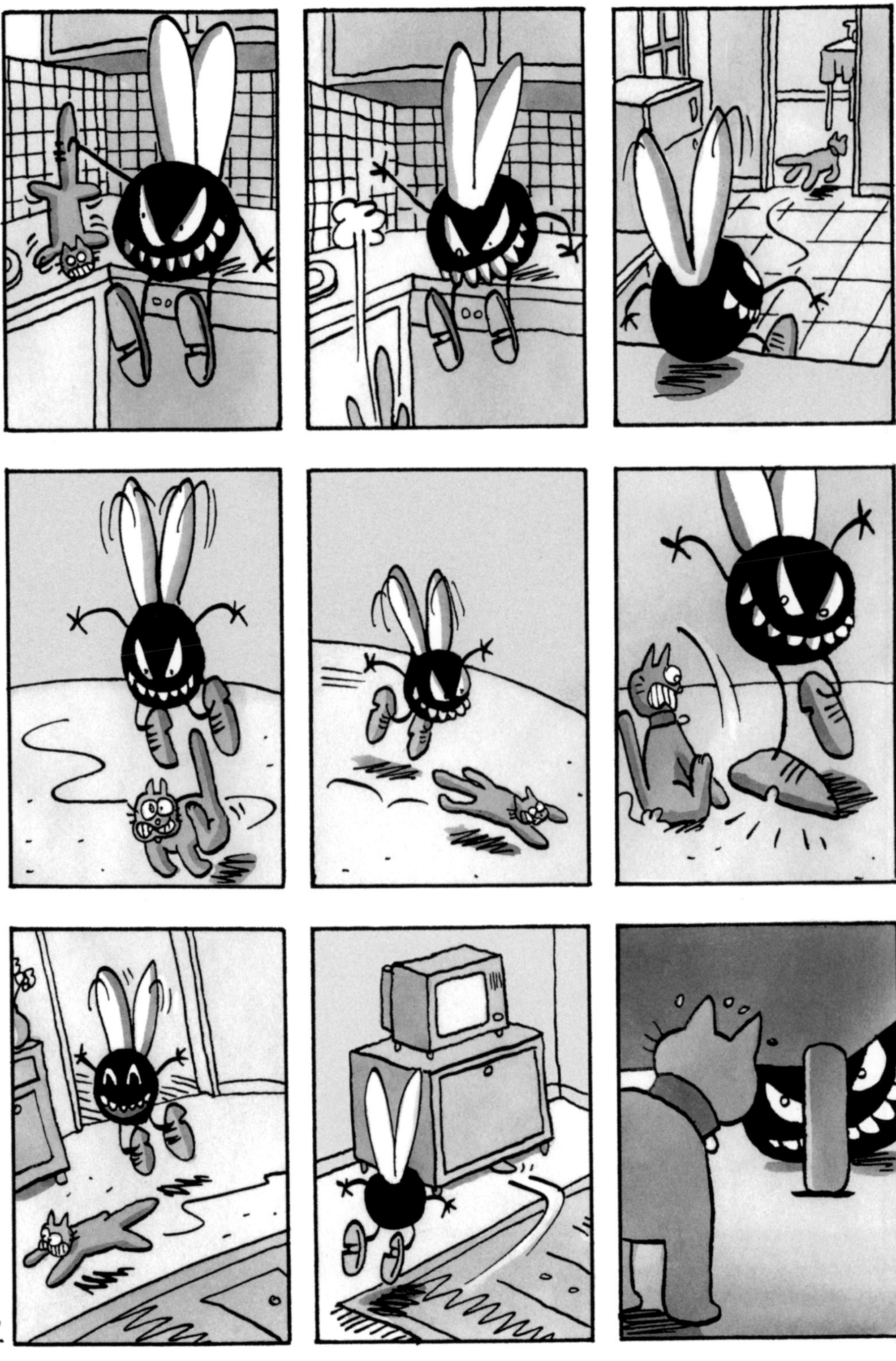

82

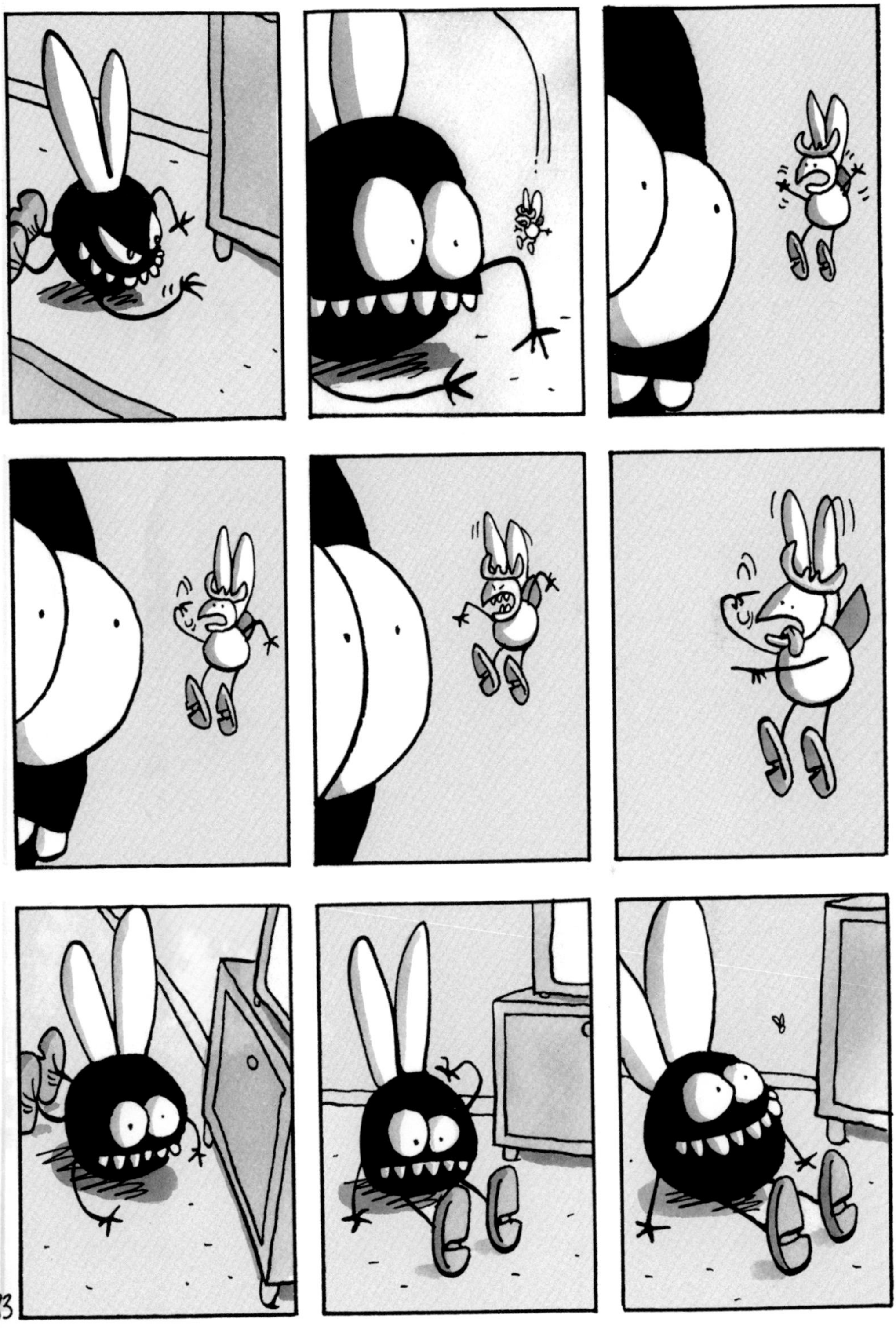

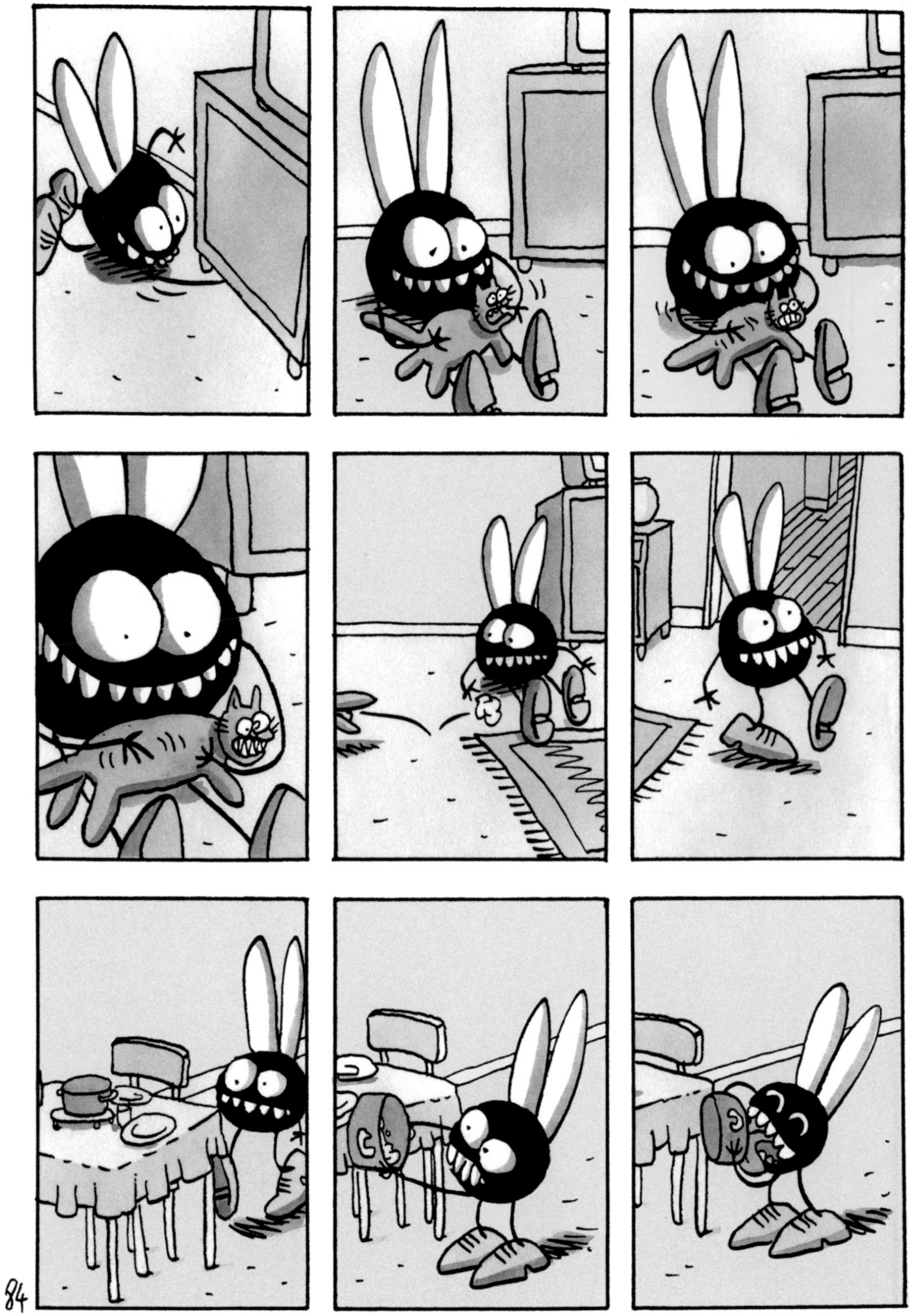
84

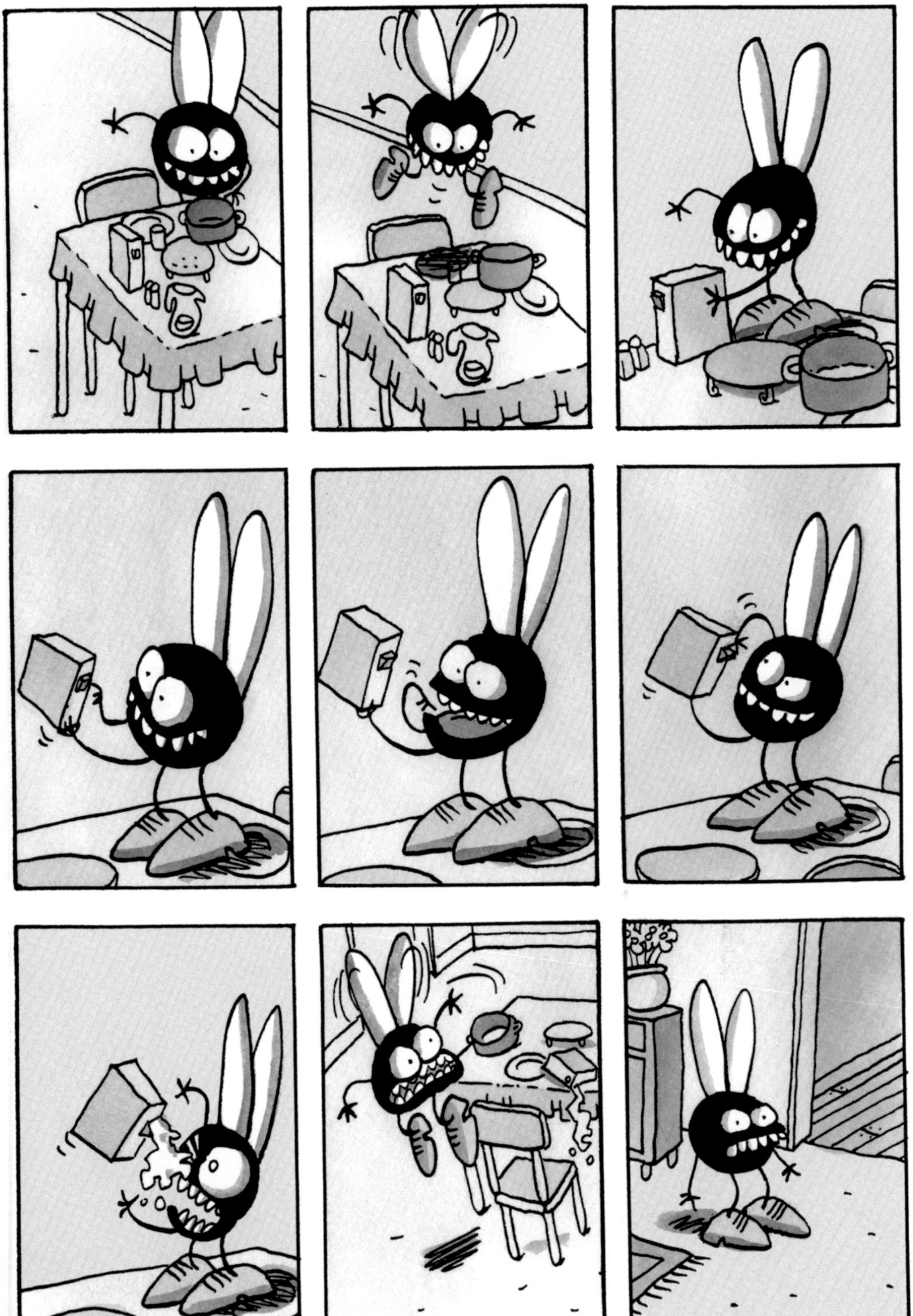

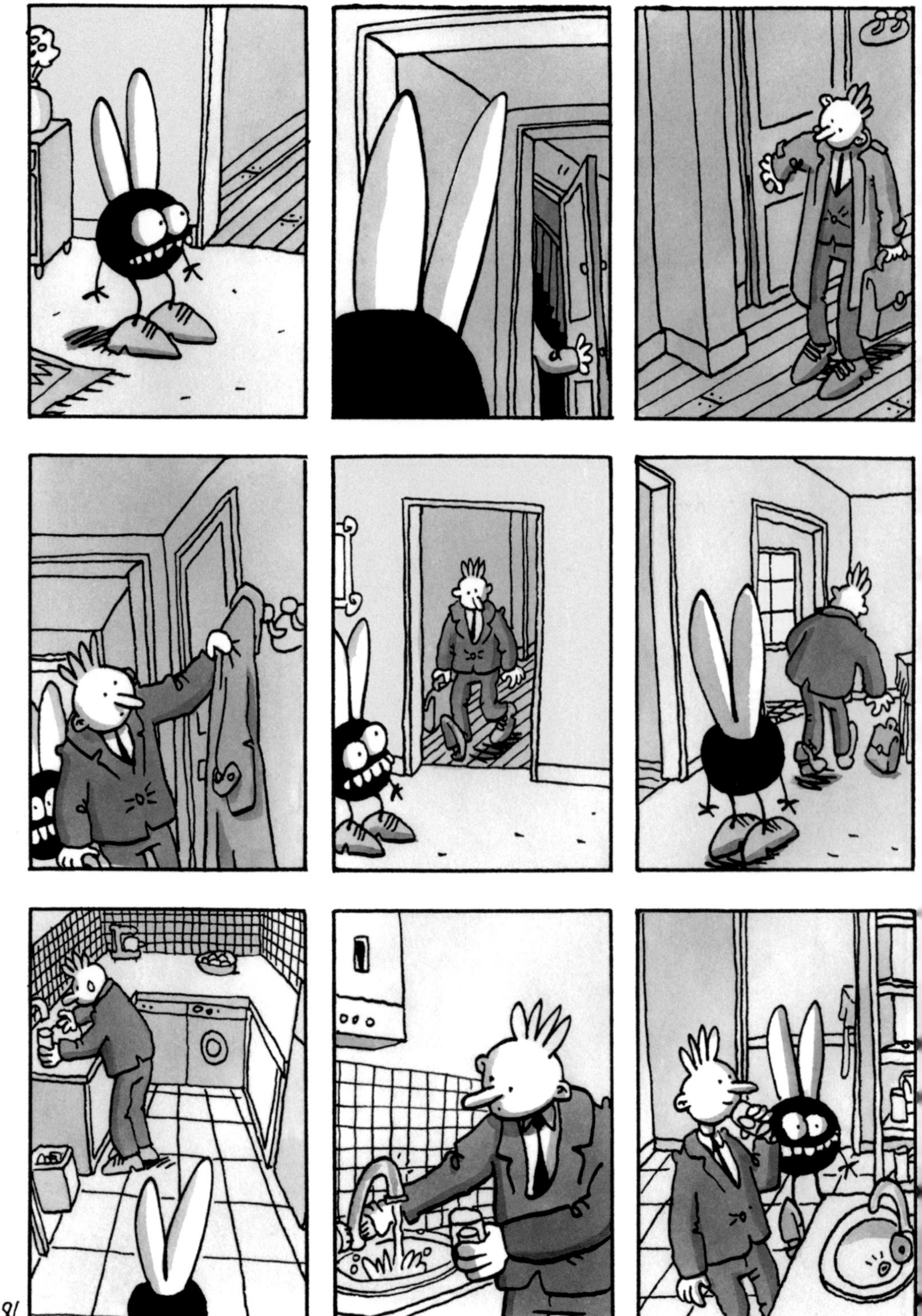
86

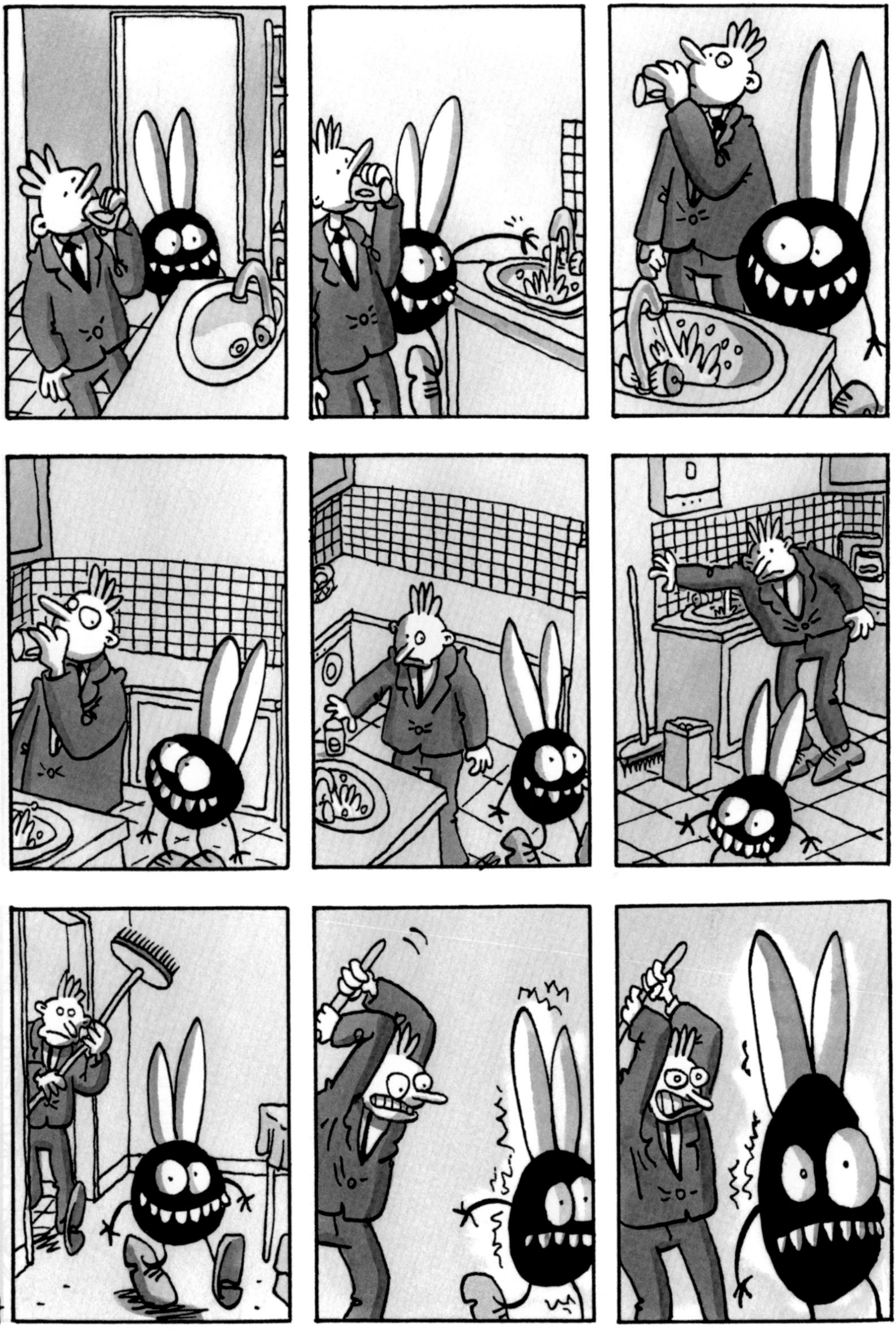

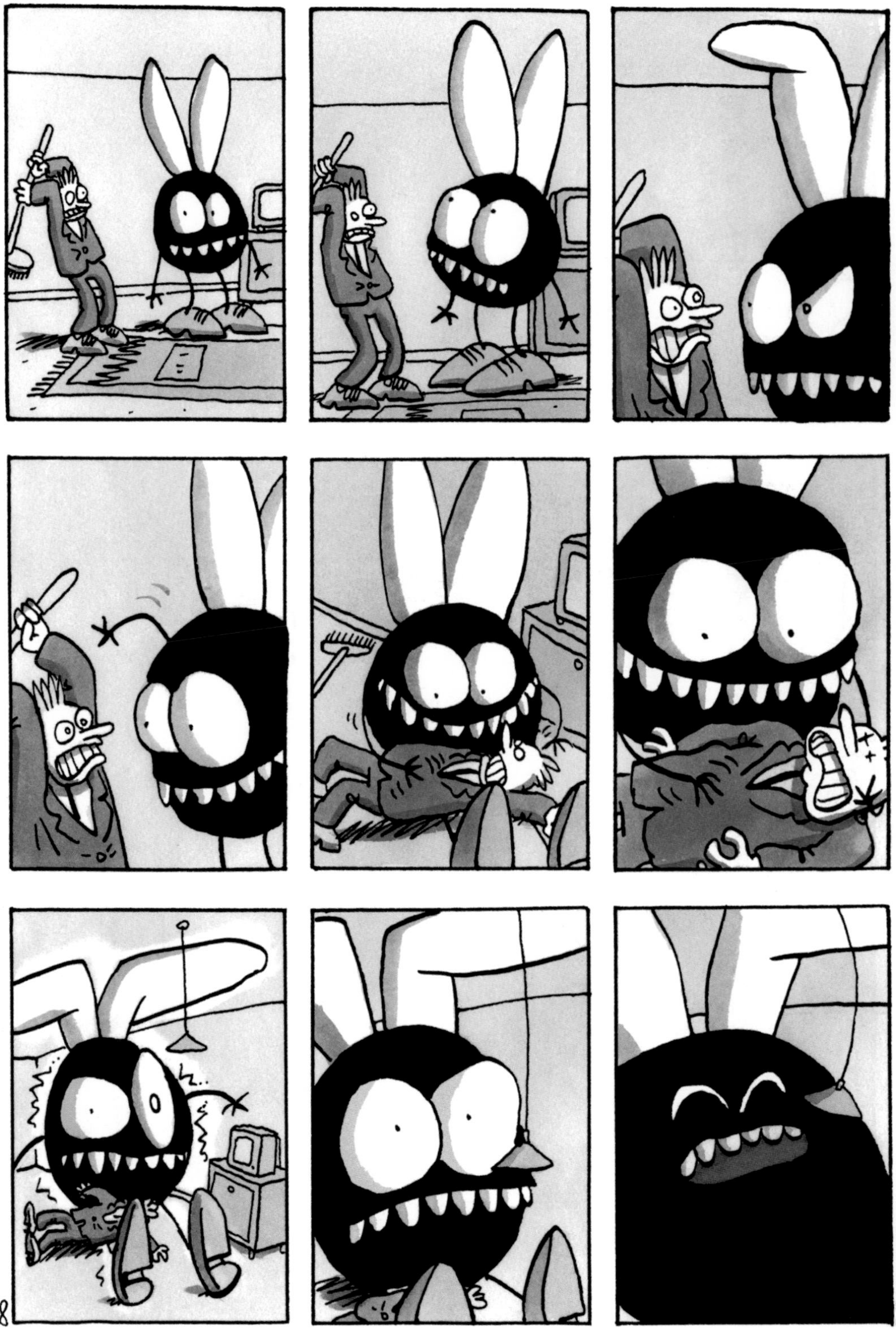

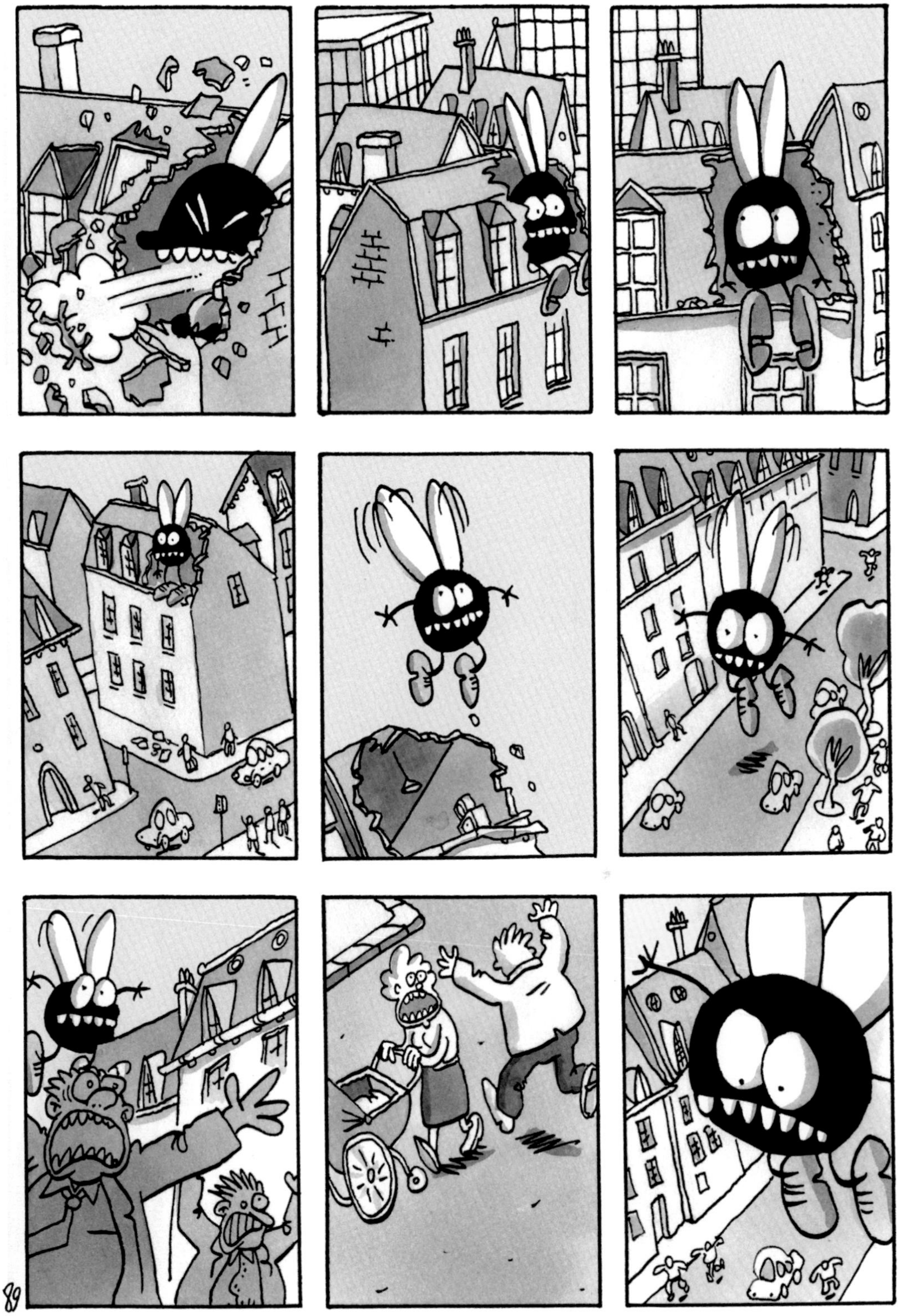
89

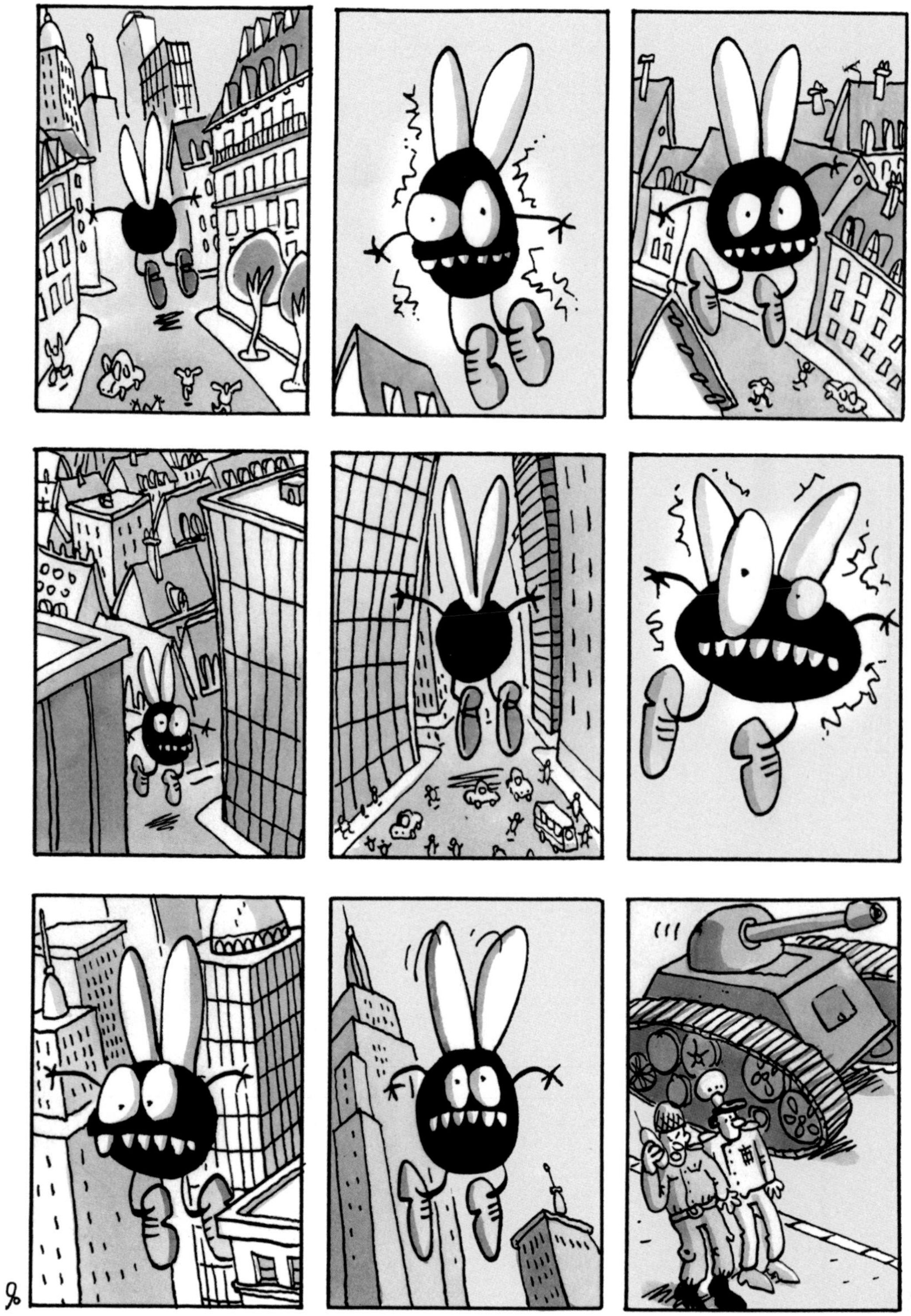

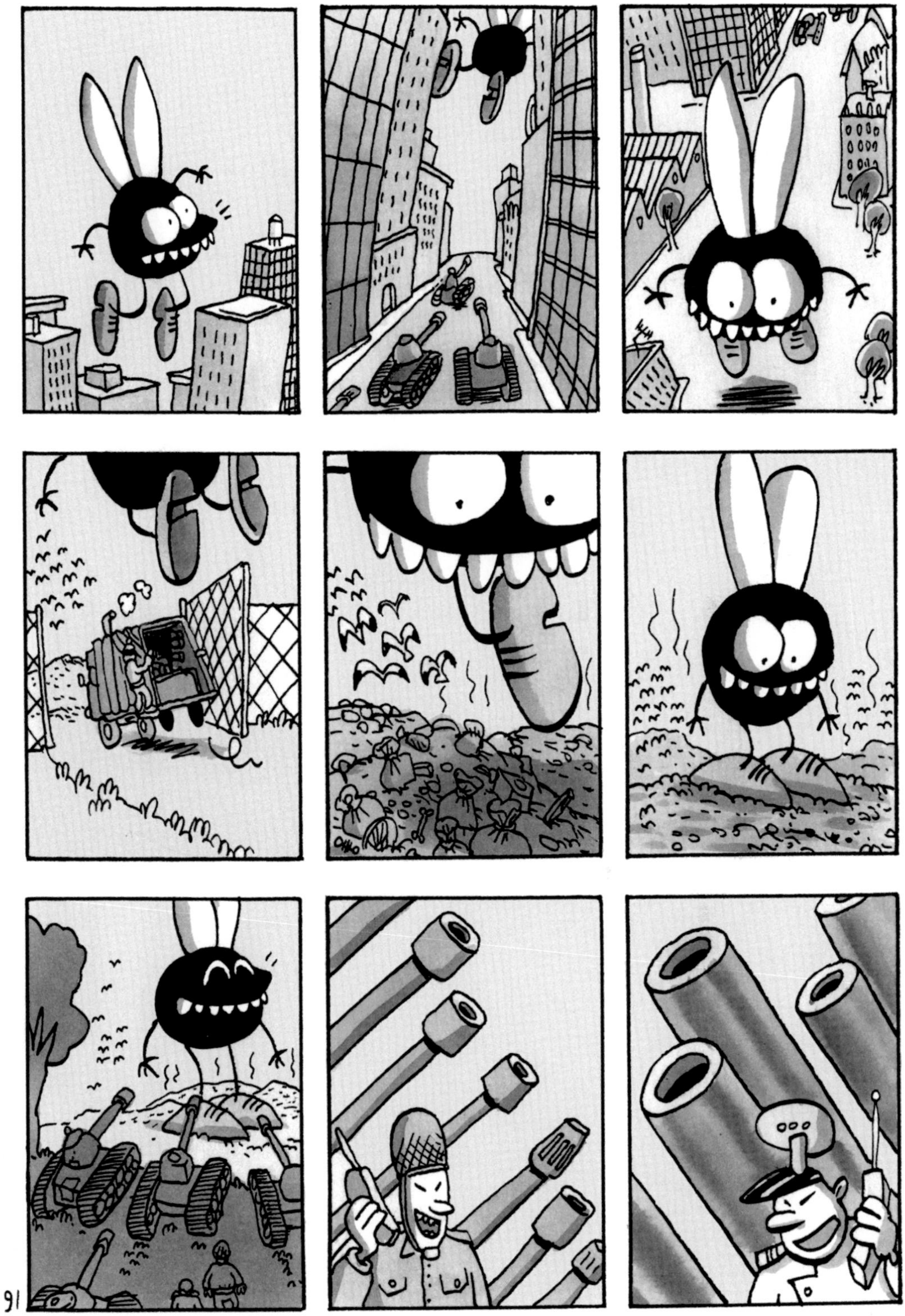

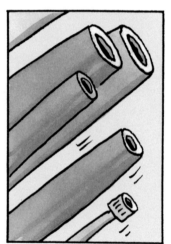

92

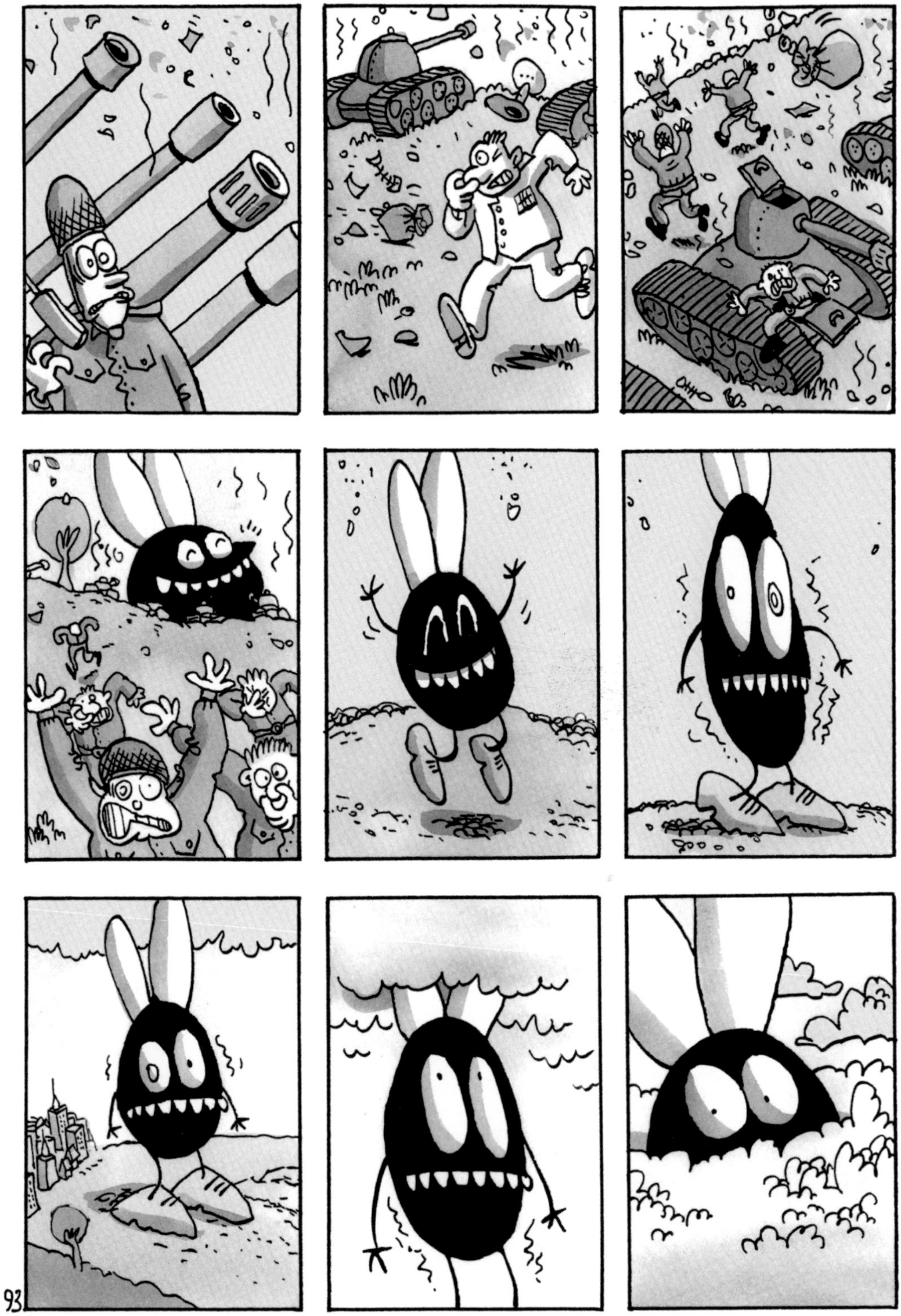
93

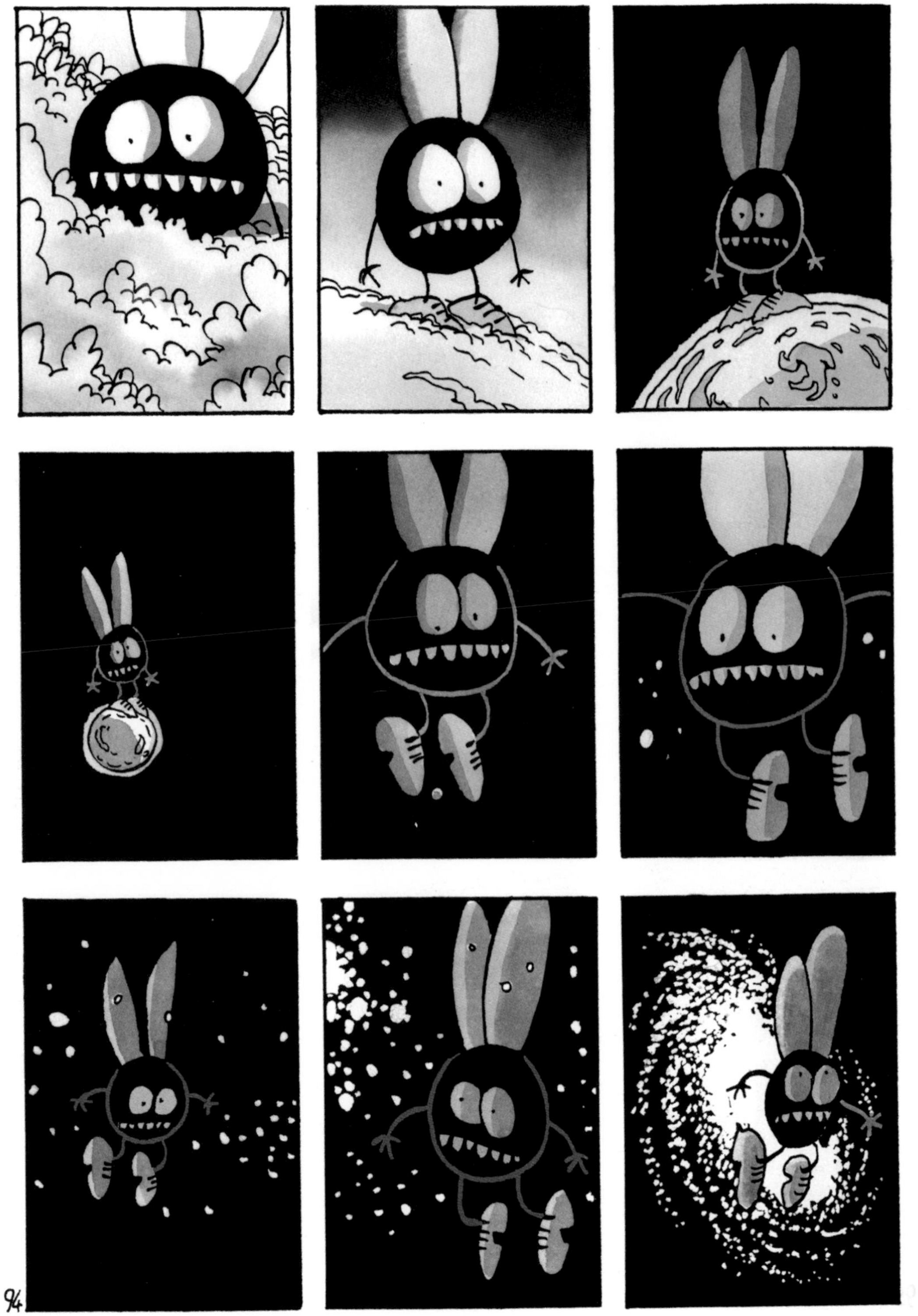

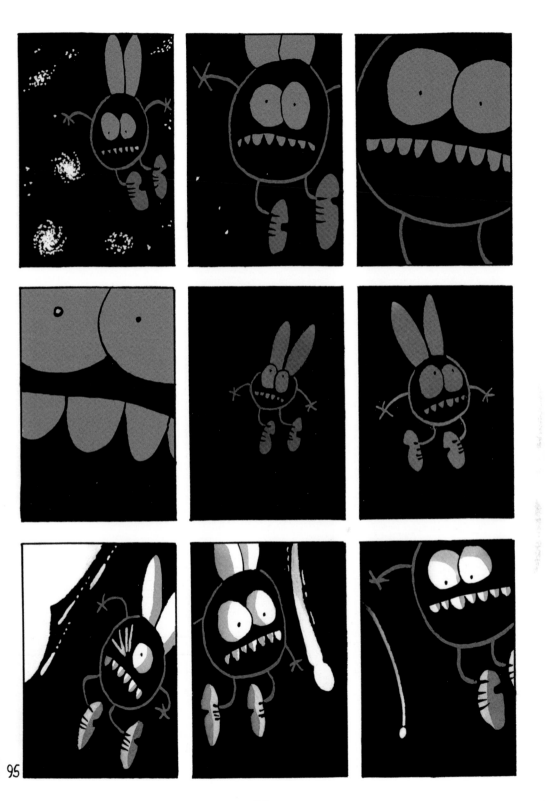

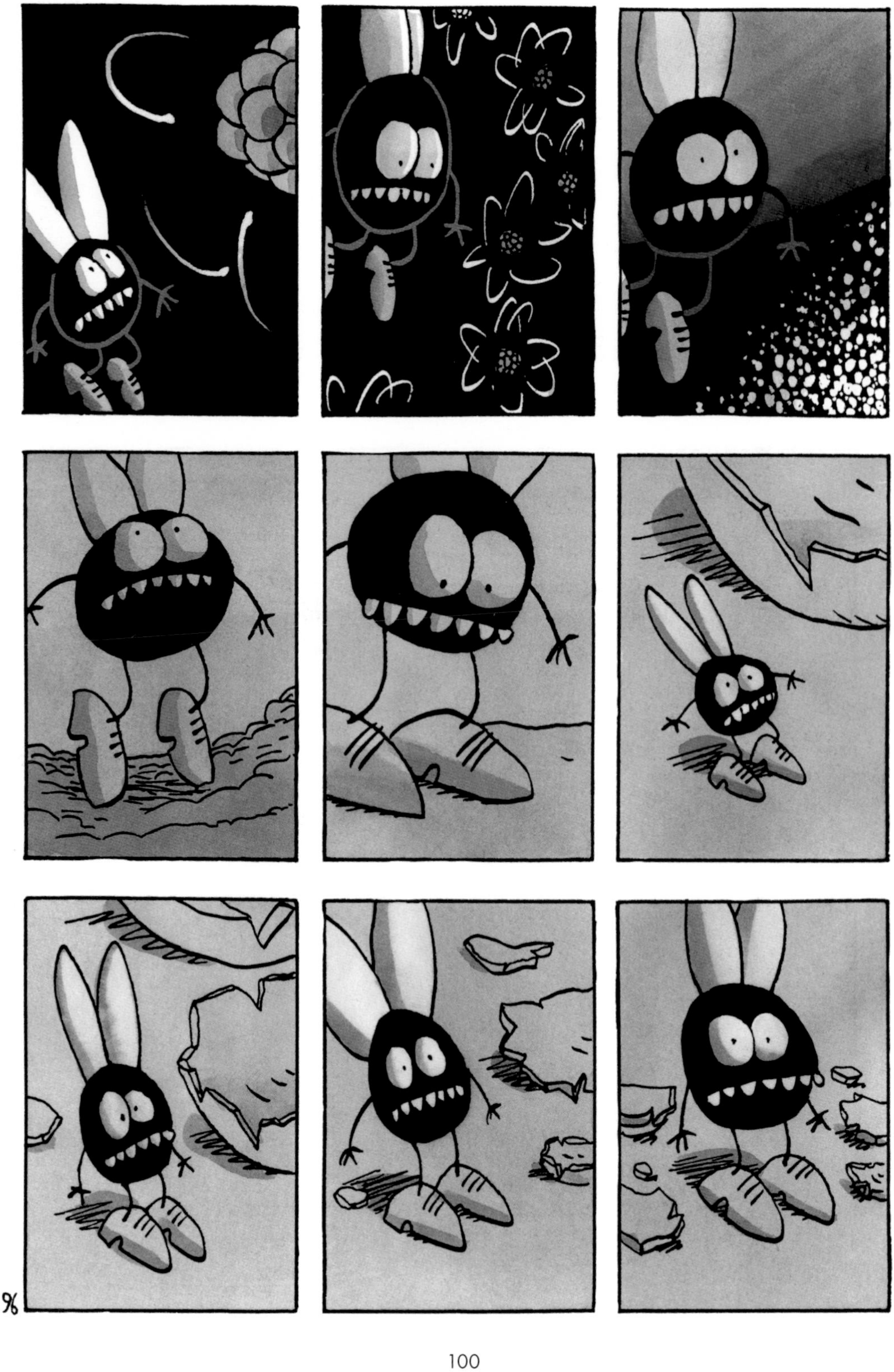
96

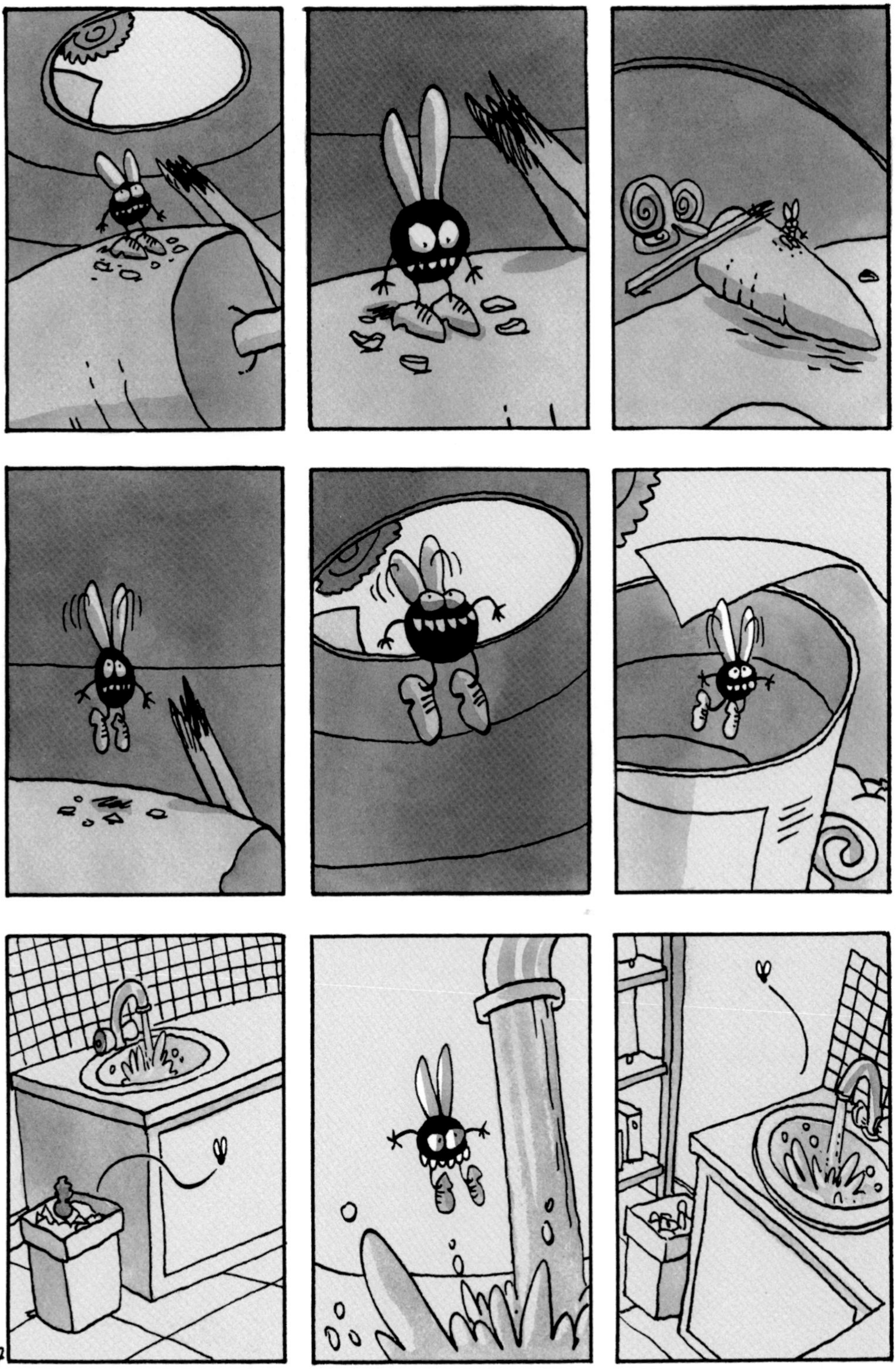
97

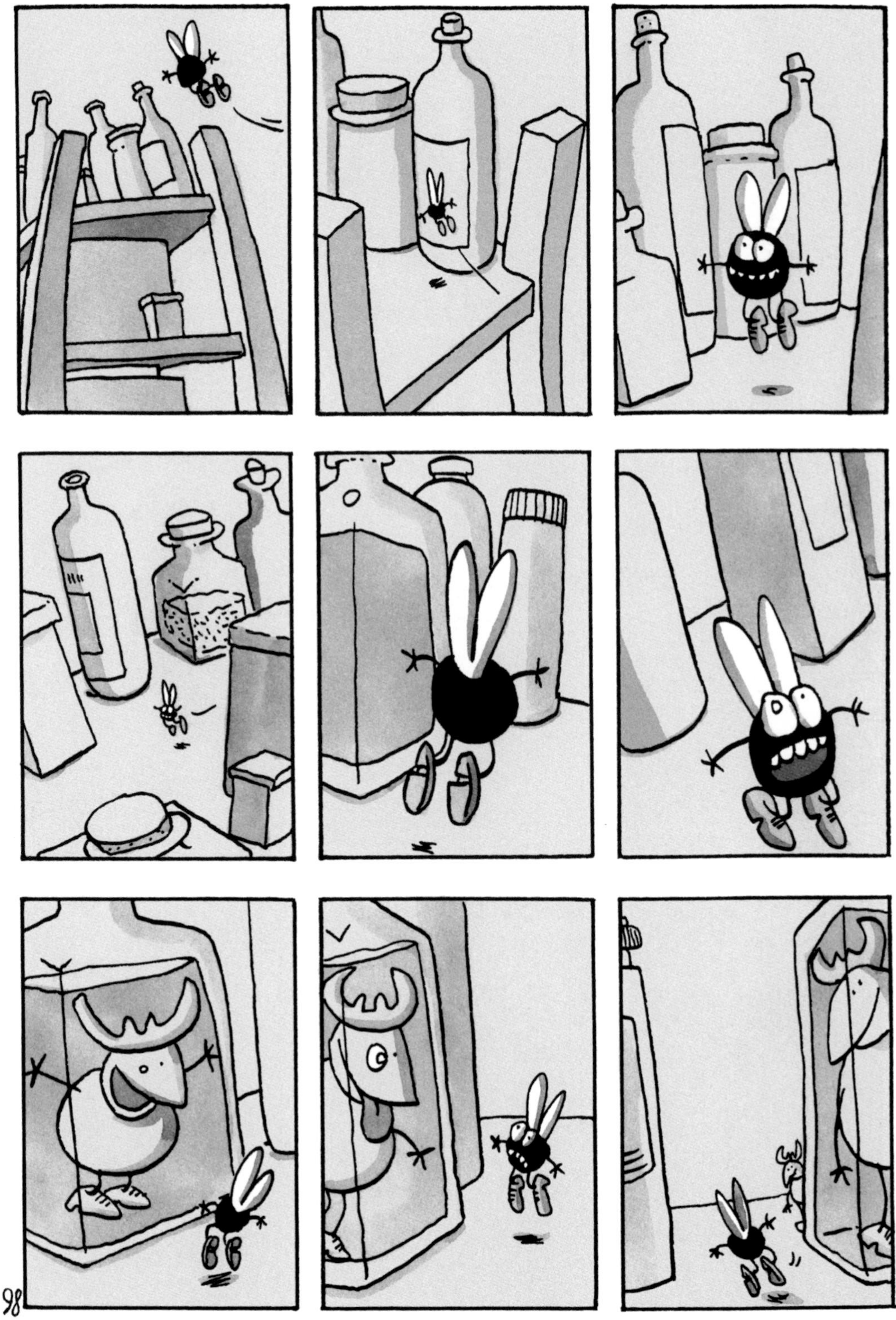
98

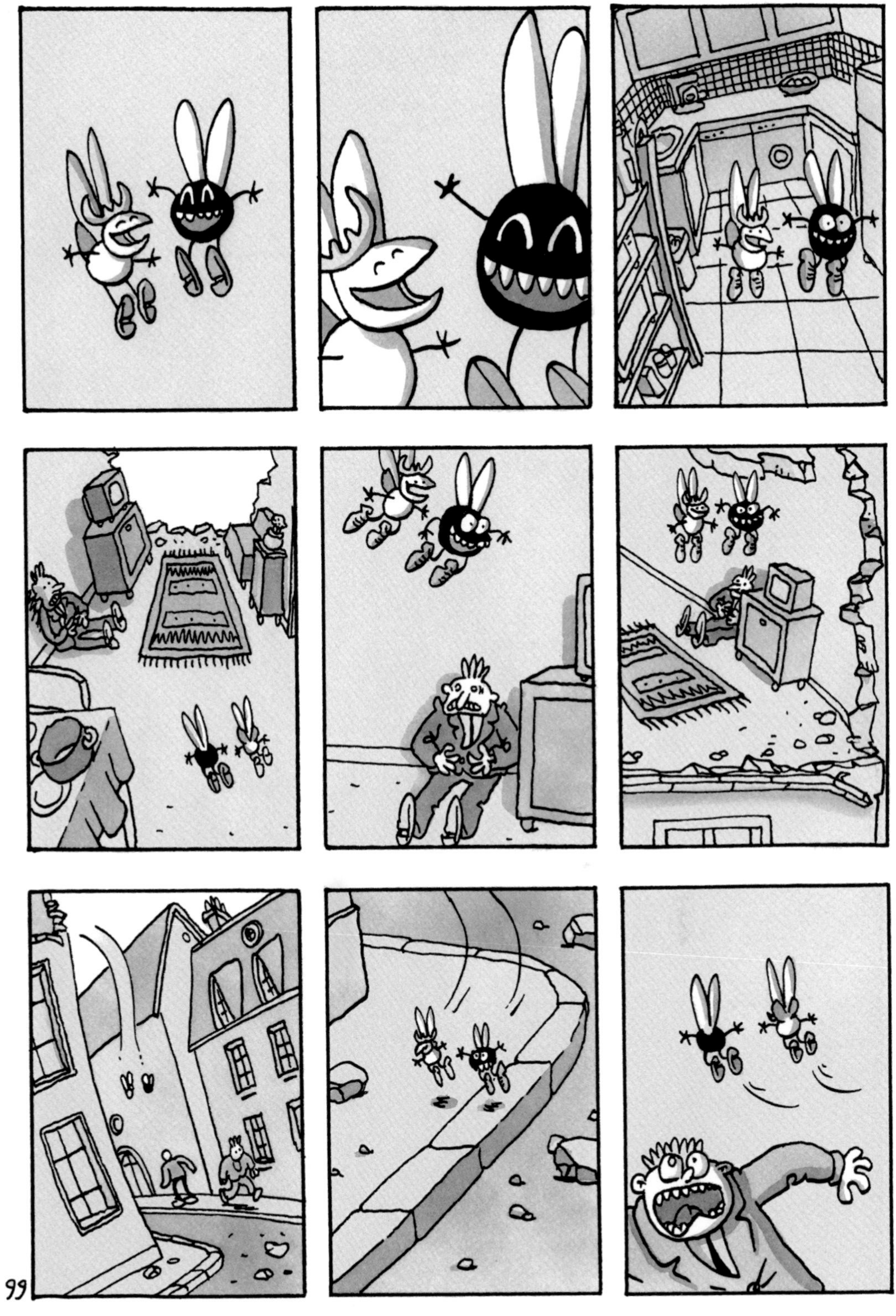
99

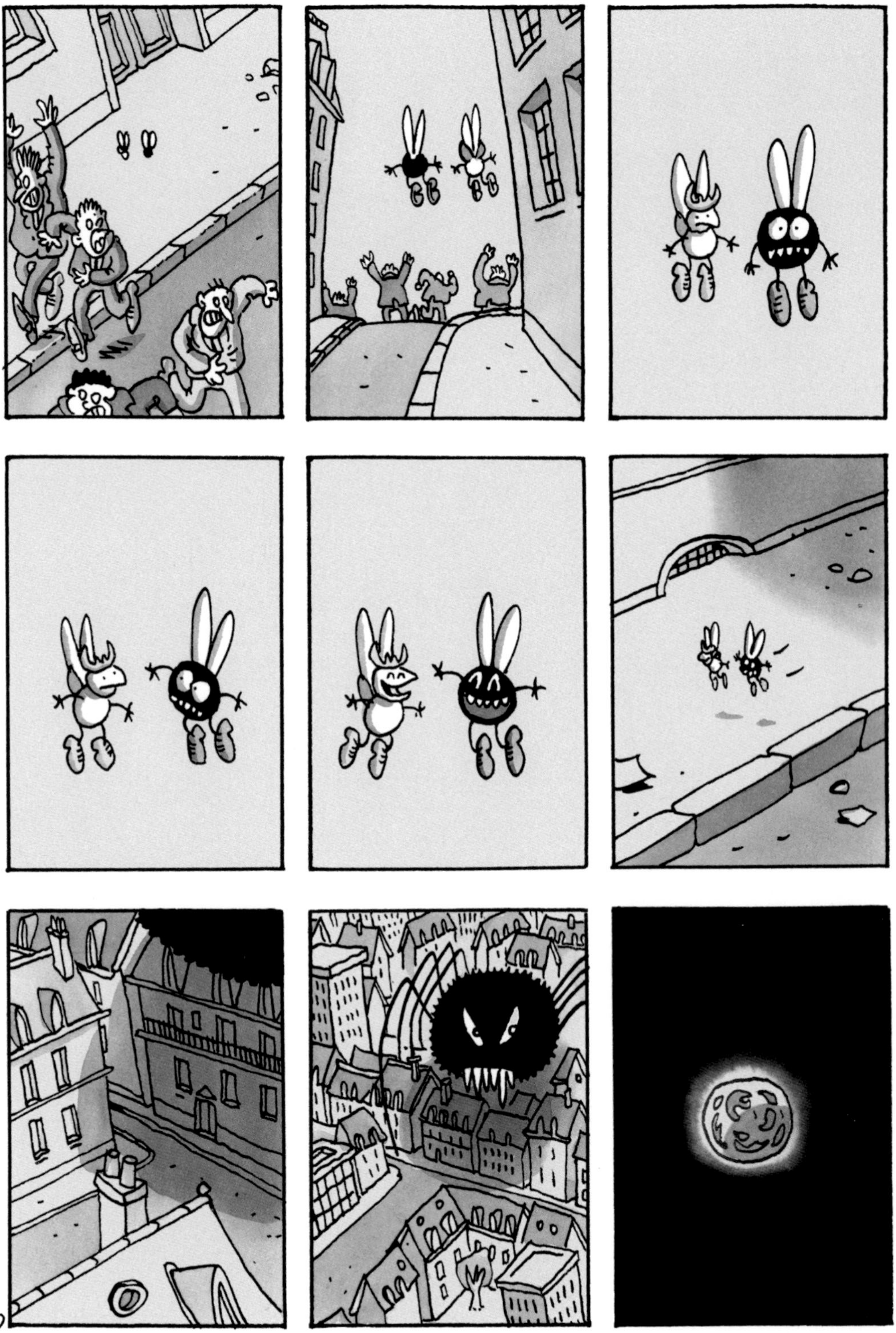
100

LEWIS TRONDHEIM

WATCH OUT FOR PAPERCUTℤ™

Welcome to THE FLY graphic novel by award-winning cartoonist Lewis Trondheim, brought to you by Papercutz, those fannish folks dedicated to publishing great graphic novels for all ages. And if ever there was a graphic novel truly for all ages, THE FLY is it! Whether you're 8 or 88, you'll be able to enjoy this timeless tale. I'm Jim Salicrup, the Editor-in-Chief and Lewis Trondheim fan, here to offer a little behind-the-scenes peek at how Papercutz finally was able to bring you THE FLY…

Back in 2011-2012, Papercutz published four great graphic novels—MONSTER MESS, MONSTER CHRISTMAS, MONSTER DINOSAUR, and MONSTER TURKEY, all written and drawn by the great Lewis Trondheim. Our sister company NBM graphic novels had published even more Trondheim graphic novels (The DUNGEON series, for example), as did First Second and Fantagraphics. This Trondheim fellow is nothing if not prolific. And I couldn't get enough of Trondheim.

In 2001, one of the greatest graphic novel publishers of all time, Fantagraphics, brought out a book entitled *Approximate Continuum Comics* by Lewis Trondheim, and it was an amazing autobiographical look at the young French cartoonist at a point in his life where he was about to get a house with his wife and start a family. This graphic novel essentially featured Trondheim confronting all his personal demons—exploring his fears and hopes for his future. Like everything Trondheim writes and/or draws I simply loved it. He was surprisingly candid, revealing all sorts of stuff about himself, but incredibly entertaining as well. I should also mention that Trondheim usually portrays himself graphically looking somewhat like a humanoid duck (see page 107), as well as drawing all his friends and family as various animal/human hybrids. Within the story, Trondheim talks about a project he was working on called *La Mouche*, or in English, THE FLY. In the back of the book, many of the cartoonists featured within the story comment about their portrayal by Trondheim, including Trondheim. Here's what he said:

"Originally, when Jean-Louis suggested that I create a quarterly comicbook, I did not think I would end up drawing the 144 pages that comprise this collection. My idea was to alternate fictional stories and gags with bits of dreams or true-life stories, and ultimately what I ended up with was almost exclusively autobiography. Once again, improvisation caused me to wander off in a direction different from the intended one. Ah well, so it goes. Oh, I called up Jean-Louis to ask him if my memory is accurate and he said it was seeing the first pages of THE FLY that made him suggest I make a comicbook out of it, and I was fine with this, but since it was wordless, it would've been a rather quick read, so he said I could interpolate bits of real-life stories to flesh it out, and then we agreed we'd call it *Bzz* but I became aware there already was something called *Bzzz* in Italy but fine, we'd do it anyway, and then ultimately, when I brought Jean-Louis my pages it was something totally different.

And then fifteen years later, when Kim Thompson suggested that as a follow-up to the US edition of this book Fantagraphics put out its edition of THE FLY (which I eventually drew as a separate book anyway) under the title *Buzz Buzz*, I said, 'Sure, why not?'"

Why not, indeed? As a fan I eagerly awaited *Buzz Buzz*, but years passed and it never came out. After *La Mouche* was originally published, there was a Canadian-French animated series called *Fly Tales* produced in 1999. Sixty-five 5-minute episodes were created, and you can see them on YouTube if you search for *Les Adventures d'une Mouche*. But I wanted the original graphic novel. I'm sure it didn't help matters when Fantagraphics editor Kim Thompson passed away.

More recently, we launched a series at Papercutz called MAGICAL HISTORY TOUR that is co-edited by Lewis Trondheim (Is there anything he doesn't do?), and that got us thinking about Trondheim again. We had thought about publishing THE FLY ourselves before, but we had trouble figuring out who had the rights to the material. Enter Papercutz Managing Editor Jeff Whitman. After everyone else gave up, I asked Jeff to track down the rights—and he did!

So, here we are, twenty-six years after *La Mouche* was originally published, twenty-two years after *La Mouche* was adapted into animated cartoons, two decades after I read *Approximate Continuum Comics*... and THE FLY is finally in print in North America from Papercutz. We hope you enjoy it as much as we do.

And if that wasn't enough, Super Genius, the Papercutz imprint for older audiences, will soon be continuing another Trondheim series that Fantagraphics had begun back in 2012, RALPH AZHAM. Go to supergeniuscomics.com for more information about that exciting series.

Thanks,
Jim

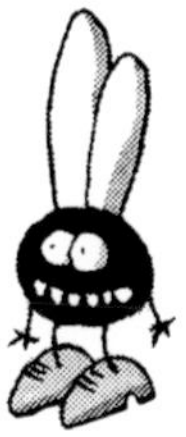

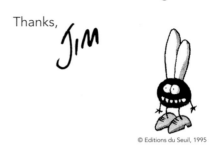

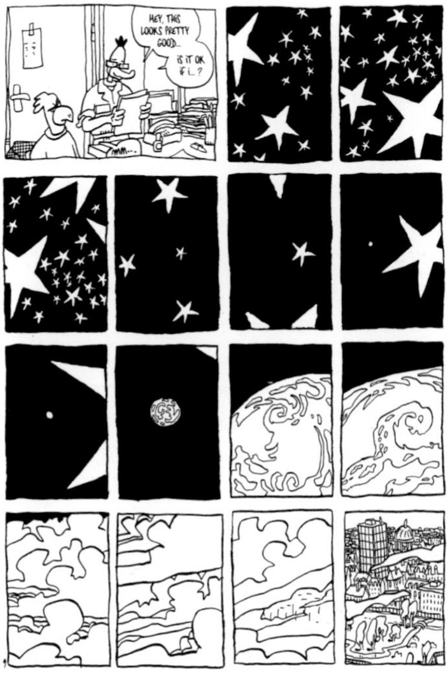
HEY, THIS LOOKS PRETTY GOOD...
IS IT OK IF I...?
MMM...

Page 9 from *Approximate Continuum Comics*. The Fly appeared in this sequence of Trondheim's auto-biographical graphic novel. Special thanks to Gary Groth and Fanatgraphics.

STAY IN TOUCH!

EMAIL:	salicrup@papercutz.com
WEB:	www.papercutz.com
TWITTER:	@papercutzgn
INSTAGRAM:	@papercutzgn
FACEBOOK:	PAPERCUTZGRAPHICNOVELS
FANMAIL:	Papercutz, 160 Broadway, Suite 700, East Wing, New York, NY 10038

Go to papercutz.com and sign up for the free Papercutz e-newsletter!

THE FLY

CREATOR LEWIS TRONDHEIM SPEAKS

Self-portrait of Lewis Trondheim, the artist at work.

One of the founders of L'Association in France which turned comics publishing there on its head, Lewis Trondheim is a prolific and incredibly imaginative creator in comics. From wordless strips such as *Mr. O* to the darkly tongue-in-cheek loving spoof of heroic fantasy *Dungeon* which he co-writes with Joann Sfar, his breadth of contributions to comics is staggering. He's also known for *McConey Rabbit*, *A.L.I.E.E.E.N.* and Papercutz's MON-STER, among other goofy kids comics and heads a very unusual imprint called "Shampoing" in one of France's largest publishing companies, where he continues to expand this art form's horizons. Both his silent comic THE FLY and *Kaput and Zösky* have been made into animated cartoons.

For this edition of THE FLY, Lewis Trondheim graciously agreed to be interviewed via email by Papercutz Editor-in-Chief Jim Salicrup. Lewis answered in French, which was translated by Papercutz Managing Editor Jeff Whitman. Papercutz thanks Lewis

Trondheim for taking the time to answer our questions.

Jim Salicrup: Where and when were you born?
Lewis Trondheim: I was born in 1964 in Fontainebleau. A small city 60 km from Paris, with a castle and a very big forest. Well… for the French, it is really big.

JS: Why did you decide to change your name to Trondheim? (He was born Laurent Chabosy.)
LT: Because no one had asked me my opinion at birth, but I don't blame my parents.

JS: What was your childhood like?
LT: I got bored a lot. This certainly developed certain creative capabilities. It must be said that there was only one television channel when I was born. When I was 12… no Internet. No social media. A pinecone battle was the highlight of my entertainment.
JS: Did you read comics? If so, what

108

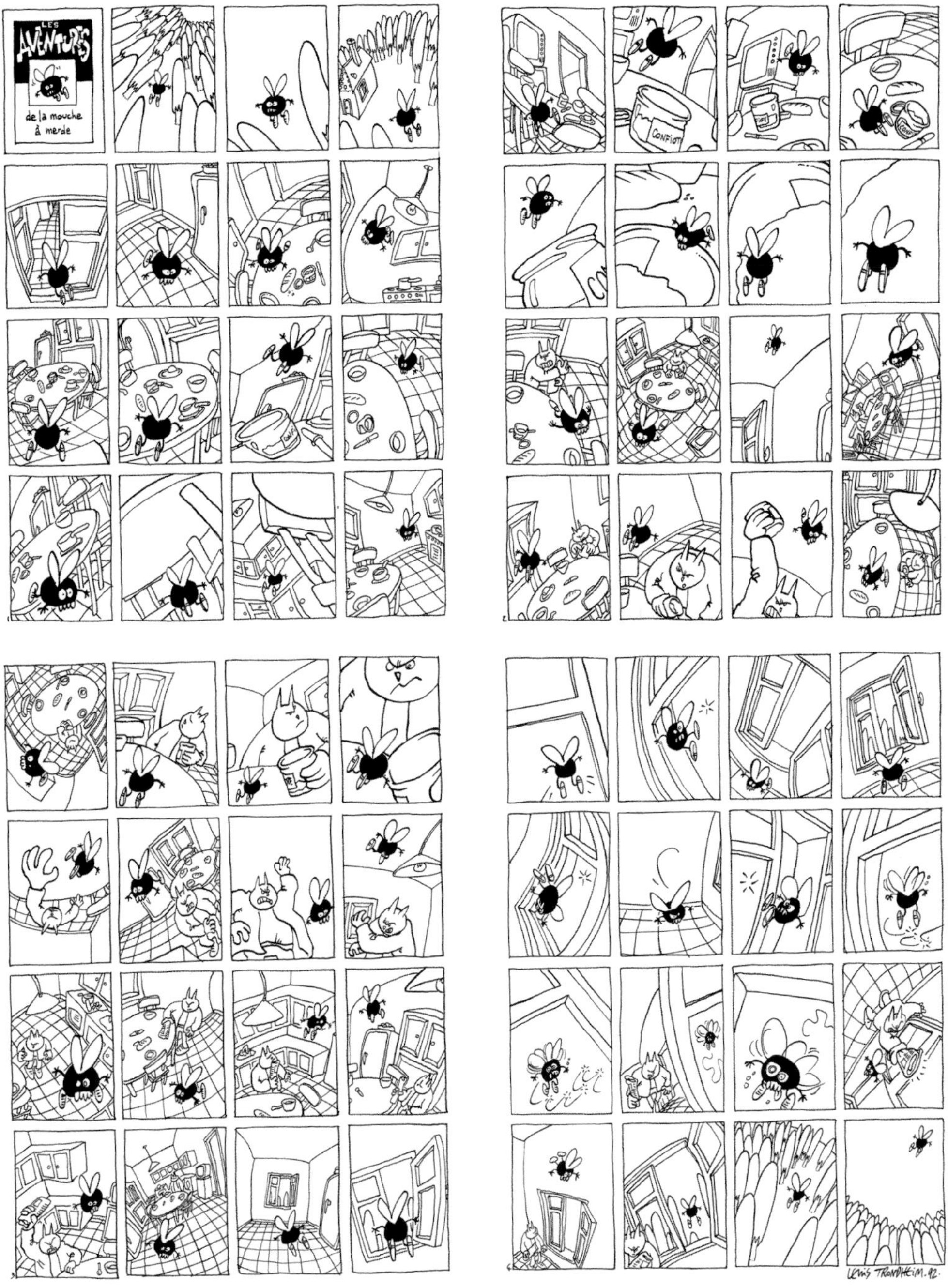
LES AVENTURES
de la mouche à merde
CONFIOT
LEWIS TRONDHEIM.92.

Here are the very first pages of THE FLY ever created by Lewis Trondheim.

were your favorites?

LT: My dad was a bookseller and I would regularly check out Franco-Belgian classic comics. My parents had taught me to open the book at 90 degrees maximum to not damage it so we could then sell it after I read it. *Tintin* and *Gaston Lagaffe* were my favorites.

JS: Did you go to art school? If so, where and what was that like?

LT: No. I went to a school for graphic design. But this helped me later to set up files and create book covers.

JS: When did you decide you wanted to create comics?

LT: The day I understood that I didn't need to know how to draw very good in order to do comics. All I had to do was be interesting and catch the readers with the first word balloon and then never let them go.

JS: Who were your greatest artistic inspirations?

LT: Moebius, Tolkien, Lovecraft, Philip K. Dick, Fredric Brown.

JS: How did you break into comics?

LT: I started by doing a fanzine, all by myself. Every two months, then monthly. I started to get noticed by photocopying panels where I just changed the dialog. Some funny and absurd stories there.

JS: Do you prefer working in a studio with other artists or working at home (with your wife)?

LT: I prefer working from home because I wake up at 11AM.

JS: How do you keep coming up with so many great ideas?

LT: I improvise a lot. I'm my first reader and I want to surprise myself and to find out how the story will end. I always get very surprised that the readers always like my stories.

JS: What inspired you to do THE FLY?

LT: Before I hid behind a lot of dialogue in my stories. The art didn't really matter. Well, to improve, I told myself that it wouldn't be a bad idea to do a story without dialogue, like this, and I would be forced to design the backgrounds and to work on changing camera angles. I really like working under pressure. I am very playful and pressure always lets me surprise myself.

JS: Were you involved with THE FLY animations?

LT: Not at all. I am quite pragmatic and I knew where I would be best, and that was doing new comics, not working on the adaptations of my comics.

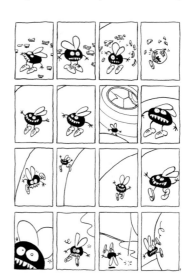

Page 10 from *Approximate Continuum Comics*.

JS: Do you think you'll ever bring back THE FLY?

LT: No. There are still plenty of potential worlds to discover with comics.

I don't like redoing the same things over and over again.

JS: What inspired MONSTER?
LT: When I became a father, I wanted to write stories for my two children. Stories where they would be the main characters.

JS: What made you end MONSTER?
LT: My children became too old for this series, alas.

JS: Do you enjoy writing for other artists?
LT: My capacity as an artist is quite limited. My art is minimalist and animalistic. Working with other artists allows me to create stories that wouldn't work well with my art style. Besides, I always wanted to be a writer. I became an artist by accident, by staging my stories.

JS: Do you enjoy editing *The Thread of History* (MAGICAL HISTORY TOUR) series?
LT: Yes. It's a great power to give young readers the keys to understand our world. And this does that, without lecturing too much, with a drop of humor, but remaining factual. It's a very exciting challenge. Basically, I try to be the teacher that I would have loved to have when I was 10.

JS: What's your next project?

Page 11 from *Approximate Continuum Comics.*

WHAT'S THE FLY STORY? I THOUGHT YOU ALREADY DID ONE OF THESE?
THERE WAS ONE IN THE SECOND ISSUE OF "LAPIN." PIERRE-ALAIN, WHO WORKS FOR KODANSHA, SAW IT AND ASKED ME TO DO SOME 'FLY' SAMPLES TO PITCH TO THE JAPANESE.
BUT THE ONE YOU'RE LOOKING AT IS THE "WESTERN" VERSION I DID JUST FOR MYSELF. THE MANGA VERSION'S GOT LETRATONE ON IT AND IS DRAWN BACKWARDS.
WHY ARE YOU DOING YOUR OWN VERSION?
BECAUSE THE JAPANESE HAVE REQUESTED SOME ANNOYING CHANGES.
FOR EXAMPLE, THE FLY IS BLACK, WITH WHITE TEETH. THEY WANT IT TO BE CUTER BECAUSE THEY THINK "THE FLY" IS MORE FOR A FEMALE AUDIENCE, SO THEY WANT TO GET RID OF THE TEETH, AND MAKE IT WHITE. AND FOR THE BIRTH SCENE, THEY WANT IT TO TAKE TWO PAGES TO GET OUT OF THE EGG -- YOU KNOW, FIRST ONE HAND, THEN THE OTHER HAND, THEN AN ARM, THEN A FOOT, THEN THE LEG, ETC...
IT SUCKS, BUT PIERRE-ALAIN SAYS DON'T TRY TO SECOND-GUESS THE JAPANESE.
SO I DON'T.

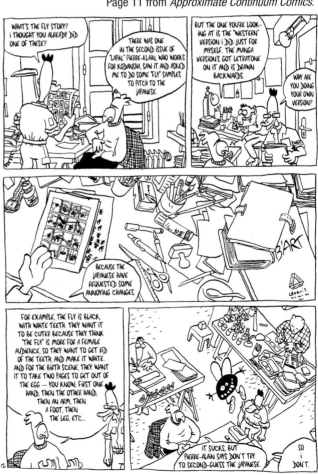

Page 12 from *Approximate Continuum Comics.*

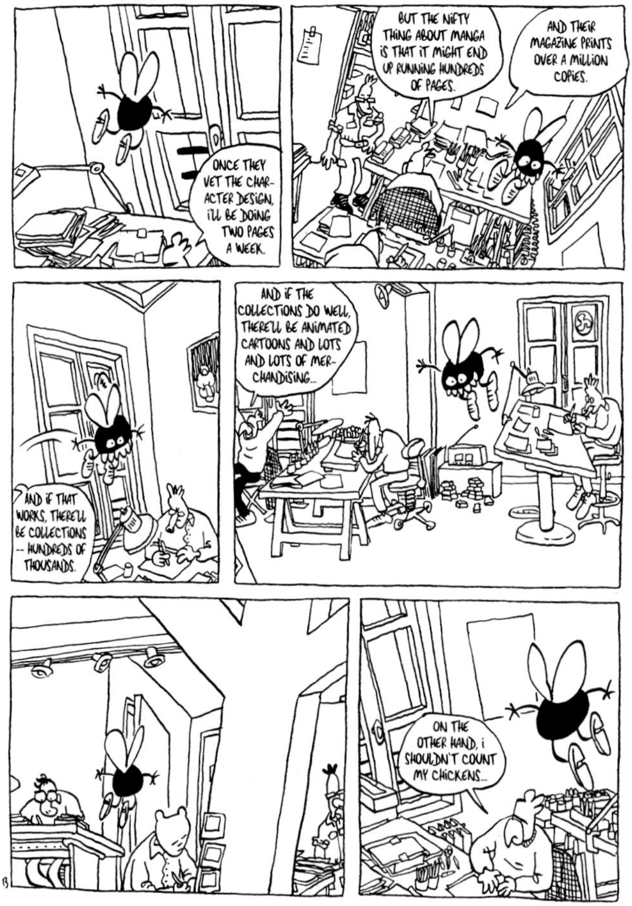
ONCE THEY VET THE CHARACTER DESIGN, I'LL BE DOING TWO PAGES A WEEK.
BUT THE NIFTY THING ABOUT MANGA IS THAT IT MIGHT END UP RUNNING HUNDREDS OF PAGES.
AND THEIR MAGAZINE PRINTS OVER A MILLION COPIES.
AND IF THAT WORKS, THERE'LL BE COLLECTIONS -- HUNDREDS OF THOUSANDS.
AND IF THE COLLECTIONS DO WELL, THERE'LL BE ANIMATED CARTOONS AND LOTS AND LOTS OF MERCHANDISING...
ON THE OTHER HAND, I SHOULDN'T COUNT MY CHICKENS...

Page 13 from *Approximate Continuum Comics.*

LT: Keep my childish soul intact and still enjoy drawing comics for a few more years.

JS: Any advice for kids who wish to become cartoonists?
LT: Write the texts so they can be read properly. Enjoy yourself. And always have a notebook on hand to sketch what surrounds you in life.

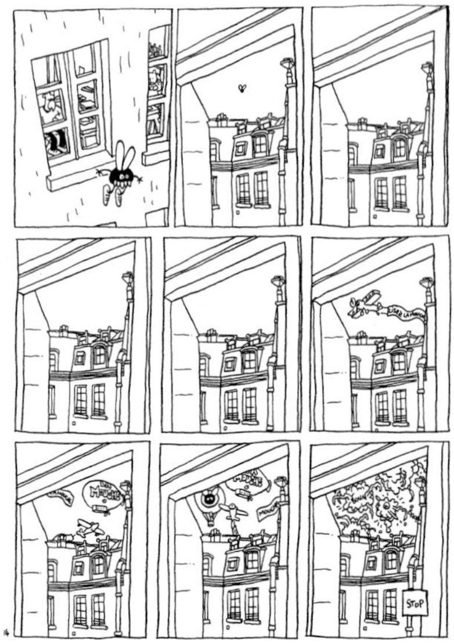
STOP

Page 14 from *Approximate Continuum Comics.*